"Zach is my husband."

Shelley looked straight into Zach's mother's face and continued. "We were married three weeks ago in Las Vegas."

The older woman looked at her son. "You didn't think we might want to know beforehand?"

"We had our reasons for doing it this way," Zach replied.

His mother turned back to Shelley. "But...what about Mr. Hightower?"

"I'm sorry—I thought you knew." Shelley's voice was a little shaky. "I was divorced from him six years ago."

"But you're carrying his child."

"No, Mom." Zach spoke before Shelley could. "The baby's mine."

"You mean you and Mrs. Hightower...were...are..."

"Yes, Mom. We're married. And we're having a baby."

Dear Reader,

According to a Victorian saying, "The first baby can come anytime. The rest take nine months."

Babies conceived before marriage have been a fact of life since the beginning of human society. The emotions associated with sex—the desire to be wanted, to be accepted, to be loved—wield great power in our lives. Even in this age of reliable birth control, these needs sometimes, even often, overwhelm our sincere attempts to direct destiny.

In *Expecting the Best*, Zach Harmon and Shelley Hightower are determined to be cautious. And yet, in that capricious way fate sometimes employs, there's a baby on the way. This couple's story is about adjusting, accepting and appreciating the possibilities offered by an unexpected detour. That process, when I think about it, seems to be the very definition of "living."

Some books write themselves, and *Expecting the Best* is one of those. Zach and Shelley are people who say what they think. As the writer, all I had to do was listen. I've enjoyed spending time with them, and hope you will, too.

Hearing from readers is a great pleasure. Please feel free to write me at Box 17195, Fayetteville, NC 28314.

Thanks for reading.

Lynnette Kent

Books by Lynnette Kent

HARLEQUIN SUPERROMANCE
765—ONE MORE RODEO
824—WHAT A MAN'S GOT TO DO

EXPECTING THE BEST
Lynnette Kent

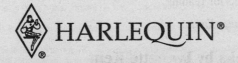

HARLEQUIN®

TORONTO • NEW YORK • LONDON
AMSTERDAM • PARIS • SYDNEY • HAMBURG
STOCKHOLM • ATHENS • TOKYO • MILAN • MADRID
PRAGUE • WARSAW • BUDAPEST • AUCKLAND

ISBN 0-373-70868-8

EXPECTING THE BEST

Printed in U.S.A.

For Lucy,
a wistful revision of history

CHAPTER ONE

THIRTY MINUTES. He would be here in thirty minutes.

Wearing only perfume and lingerie, Shelley Hightower stared at the array of dresses blanketing her bed. What in the world made choosing something to wear this Friday night so difficult?

"Black?" She fingered the hem of a beaded sheath. The dress felt heavy, and she didn't like the way the crystals winked.

"Red?" But the red was an Oriental print with gold and teal and too much braided trim. Six months ago, she'd loved the outfit and bought it just for tonight. Now the effect only seemed...loud.

"White?" As if she were a bride? Hardly.

Her stomach tightened. "Maybe I should just put on a coat and go to the banquet in my underwear," she groaned. "I don't suppose Zach Harmon will notice one way or the other."

Other people would notice, though. Accepting tonight's award for top seller at the Denver Realtors' dinner represented the pinnacle of Shelley's career. She wanted to make an impression, convey an image of class and style and success.

That's where Zach came in. Good-looking...okay, more than that, he was gorgeous. Personable. Funny *and* a great dancer. A bona fide hero with police-department decorations for proof. In other words, the perfect date to complement her career.

Even better, they barely knew each other. The wedding of mutual friends and a few parties were the only times they'd encountered each other over the last couple of years. Three hours of superficial conversation at tonight's social function with hundreds of other people wouldn't require any kind of commitment beyond good manners.

So why did she care what he thought of her dress?

The image that slipped into her thoughts twisted her insides even further…the image of a beautiful, elegant woman whose every move telegraphed class. An accomplished, intelligent woman who could hold her own with senators and CEOs and saints.

That was Claire Cavanaugh, the woman now married to Shelley's ex-husband. The same woman who had introduced Zach Harmon into Shelley's life. Zach and Claire might even have been lovers at one time, and they were still close friends. With that level of competition, how could a merely mortal woman possibly choose a dress?

Shelley glanced at the clock—twenty minutes—and looked back at the bed. Pink?

"Good grief!" She stomped into her closet and glared at the rack of gowns there, all of which looked gaudy, dated, ridiculous. She couldn't possibly wear any of them. She would be accepting the award in her underwear after all.

Having disqualified every dress in her closet, she took the only option left. Closing her eyes, she spun in a circle three times and stretched out her hand.

Whichever dress she touched first would be the one. No arguments.

Ten minutes later, with less than that to spare, she opened the jewelry box. Diamonds? Gold? Silver? "Damn!"

The doorbell rang before she'd decided which shoes would work. Should she leave him standing in the cold? Choose anything, then come back up to change them? Go down barefoot?

All Shelley knew for sure was that if she gave in to the angry tears in her eyes, her mascara would run. Then the whole evening would fall apart, and she couldn't afford to have that happen. She wanted this award, wanted recognition from the people she worked with—and against. She'd established an enviable career, one that mattered more than almost anything else in her life.

Because the career was the only thing she'd ever done *right*.

ZACH RANG the doorbell a second time and plunged his hands into his overcoat pockets. The sky was spitting snow, with a windchill of barely ten degrees. When would somebody open the damn door?

At his thought, the blue panel swung back. Zach blinked against the light flooding into his face. "Shelley?"

"Come in, Zach. Sorry I kept you waiting."

"No problem." His eyes adjusted as he stepped inside. When he turned, his first look at the woman by the door hit like a solid punch beneath the ribs.

She wasn't what—who—he'd expected. The Shelley Hightower he knew was bright and brittle, smart and savvy, but just a little too much of each.

The woman before him seemed, well, kinder and gentler. A dark blue dress skimmed her petite curves, covered by a jacket in the same blue with a white satin collar and cuffs. Her hair was longer than when he'd seen her last, framing her face with white-blond curls. Her makeup accented big dark eyes and a kiss-able mouth to perfection.

"Wow." Zach pulled his hands out of his pockets. "You look great."

Those eyes widened, but she didn't smile. "Thanks. Let me get my coat and we'll go." She crossed to a closet, and Zach welcomed the opportunity to run his gaze over her one more time.

"Uh, Shelley?"

She pulled a thick fur coat off a hanger and brought it to him. "Yes?"

"I don't mean to be critical…"

"What? What's wrong? You don't like the dress?"

He quieted her with a lifted finger. "No, the dress is perfect. But are you sure those are the shoes you want?"

They both stared down at the slippers on her feet—backless pink satin with frothy pink feathers across the toes.

When Zach looked up, the horror on Shelley's face suggested she'd seen a mouse. Or a snake.

"Hey, it's not that serious." He knuckled her chin higher. "Just run and change. I don't mind waiting— I'm at your beck and call tonight. Or I can carry you to the car, if these are your choice. They look comfortable, at least.''

Shelley gave a tiny laugh and shook her head. ''No, thanks. I'll be back in a minute.''

She left him holding the coat as she tripped up the staircase. Mink, perfectly matched, tickled his palms. That was more like the Shelley he expected. In the battle between status symbol and political correctness, status would win with her, hands down.

The house indicated status, too. Zach stared up two stories at an awesome crystal chandelier, wondering how one tiny woman could live alone in all this space and not get lost. Or really lonely.

The solemn look on Shelley's face when she'd opened the door made him wonder about the latter. As far as he knew, she'd lived by herself in the two years since she'd given up full custody of her now-eight-year-old daughter. What kind of social life did she have, if her only escort option for a big night like tonight was a cop she'd seen maybe five or six times?

And what did it say for *his* social life that he'd accepted the invitation?

''Better?'' She came halfway down the stairs and stopped, one foot on the step behind her. Zach took another body blow as he realized the dress wasn't quite as conservative as he'd thought—a slit up the side gave him a long look at the excellent shape of Shelley's leg.

Clearing his throat, he focused on her feet. ''Definitely an improvement. You might even stay warm for the duration—unless the snow gets deep.''

''It's snowing?'' She ran the rest of the way down

and peered out the faceted glass pane beside the door. "That's sure going to keep people home tomorrow, just as we're getting into the spring selling season. March is a big month."

She came back to him, and Zach straightened out the fur, holding it as she slipped her arms into the sleeves. Her perfume drifted between them, a scent of exotic woods and lemon.

He shook his head clear. "Yeah, but it gives all the home owners another weekend to get their paint touched up, their carpets cleaned. That'll make your job easier."

Shelley looked up at him over her mink-cloaked shoulder, a puzzled frown around her eyes. "Are you an optimist or something?"

"Why not? Pessimism takes more energy."

"An optimistic cop has got to be a rare character."

"One of a kind, that's me." He grinned at her and finally got a real smile back. Zach wasn't sure he'd ever seen Shelley Hightower smile before, but he decided she did it very nicely. He would have to see about getting a few more before the evening ended.

By the time dessert arrived, he could congratulate himself on reaching that goal. Shelley had smiled several times, thanks to some gentle flirting on his part, combined with the gradual consumption of reasonably good champagne.

He refilled their glasses as the dinner plates were cleared. "Allyson couldn't get down to be here tonight? I kinda hoped to see her."

She shook her head. "I didn't mention this to her or Dexter—she's got a science fair at school this weekend. She'll be down next week."

Zach remembered the days when Shelley's agenda would have come before anyone else's, even her daughter's. Since he'd just gotten her to relax, now didn't seem the right time to point out the change, so he switched subjects. "I had no idea Denver supported this many real estate agents." He murmured his comment into her ear, to avoid being overheard. "Are there enough houses for sale to go around?"

When she turned her head, their faces were close. "Like any sales job, you make your own business."

Zach returned her solemn gaze and pondered the lack of laughter there. "There's more to life than business, Shelley."

"Not if you want to win."

"And you want to win?" The skin of her face was smooth and pale. Touchable.

"Would you ask that if I were a man?"

He lifted his hands in a gesture of surrender. "Acquit me of sexism. I'm not convinced the world needs any more winners of either sex. How about just being happy?"

"Happy doesn't pay the bills."

"Sure it does. Maybe not as many as you'd like. But you can get by without giving your life over to work."

"That's assuming," Shelley said, "you have other options." Before Zach could reply, she shifted in her seat to watch the president of the Realtors' association begin his speech.

The awards presentation went on forever. Zach had long ago perfected an interested stare and the ability to let his mind drift while applauding at all the right moments. The bottle left on the table between his glass and Shelley's made that task even easier.

He brought his attention back when the president held up a huge plaque. "Last but certainly not least, I'd like to present the award for top seller of the year to...Ms. Shelley Hightower!"

Beside him, Shelley took a deep breath. Zach saw a flash of...sadness? regret?...cross her face. The audience applauded with enthusiasm as she walked to the podium. Zach joined in. The lady looked great under the lights—poised and polished. Smiling, she shook hands with the president and stepped forward when he motioned her to the microphone.

"Thank you," she said. Her clear voice carried easily over the sound system. "I'm sure all of you know that this is not something I did by myself. I want to thank the staff at my office and the agents in the company for their dedication and hard work." She paused for a glance at the award. "And special thanks go to my daughter, Allyson, for being my biggest fan and constant cheering section. She'll be thrilled to hear about tonight." Serenaded by more applause, she left the spotlight.

Zach leaned toward her as she sat down. "Do you have space on your office wall for a plank that huge?"

"Definitely." She patted the edge of the plaque. "I've waited more than ten years for tonight. I plan to hang this where everybody can see, if I have to build a wall to do it."

The closing remarks also lasted forever, but at last the banquet broke up. Zach escorted Shelley to the coat-check desk, where she stowed the plaque, and then to the hotel ballroom. They reached the edge of the floor as the band started playing. Without a word, he held out his left hand. Her right palm lighted on his. He took her onto the parquet surface—she caught his rhythm immediately. Just like that, they were dancing.

"Mmm." Zach grinned with satisfaction, swinging her through a turn. She followed like a pro. "I haven't had anybody to dance with in a long, long time." Not since his best friend, Claire Cavanaugh, had married Shelley's ex and moved to Wyoming.

His partner stepped close and tucked her head just beneath his chin. "How many cops dance as well as you do?"

"Don't know. Don't dance with many cops." He enjoyed her responding chuckle. "You should do that more often."

"Improvise?"

"Laugh." He didn't expect an answer and moved her into another turn. When she came back, his hands automatically found their place.

Two years, he realized at that moment. He hadn't made love to a woman for almost two years. Not since Claire's wedding, when the realization of what he'd lost had hit him with the power of an avalanche. He'd needed someone to hold that night, and his date for the reception obliged. They went their separate ways the morning after, and he'd kept to the company of guys since. His handball game had really improved.

Tonight, he wasn't thinking about handball. Shelley's thigh brushed his legs, her fingers played across his shoulder. Her back arched as he drew her close for a dip and she looked up at him from under her lashes, smiling.

At the sudden rush in his blood, Zach wondered if he'd pushed the limits on his restraint a little too far.

The music slowed, ended. He forced his hands away from Shelley long enough to applaud. When the band started up again, he made himself wait and at least look at her for permission. The expectation on her face eased his mind...and raised his temperature. "You like to dance, don't you?"

She moved into his embrace. "I grew up on Fred Astaire movies."

"I'm no Astaire."

"Don't sell yourself short, Zach."

He wasn't sure, at that moment, whether or not to believe the invitation in her eyes.

The rest of the evening convinced him.

THEY DANCED to every tune, drank champagne when the band took a break. Co-workers and competitors drifted by to offer congratulations on the award. Shelley found herself smiling at them, introducing Zach with her fingers on his arm as if he belonged to her or something. At the realization, she dropped her hand.

During the next introduction, her face heated up when he put an arm around her waist. But her stomach had settled down nicely. Somehow, she didn't think she could credit the food.

At last the music started again and they could go back to doing what felt so right—dancing. Zach wasn't a tall man like her ex-husband, but she was only five-two so she didn't need tall. His steel blue eyes glinted with a smile as he engineered turns and dips and sways. While his breath warmed her ear, her temple, her cheek, his muscles responded with controlled power to every step she took.

Wise or not, Shelley couldn't ignore the pleasure of being held in a man's arms again, with his hands to guide her, his strength to lean on. She couldn't resist the kick of flirting, and having somebody as good-looking as this man flirt back. Zach wore his tux as comfortably as a pair of jeans, as precisely as a European playboy. His light brown hair was sleek and tame tonight, his face more austere than she remembered. He smelled like heaven.

Under such a potent influence, any second thoughts lasted about as long as champagne bubbles. Late in the evening, Zach's mouth brushed the skin of her temple. Desire, warm and fluid, rippled along her spine. When she looked up, his gaze asked a question. She impulsively parted her lips in invitation.

Yet his kiss took her completely by surprise. She'd never known such power, never felt so weak, as at the moment his lips moved over hers. The pleasure of being wanted tempted her to tears. Zach swept her across an entire range of emotions within seconds, and all with just the brief contact of his mouth.

He drew back the space of a breath. "Shelley." His whisper sounded as unsteady as her pulse. "Leaving now might be a good idea."

She didn't have any clever words to use, didn't intend to shatter the moment. Whatever he meant, she wanted these feelings to last as long as possible.

As if he understood, they stopped in unison and turned without a word toward the nearest door out of the dim ballroom.

The bright lights in the outer hallway couldn't break the spell. They retrieved the plaque and their coats. Zach helped Shelley into hers with a squeeze of her shoulders she knew she hadn't imagined. As they waited for the elevator, she could barely feel the press of his palm in the small of her back, but she needed nothing more to keep her aware of his strength. He filled her consciousness to the exclusion of anything else.

In the lobby of the hotel, reality cracked over her like an icicle falling from the roof.

"Oh, wow." Shelley stared out the glass front door at a foot of new snow. "Were we having a blizzard? I missed the news."

Zach stood behind her. "Me, too. Doesn't look like it's thinking about stopping any time soon, either."

"Maybe never."

They watched the heavy curtain of snow in a kind of trembling suspension of time.

And then Zach bent close. "Your house is a long way out of town."

"It is." *And dark and incredibly empty.*

"Mine's closer, but the cop in me knows better than to drive even that far after this much champagne." His breath played across her ear.

She shivered. "Definitely a bad idea."

"We could call a cab."

That would give her too much time to think. "I

dread going out in the cold." Even inside her house, it would be cold. Because she'd be alone.

He took a deep breath. "We could stay the night here."

For a thousand reasons, *no* would be the right answer. A wise woman learned from her mistakes.

Or did a wise woman take advantage of a once-in-a-lifetime chance? Shelley nodded and kept her eyes on the snow. "I think that sounds…perfect."

His hands covered her shoulders again. "Back in a few minutes."

There wasn't much time to reconsider, even if Shelley could have managed to think amidst the fireworks of anticipation exploding in her mind. Zach returned in what seemed like seconds to sweep her and the plaque into a packed elevator—obviously, they weren't the only ones who'd decided against travel. After an endless trip, he guided her out at the concierge floor. The rowdy crowd vanished behind sliding brass doors.

Walking down the hallway, Shelley registered impressions instead of thoughts. The dent of their footsteps on carpet the color of blue stained glass. A scent of flowers—lilies? And the quiet that only snow can bring, even to a tall, downtown building.

Then the click of a key card in the door lock.

The floor lamp between the armchairs had been switched on. A service tray waited nearby, bearing an ice bucket and champagne, glasses and a single rose in a crystal vase.

Shelley set the plaque down near the wall and turned as Zach closed the door behind them. "Someone works fast."

"Someone," he agreed, a smile tilting one side of his mouth. "Let me take your coat."

He lifted the weight from her shoulders and hung the fur in the closet, along with his dark wool. When he came back, he stopped far enough away that she understood she shouldn't feel coerced. "Champagne?"

But his eyes had changed, and in them Shelley saw the need she could feel tearing inside herself. She shook her head and closed the distance between them. "Later. Please…kiss me like that again."

Zach held her as if they were still dancing, one hand clasping hers, the other at the curve of her waist. Their bodies barely touched. Yet the pressure of his mouth demanded. Required. Compelled.

Shelley responded with unforced pleasure. There had been no one as real as Zach in her life for a very long time. She needed his warmth, his closeness. Needed to think that she mattered, if only for tonight.

She loosened his bow tie and felt him chuckle, deep in his throat. His palms skimmed her bare arms with a delicious friction, and she realized that the jacket for the dress was gone. The studs on his shirt gave her some trouble, so he got her zipper down first. Then she stood in front of him wearing just her slip and stockings.

His blue eyes blazed as he slowly looked her over, and he whistled low and long. "Lady, as far as I'm concerned, you could have come dressed like this tonight!"

CHAPTER TWO

ZACH DIDN'T KNOW why Shelley was laughing, but he liked the sound. He liked the sight of her just within reach, wearing dark blue satin and lace. He liked the feel of her skin under his palms. And he loved the way she smelled.

But she was too far away. "Come here," he murmured, catching her wrists to draw her close.

Her arms curved around his waist under his shirt, cool against his heat. "Better?"

"Oh, yeah." Zach dipped his head, found her mouth and settled back into her scent and taste, letting his mind shut down in favor of other systems. He skimmed his lips over her cheek, her ear. "Definitely better than champagne. I'm drunk on you, Shelley."

With a tilt of her head, Shelley's mouth recaptured his. She eased his shirt off without breaking the kiss. Her hands lingered on the balls of his shoulders, then stroked the fabric down to his elbows. There she stopped.

"Gotcha," she whispered, trapping his lower arms inside the sleeves with the cuffs still fastened.

"I'm not as talented without my hands." Zach backed up as she put a palm against his chest and pushed. "But I'm certainly willing to give it my best shot."

"Later," she said again. This time she pushed with both hands. Abandoning his halfhearted protest, he fell backward onto the bed.

She came down after him, a featherweight on his chest, and took him into another kiss. Hunger flared up fast, edging him toward the limits of control. They were both panting by the time Shelley tore her mouth away.

Slipping to the side, she ran a hand through the hair on his chest. "We've got all night. No hurry."

"Speak for yourself," he muttered, straining his wrists against starched cotton, but without enough force to actually break free. "I was considering the priesthood until I saw you tonight."

"A long time, hmm?" Her fingers traced over his skin, just above the waist of his slacks.

"You're killing me."

She lowered her head, nuzzled his collarbone. "Good."

Crazy with need, Zach surrendered. If Shelley wanted the power, he'd let the lady have her way— for now, at least. Her small hands stroked and kneaded, and his breath got shallower with every touch. Her mouth scattered sparks across his skin. The woman was too dangerous to be safe. Too good to be left alone.

She eased his zipper down, and Zach thought he'd lose his dignity right then. He focused on Shelley for distraction, the way her lips pressed together as she concentrated, how her lashes fanned dark across the curve of her cheeks. White-gold hair fell around her face like angel glass, but if she was an angel, he'd bet on her being one of Lucifer's crowd. What she was doing to him tonight could only be classified as absolutely wicked.

His socks, slacks and shorts disappeared, and her warm palms covered him. Zach groaned and closed his eyes. "I swear, Shelley, this isn't going last if you don't—"

He shut up and opened his eyes as she rolled on a condom.

"There are toothbrushes in the other pocket," he pointed out between clenched teeth.

She rose above him—delicate, provocative as hell, with one blue satin strap slipping down over her shoulder. "I figured you'd be prepared."

Zach grinned tightly. "I made Eagle Scout, once upon a time."

She nodded. "I'm not surprised." Then, holding his gaze, her own sultry and smiling and serious all at once, she took him inside.

Blood pulsed through his bound wrists, behind his eyes, in his belly. He wanted to slow down, get his breath, control the aching, pounding craving to get *there*...

But Shelley's face mirrored his struggle, reflected the agony and the need and the yearning. Zach knew he wouldn't last another second...and then she cried out and gripped him, with a strength that thrust them both into the heart of a shattering star.

WRAPPED IN THE HOTEL'S thick red robe, Shelley curled up in the armchair by the window and stared through the predawn darkness at a snowstorm that hadn't slowed in the least. Bumps and clumps on the curbs hinted that an effort had been made to clear the street at some point, but another foot or so had fallen since then. Not many people would be shopping for a house today. She didn't need to go to work.

At the thought, she turned her head toward the bed. Zach breathed deeply and stirred, but didn't wake up. He lay on his side, bare chested and adorable, his arms still holding the space where she'd slept.

Unbelievable. She'd spent the night with Zach Harmon. Seduced by his charm, enchanted by the charisma of a man who knew just what a woman wanted, she'd stopped thinking and let her needs carry them both away.

Now…the moment for regrets. This incredible connection between them wouldn't last. Shelley knew she didn't have a recipe for the glue that welded relationships. No matter how wonderful the guy appeared to be—and Zach came across as damn near perfect—she couldn't make love, or even lust, stick.

Her heart sank with the admission. Zach would be fun to keep around, at least a little while. During the two years she'd known him, they'd met maybe five or six times. She'd always thought about him afterward, in more detail and for much longer than was smart.

The result of those silly daydreams was this. *This.* A weekend fling, a moment out of time. He would walk out the door of this room and, no doubt, forget all about her, as he'd done after their other encounters. He'd never called her, had he? Never asked for a date?

And she would resume her own life, presenting deals and negotiating contracts, cajoling stubborn buyers and obstinate sellers. Late at night, she'd go back to an empty house, turn on the television for noise and wait for the dreams to keep her company.

"Hey." At the word, Shelley opened her eyes and found Zach awake. "What are you doing over there?" The rumble in his voice reminded her of a drowsy lion's purr.

Aware of his gaze, she stretched slowly. "Watching the snow."

"Still?"

"More than two feet now."

"Too bad." He grinned, and the sexy message revved up her heartbeat. "We'll just have to stay inside and play games."

"Parcheesi?" She decided she might as well get as much of Zach as she could while he was here. The more she had, the more fuel there would be for dreams when she was alone again. "Monopoly? I'm very good at Monopoly." Walking toward the bed, she untied her belt and let the robe drop to the floor.

"Oh, yeah? So'm I." His gaze stroked over her as she came closer, and her skin heated everywhere he looked. "We'll have a playoff sometime. But right now…" The sheet fell to his waist as he sat up and reached for her. Shelley sighed as their bare bodies touched. "Right now I've got other amusements in mind."

"Show me," she invited. And he did.

MUCH LATER that morning, room service delivered brunch while Shelley was still in the shower. "If you don't hurry, I'm going to start without you," Zach called through the door. "I'm starving!"

"I'll be right out." Turning off the water, Shelley wrapped up in a towel and used another one to wipe off the mirror. The woman there wasn't wearing her usual mask, but she didn't have the supplies to re-create the image. No makeup, except powder and lipstick, no rollers and mousse and spray, no jewelry. No clothes, except the blue dress. And the robe.

She dried her hair and combed it as best she could, donned the robe and then gazed at her naked face. How could she go out there like this? What would he think?

This time, Zach knocked on the door. "Shelley, come on. Your eggs will be cold."

"Okay, okay!" Maybe he'd be too busy eating to notice her. She took a deep breath and opened the bathroom door.

Zach waited for her outside, wearing an identical robe. He curled his fingers into her hair. "You look great." His kiss was sweet and soft and so gentle she wanted to cry. When she opened her eyes, he grinned. "Now," he said, "let's eat."

They sat beside the window, watching the storm. "I called my mom, just to check on her." Zach crunched his bacon. "She's fine. The TV's saying this is the worst spring blizzard in twenty years."

She suddenly remembered what he did for a living. "Do you get called into work on days like this?" Would the end come so soon?

"Sometimes. I checked in there, too. So far, the

power's stayed on and the situation's under control. I left the station this number if they need me.''

So she could keep him for a while. Shelley relaxed a bit. ''I'll bet the ski slopes stay open until the end of April, now, even into May.''

''We can hope. I'll have to see about taking my sisters up for a weekend.''

A chance piece of information she'd overheard long ago came to mind. ''How many brothers and sisters do you have?''

''Eleven of us, plus two parents. We never went anywhere all together because there wasn't enough room in the car.'' He winked at her over the breakfast dishes. ''Lucky thing church was within walking distance.''

His grin drove good sense out of her head. With his hair mussed and his blue eyes bright and the red robe setting off his tan skin, he looked like a magazine centerfold. His bare legs had somehow tangled with hers under the table, so even getting a decent breath took concentration.

Shelley struggled back to sanity. ''That must be why you have such magic with kids. Allyson is always talking 'Uncle Zach.'''

''Your daughter is a special case. I manage to see her whenever Dex and Claire bring her to town—we always have a good time.'' He toasted Allyson with his coffee cup. ''She reminds me of my 14-year-old baby sister, Carol. Both of them are bright, impulsive, a little hard to control.''

The description certainly fit Allyson. ''Your parents have trouble with Carol?''

Zach's smile faded. "My dad died of lung cancer four years ago. That's when I left the army."

"I'm sorry. I didn't know."

He nodded. "No reason you should. Carol took it really hard, and she's been tough to reach ever since. I get called in whenever there's a problem—she listens to me more than anybody else. But that's not saying much."

"A big family must be fun. I didn't have brothers and sisters."

"There were plenty of times I wished I could be an only child." After thinking a second, he shrugged. "Still are, for that matter. These days, at least, I can go home and get away. You couldn't pay me enough now to give up my privacy."

"You don't want kids of your own?" That surprised her. She'd never seen more perfect dad material.

"You'll have noticed I make pretty damn sure that's not going to happen." He flashed that sexy grin. "Families mean complications, and I've already got enough of those—along with plenty of brothers and sisters to carry on the family genes. I figure I'll be known as eccentric Uncle Zach, who spent his life standing the line between right and wrong but wasted his free time on wild, wicked women."

He shoved the table out of the way, drew her into his lap and loosened the belt on her robe. "Like you, lady," he whispered roughly against her skin.

Shelley gripped his shoulders, shuddering as his tongue traced the arch of her throat. "I admire a man with a long-range plan," she managed to reply before his wandering hands made words impossible.

THEY GOT new towels, shooed the housekeeper away and watched movies late into Saturday night. Zach picked the first one, a big budget historical he'd missed in theaters. Shelley's choice was romantic comedy.

"Aha," he crowed as the credits rolled. "You're a closet romantic. The pragmatic and successful Ms. Hightower enjoys love stories. I bet you read them, too."

She sat up, pointed the remote and clicked off the TV. "Who has time to read?" But her cheeks reddened.

"I like historical romance myself," he said casually. "I'm into history."

"You read romance novels? You're kidding, right?"

Zach grinned at her skepticism. "Why wouldn't I?"

"But—"

He stretched out on his side and propped his head on his hand. "Good stories, good research, an interesting relationship. Is that strictly female territory?"

"Maybe not." Her gaze sharpened. "But you're not planning 'happily-ever-after' for yourself?"

The lady had a way of getting to the heart of things. He turned the tables to make his escape. "Are you?"

She fell back against the pillows and put her arms over her eyes. "Not likely. I have lousy judgment when it comes to men."

Zach decided to assume present company was excepted. "Hightower is a good guy." He'd better be, since he was now married to Claire.

Lowering her arms again, Shelley sighed. "Dexter and I were terrible for each other. If Allyson hadn't come along, we wouldn't have stayed together at all."

"You can't count her as a mistake."

"Oh, no. She's the best thing I ever did." The smile she'd started faded away. "I know she's doing great in Wyoming, but I really miss having her with me."

Zach put his free hand on her arm, stroked the soft skin on the inside of her elbow with his thumb. "Dex and Claire would probably bring her down even more often, if you asked."

"My life's so crazy, so...relentless." She shrugged. "And Allyson's happy on the ranch, or at their second home in Cheyenne. I'd feel bad to tear her away from her friends and life there."

"That still doesn't mean you have to be alone all the time."

Her dark gaze hardened and she pulled her arm away. "So which wonderful candidate should I choose? The guy who steals my credit cards? Or the one who hits and threatens me and, incidentally, cost me custody of my daughter?"

"Shelley, those aren't the only men who'd go out with you." What the hell did she think *he* was doing here? Maybe she did put him in the same class with those jerks.

She wrenched away to the edge of the bed with what sounded like a snarl, found her robe and pulled it around her. Yanking the belt tight, she stalked to the window—a delicate, determined silhouette against the black sky outside. Zach waited out the tension.

Eventually, her shoulders drooped.
"Some women are just not cut out for happily-ever-after." She rested her forehead against the glass. "My mom made a choice once, and he dumped us both when I was three months old."

"That classifies him a bastard, but it doesn't say anything about your mom, or you."

"Yes, it does!" Her head came up and she turned, dark eyes glittering. "My mom built a life for us all by herself. The rest of her family helped out, but Mom worked two jobs and went to secretarial school, then spent twenty years taking orders from men with half her brains so that I could have clothes and a car and…and skiing. And a decent career."

"I didn't say—"

She lifted a hand. "I know. But she managed her life without a man, and did a damn good job. Now I'm doing the same. I mean it—some of us are better off alone."

Zach pondered for a minute. Was that an invitation to exit? He was surprised by how much the prospect bothered him. Still, when a lady said no… "Well then, maybe I should leave."

He rolled to the near side of the bed and sat up, feeling around on the floor for his robe. Just as he found it, Shelley's scent reached him. Her small hands slid over his ribs and her soft breasts, bare and aroused, pressed against his back. His breath left him in a rush.

"You don't want to go out in the middle of a cold,

snowy night," she whispered over his ear. "Do you?"

He chuckled. "I think the answer to that is pretty obvious."

"So, don't." She laid kisses across his shoulder while her hands—her warm, clever hands—roamed south. "I don't want you going anywhere right now."

"That's good," Zach sighed, relaxing under her caress. "That's really, really good."

SUNDAY MORNING, the snow had stopped and the plows were out in droves. While Shelley called Allyson in Wyoming, Zach made a visit to the hotel shops and came back with clothes for them both. They ate lunch downstairs in the dining room.

"I'll bet Allyson's loving this snow." He poured coffee into Shelley's cup and then his own. "I went up last winter to visit Claire, and they had snow-maidens all over the lawn in Cheyenne."

Shelley stirred in cream and artificial sweetener. "She could barely talk this morning for all the excitement. We E-mail several times a week—I've probably got hourly updates waiting in my mailbox." Her smile was part sigh. "I can't deny she's happy where she is. Claire and Dex are doing a great job."

She didn't look exactly happy, but she wasn't bitter, either—she'd come a long way in two years. "Sounds like you've accepted the situation. That's a big step."

Her calculating gaze pinned him to the wall. "And you haven't."

im swear in front of a woman. But then, his mother
would kill him for almost everything he'd done since
7:00 p.m. Friday night.

And why was he thinking about his mother? "I
thought we were enjoying the moment and each
other, Shelley. I wasn't making plans."

She turned to look out the window at the cleared
streets. "We were. But we both know this isn't going
anywhere. I just wanted to let you off the hook."

"Gee, thanks." He couldn't think, couldn't see
how to turn the situation. She might relent if he
touched her, but he would still be irritated, which
wasn't a good prelude to sex or anything else.

"So," she said, in that same calm, impersonal
tone. "I think I might be going, now that the streets
are passable."

Now he had her. "You came in my car."

She stared at him, her eyes wide with panic. "I
can get a cab."

Another point for his side. "Good luck finding a
driver who'll take on a snow-covered interstate."

She knew the truth when she heard it. "Great. Just
great." Her disappointment was so real, Zach almost
laughed.

"So you can't get away from me yet. Come sit
down." He pointed her to the chair on the other side
of the table. She gazed at him with a question in her
eyes and he repeated the motion. "Yes, sit down."

He opened the dresser drawer and found a notepad
and pen. Desperate situations called for desperate
measures. "Did you ever play Battleship?"

THEY SHARED the pen through four games, when the
ink ran dry. Zach called down to room service for a

Zach retreated behind his own coffee. "[I] [don't have]
a clue what you're talking about."

"At least I didn't love Dex anymore. But [you were]
still in love with Claire when they got [married.]
Weren't you?"

He stared into his cup for a speechless s[econd.]
"I—"

"She's an unforgettable woman. I don't blame [you]
for wanting her back."

"Shelley—" Denial would be good, if he co[uld]
get his mouth around the words. But he wasn't use[d]
to lying.

"I realize I'm a substitute." He glanced up to find
her watching him with a calm, impersonal stare.
"But that's okay. This is just for kicks, right?"

Zach waited for the red haze to clear out of his
vision before trusting his voice. "Are you finished?"

"With my lunch?"

"And your ridiculous…"

"It's not—"

He got to his feet. "Coming back to the room?"

No was on the tip of her tongue, he could see it.
But she stood as well, and put her napkin on the
table. "Why not?"

Upstairs, they faced each other across the newly
made bed. Zach didn't let the lady go first this time.
"Have you decided this one's over, too, Shelley?
Time to move on?"

"I thought I'd say it before you had to."

"Nice of you. What if I had other plans?"

"Do you?"

"Hell, I don't know!" He shoved his hands into
his pockets. His mother would kill him if she heard

bottle of champagne, cheese and crackers, and a box of pens. The war escalated as the room darkened until they could hardly see their marks on the paper. Shelley finally stood up to turn on a lamp.

"That makes us even." She looked across at Zach, sprawled in a chair with his head back and a half-full glass of champagne dangling from his hand over the arm of the chair. "Twenty games each."

"We need a tiebreaker."

"World War Three?"

"Or something like that." His voice had gone back to the leonine purr she'd followed for two days now.

Her pulse jumped, but she fought to stay sane. "Zach, that's not a good idea."

"Why?"

Because I'm already in too deep, she wanted to say. "Let's...let each other go easily."

"Okay."

Shelley took a deep breath of relief.

He stood up. "Tomorrow morning."

The breath blew out in exasperation. "Zach—"

But he was already kissing her. He warmed her lips with his breath, filled her mouth with his taste, and she had no hope of anything except holding on and enjoying the ride. With Zach, she knew that's all she could count on. The ride of her life.

MONDAY MORNING, the weather thawed. Shelley froze.

Zach didn't attempt to break the ice. The next move, glacial or otherwise, would have to be hers.

"Here's my number." He handed her a piece of paper. "Call me. I always return my messages."

Now that she'd summoned a cab, she wouldn't even look at him. "Sure." She gathered up her clothes and lingerie and folded each item carefully into a shopping bag. "You can reach me anytime at the office. I have call forwarding."

"Okay."

He watched as she put her blue dress shoes on top of the clothes and folded the handles of the bag together. When she looked over, her eyes were wide and bright. Was she trying not to cry?

She succeeded. "Thanks, Zach, for...for everything. I'm not being very graceful, but this was a wonderful weekend."

"For me, too. Kiss me goodbye?"

"Of course." She meant to give him a buss on the cheek and run off. But Zach turned as she reached him, slipped his arms around her and gathered her close. Her body pressed into his and their mouths touched.

When Shelley pushed at his arms, he forced himself to release her. "Bye," she whispered. Without another glance, she hurried out the door.

"Bye, lady," Zach murmured after her. Alone again, he looked around the room, at a loss...and caught sight of the giant plaque. He grabbed it and shot out the door. "Shelley? Shelley!"

She stopped in the process of getting on the elevator and looked his way. "Oh." Pulling her foot back, she let the doors close. "I—I forgot." Her hand came up to grasp the award.

Zach let go, reluctantly. "Are you sure you can manage? I could carry it down for you."

"No!" She glanced into his face and quickly away. "No, thanks. I'll be fine."

He relinquished the plaque. "Well, then. Goodbye." Retreating toward the room, he lifted a hand. "See you."

Shelley pressed the down button and sent him another cool smile. "Sure." Then she turned her back on him, which left her facing a wall. But the message came through loud and clear.

With a sigh, Zach returned to the room and waited a meticulous thirty minutes to give her time to get away. Then he picked up his wrinkled tux and headed for home.

CHAPTER THREE

THREE MONTHS LATER, Shelley stared across a tidy desk at the woman facing her. "*What* did you say?"

Dr. Deb Bryant didn't blink. "I said your pregnancy test is positive. You're going to have a baby."

"No, I'm not."

"Does that mean you're considering an abortion?"

"No!" The idea made her sick. But then, she'd been sick a lot lately—that's why she'd come to the doctor. "How could this have happened?"

"The usual way, I imagine. What were you doing around the first week in March?"

"Working myself to death as...oh." All except for one weekend. *That* weekend. The awards banquet. The blizzard. Zach.

She took a deep breath. "But I...we...used protection. Every time." Not that she could remember how many times they'd made love between Friday night and Monday morning.

"All methods have a failure rate. Now, what do you plan to do?"

Staring at the doctor across the desk, Shelley tried to think and failed. She could only give a gut reaction. "Have a baby, I guess."

"Then we should choose an obstetrician. Since

you're close to thirty-five, I'd like to recommend a specialist in high-risk pregnancies, just to be on the safe side. We need to get you on iron tablets and vitamins, improve your diet..."

Shelley walked out to her car half an hour later, shaken to the very roots of her soul.

A baby. Zach Harmon's child.

She went so far as to pick up the car phone, punching out the number she'd memorized twelve weeks ago. But with her finger on "send" she stopped, then ended the call.

They hadn't seen each other since that Monday morning when she'd rushed off to work, promising to get in touch. She'd never worked up the nerve to call him. Zach hadn't made contact, either...hadn't wanted to, she assumed.

Was she going to phone him now and start a chorus of "Hello, Daddy?"

With a moan, Shelley put her head back and blinked away tears. Whatever memories of that weekend remained a blur, Zach's comments on family had been clear. He emphatically did not want children.

"Oh, baby." She put a hand low on her stomach. "What in the world am I going to do about you?"

That question became even more crucial when the phone rang about nine that night. Caught in the middle of cleaning out her refrigerator, Shelley answered the phone with some impatience. "Hello?"

"A little tense, aren't we?"

"*Zach?*" She held the phone in front of her and stared at it, half hoping she'd conjured his voice out of her imagination. Putting down a bottle of salad dressing, she brought the phone back to her ear. "Zach, is that you?"

"In the fiber optically transmitted flesh. How are you?"

She choked back a hysterical laugh. "Fine, just fine. How are...things?" Why was he calling? He couldn't possibly know about the baby. She'd just found out. Right?

"Great. But I woke up this morning and realized that June had arrived and I hadn't heard from you, so I thought I'd see if you were free for dinner."

"Tonight?" She couldn't possibly face him tonight.

"Actually, I'm on duty in a couple of hours. I was thinking about the weekend, if that works for you."

"Um..." How was she supposed to think? What should she say? Could she sit through a meal with him and not blurt out the truth? "I don't know..."

"Okay." His voice took on a cooler tint. "I probably caught you at a bad time. Maybe later—"

"No, Zach, wait." Shelley drew a deep breath. "How about Saturday? I've got appointments all week, and I was saving Saturday night for a break."

"Sounds good to me. I'll pick you up about seven-thirty. Wear the pink slippers, if you want. They were cute."

He disconnected before she could think of a clever retort.

SATURDAY MORNING, the Crushers baseball team went into the final inning ahead of Zach's Falcons, six-two. But the Falcons loaded the bases. With one more good hit, they could win.

Zach squatted beside his star batter as she waited on deck. "Okay, Cinda. All you gotta do is relax and keep your eye on the ball. Cool?"

"Cool, Coach." The beads on the ten-year-old's many braids clicked as Cinda nodded her head. "I'm ready."

"Go for it." He stood up and backed into the dugout, just as Tim Johnson swung for his third strike. "Good job, Tim! Way to swing!" Zach ruffled the boy's hair as he dropped onto the bench to pout. "Can't hit a homer every time."

"Cinda does."

"Just seems like it, Tim." The pitcher stretched and threw. Cinda swung and missed. "See?" But with the bases loaded, he really wouldn't mind if this were one of the times she hit big.

Another pitch and another strike for Cinda brought the Falcons one swing away from a loss—or a win.

Beside him in the dugout, the Falcons had set up a cheering squad. Zach joined them. "Good try, Cinda. Keep swinging!"

He heard the crack of the bat before he saw the hit. The ball sailed in a beautiful arc over the pitcher's head, beyond the second baseman. Cinda galloped toward first, rounded and touched the base, headed for second. Their runner on third crossed home.

The center fielder ran backward, glove high. Cinda's tremendous hit began a downward curve.

Zach held his breath. The Falcons grew silent, the crowd waited in suspended animation, while the ball fell and the fielder backed up.

With the definitive smack of leather against

leather, ball hit glove. The fielder juggled a second, brought his other hand in for help and held up the captured prize. Not a home run—a fly ball, making the third and final out.

The Falcon bench groaned. Zach let out his breath. "Okay, guys, line up for handshakes." He glanced at one of the more disappointed players. "When you throw that glove in the dirt, Joey, you're the one who has to clean it."

Cinda ran in from third with tears in her eyes. "Great hit," Zach said, clapping her on the shoulder. "Too bad he didn't step in any of the holes I dug out there before the game."

She smiled tremulously. "You're such a goof, Coach." Then she ran to take her place in line to congratulate the other team.

"Tough break," said a voice behind him. He swung around to see Jimmy Falcon, their team sponsor, standing behind the fence.

Jimmy had been Zach's first partner on the police force. Three years ago, they'd been caught in the middle of a gang fight that had left Jimmy with a shattered leg and a stalled career. "We appreciate your support, though. Those shirts are great."

"Hey, these games get me out of bed on Saturday morning. What's the record now?"

Zach picked up bats and helmets. "We're three and four. This was the team to beat from last year. I'm hoping for an easy win next week against the Terminators."

They talked baseball on the walk to Zach's Trans Am to load equipment into the trunk. Parents stopped to shake a hand and commiserate. Cinda ran by, waving.

"See you at practice Monday," Zach called.

"Right, Coach!"

"So what's the rest of the your weekend like?" Jimmy leaned against the side of the car. "I've got a hot new group at the club tonight. I'm betting they'll be a name before the year's out."

Jimmy's jazz and blues club, Indigo, was well known in Denver music circles. "I might just show up." Zach used the tail of his sweatshirt to wipe a bug splat off the trunk's glossy black finish. "I've got a dinner date first."

"Bring her along."

"Maybe." He knew a lot about what Shelley liked…in bed. But what kind of music did she listen to? "I'll ask the lady."

"I'll save you a table. You missed one." Jimmy grinned and pointed to an even bigger bug blotch on the hood.

"Thanks, pal. Don't do me any favors."

An afternoon spent washing the car didn't provide much mental distraction. Zach waxed and buffed and thought about the woman he'd see tonight. The woman he hadn't seen in three months, because…?

Working the night shift made dating in the evenings a real challenge.

Still, even cops got time off.

His basketball league took up a lot of spring nights.

But not all of them.

Coaching the Falcons kept him occupied in the

late afternoon on Mondays, Wednesdays and Fridays, with Saturday-morning games.

So what about the rest of the week?

No answers. "Okay," he muttered, crouching down to clean a hubcap. "Why did I call her now?"

After that incredible weekend with Shelley, he'd waited an agonizing month to hear from her, and managed to survive sixty restless days after that. He'd kept the memories at bay, most of the time, and tried to take a stoical view of the situation. If they happened to run into each other, he'd figured, he'd be able to tell whether he should see her again. If not, well, they didn't move in the same circles, really. And they'd already gone too far to be "just friends."

So why be surprised when she didn't call? She'd probably dropped his number in the first trash can she came to. The lady wasn't interested. Pure and simple.

Zach gave the rear fender a final swipe and stepped back. The car looked good. He, on the other hand, smelled like a car wash. Time to hit the shower.

A few minutes later, facing himself in the mirror as he shaved, he asked the question again. "So why call her now?"

The answer shamed him. Wanting to forget one woman was absolutely the worst excuse for seeing another. But he couldn't deny the truth.

Claire Hightower had called. She wanted Zach to know she was pregnant.

The news hit him like a truck without brakes on a steep mountain downgrade. He'd never imagined

Claire pregnant. Dance partner, debate opponent, movie critic and dinner companion, sure. Dynamite lawyer and advocate for women's and children's rights, of course. She made a great stepmother for Allyson Hightower.

But pregnant?

Yes. He had heard the contentment in her voice. Loving and living with Dex Hightower made Claire happy. She'd confided that carrying Dex's baby was the best achievement of her life. Zach sincerely wished her well, even as he wondered why the news shook him up so much.

The reason wasn't buried too deep. Shelley's accusations came damn close—Zach had loved Claire, easily and lightly, because she wanted it that way. He'd had hopes of getting her to change her mind, until Dex Hightower showed up in their lives. And now Claire was married and happy and Zach was…

Free, as usual. Alone, a state he'd looked forward to for eighteen years at home, four years at college, and ten more in the army. Just what the hell was wrong with his life, anyway? What more did he want?

Those questions buzzed at him for a couple of days after Claire's call, breaking up his sleep, interfering with his work and play. He needed a distraction and thought about Shelley. She made him laugh, she made him ache, she made him crazy. What better way to spend an evening?

His first glimpse of her at the door that Saturday night brought his brain functions to a screeching halt. Zach gave a long, low whistle. "You're gonna stop traffic, lady."

She wore a sunny yellow dress, long and straight, with tiny straps and a big splash of red over one hip. Her skin glowed with a light tan, her hair was a little shorter than he remembered, her nails and sandals matched the splotch on the dress. For a diversion, he couldn't have picked better—she might well be the sexiest woman he'd ever seen.

She smiled. "Good thing I'll have a cop with me, isn't it? Want to come in for a drink?"

"Sure." He followed her inside and waited close by while she shut the door. Then, he put his palms on her shoulders and kissed her hello.

The intense jolt of desire took him by surprise. Her taste and her scent were familiar, the feel of her mouth against his welcome and right. Her small sigh, as he shifted his head to deepen the kiss, was a sound out of his dreams.

Before he was ready, Shelley drew back. Her gaze was soft, vulnerable, as she stared at him while they both recovered their breath.

But in the next second he lost her. Her face changed, almost hardened. She stepped away from him. Not even her fingertips lingered. "Can I get you something to drink?"

Disappointment flooded him, but he managed a casual nod. "Beer?"

"You've got it. Come to the kitchen. What have you been doing lately?"

From another woman, the comment might have demanded an explanation of his absence. But either Shelley was a damn good actress, or she didn't care—her face showed nothing but mild interest as she brought him a bottle and a chilled mug.

He sat at the breakfast bar, fighting down his injured masculine pride. "Keeping Denver safe for women and children, mostly. I played department intramural basketball this spring and now I'm coaching Little League. How about you?"

She took the chair next to his. "Work, of course. My spring house sales are just starting to close." She sipped from a glass of bottled water. "Getting some of these buyers and sellers to the table takes real effort."

"Believe it or not, I've had to break up closings that got violent."

"You don't have to tell me. One of my clients tried to walk out recently, because the buyer wanted to change the terms of the contract. The buyer jumped up to stop him, and the next thing I know, they're crashing though the glass window of the conference room, rolling all over the floor, making ugly noises and swearing a blue streak. We managed to stop them without the cops, though."

"Takes skill, ending fights. You could get yourself hurt."

"I let the lawyer do it—I figured if anyone deserved a punch, it was him."

Zach laughed. "Good thinking. Are you hungry?" Her wrists, in red bracelets, were sparrow-small, her collarbones a little obvious. He wondered if she'd been working too hard and forgetting to eat.

She slipped off the chair. "I'm always hungry. Where shall we go?"

CAROL HARMON HELD BACK against the tug of her friend's hand. "This is a high-end store, Jen. We could get into real trouble for just touching something. Let alone taking it.''

"Don't be a wimp." Jen tightened her grip and pulled Carol through the glass doorway. "Or we won't let you join CW. Crooked Women aren't wusses."

"Neither am I!" But there were fur coats on one side of them, sequined dresses on the other. This place even smelled rich. And rich people didn't like losing their stuff.

"So, come on." Jen walked into the forest of sequins with her hands in her pockets, whistling.

Carol thought about leaving—but she didn't have a way to get home. She thought about her sisters and her brothers, the cops in her family—Rachel, Grant and, especially, Zach—and what they'd do if they caught her shoplifting. Her best friend, Sam, would beat her up before she let her do something like this.

But Sam lived in Florida now, with a new school and new friends. Carol missed her. She was tired of hanging out by herself, writing letters because there was nobody to talk to. Or going to ball games with her brothers, movies with her sisters. It was time to grow up. Get a life.

All the cool people belonged to Crooked Women. And they wanted *her* to join. Why not? What did she really have to lose?

She pushed her bangs out of her eyes and hurried across the gold marble floor. "Hey, Jen! Jen, wait up!"

SHELLEY WASN'T SURE whether nerves or the baby had affected her appetite, but she could put away a mountain of food these days. Zach didn't seem to mind when she finished her stuffed mushrooms and asked for one of his cheese sticks, and he gave her some of his steak before she even thought to ask. Dessert was cherries jubilee—she enjoyed every bite and thought she'd probably have room left for a sandwich before bedtime. Unless...

Unless she and Zach were otherwise occupied.

She couldn't tell if he expected the evening to end in bed. More than halfway through dinner, she still didn't know why he'd called. Surely he wanted more than this casual flirting, a lighthearted conversation between friends. They weren't friends. And they weren't lovers, exactly. Shelley couldn't define what she and Zach were to each other.

Besides the parents of a child.

She shook her head to clear the thought. As long as she kept the baby out of her mind, she could keep the subject out of conversation. Zach wouldn't want to know.

Would he?

"You said you're coaching Little League," she ventured as they walked to his car after dinner. "How old are the kids?"

He closed her door, came around and got in. "Ten to twelve. They're a lot of fun."

"What's your record so far?"

"Three won, four lost. Do you like baseball?"

"I played softball in high school." And she might be watching Little League games in a few years. "Coaching takes up a lot of time, when you don't get paid." She came closer to the point. "And when you don't have kids of your own."

"That's the way I like it. When they're tired and

dirty and hungry, somebody else takes them home, listens to them whine, yells at them to take a bath and fixes their dinner. Me, I pick up some fast food and a good book and stay as far away from the family trap as I can.''

And that was that. Shelley turned to stare out the window, blinking back tears and giving up on a stillborn hope.

''What kind of music do you like…? Shelley? You still with me?''

She didn't hear him for a few seconds, and had to recall his question. ''Oh…whatever's on, I guess. I don't listen to much music.''

''How do you feel about hearing some jazz tonight?''

Shelley pasted on her professional smile and turned in the seat to face him. ''Sounds like fun.''

She was surprised to find that she did, indeed, have fun. The Indigo Jazz and Blues Club bulged at the seams with people, but the owner, Jimmy Falcon, took her and Zach to a reserved table near the stage. The group they listened to played music she enjoyed, Zach kept her glass filled with ice water while he drank soda, and they shared a bowl of popcorn.

Best of all, they couldn't talk much. And she couldn't think much, with the band so close and the music loud. Jimmy came over during intermission and sat with them, preventing any personal conversation at all. More music, more drinks, two trips for Shelley to the crowded rest room. She checked her makeup in the mirror and noticed that her linen dress hadn't wrinkled too badly. She avoided thinking about anything else.

They stayed until the last set ended, until the club emptied and the staff started to stack the chairs. Jimmy and Zach reminisced about some of their funnier exploits as police partners. Shelley laughed a lot, which was better than crying.

Then she and Zach were in the car on the way back to her house. The silence begged to be filled, but avoiding the subject uppermost in her mind tied her tongue.

She fell back on professional patter. "Where do you live? Do you rent or own?"

"Southeast from downtown. I own a bungalow with lots of trees, casement windows and antique plumbing."

"You live alone?"

He flashed a grin. "Yeah. I waited almost thirty years to get my own bathroom. Now I don't share with anybody."

You shared with me, three months ago. Shelley didn't voice the protest aloud. "Property values have gone up in that area of the city. You've probably got good equity accumulating. Have you thought about moving into something with better plumbing?"

"I'm staying put. I'd like to get the place paid off in another ten years, and then I won't owe anybody."

"No credit cards?"

"I pay those off every month."

"No car loan?"

"Paid off last year."

"Impressive money management," she said, and meant it. "Living within your income is a lost art these days."

"Does that make me an old codger?" There was that grin again.

Shelley couldn't help smiling back. "If the dirt-brown sweater with darned moth holes and worn elbows fits..."

"I'm throwing it out first thing tomorrow morning!"

They laughed together, and Shelley tried to relax. But the closer they got to her house, the more her dinner started to unsettle. She planned to invite Zach in for coffee, expected him to say yes. After that, the situation would get dangerous. If he stayed for anything more, she really wasn't sure she could—or should—keep her secret.

Finally, they crossed the front lawn through a warm summer night filled with cricket songs and starshine. Shelley unlocked the door, stepped inside and turned on the lamps in the foyer. "Would you like a cup of coffee?"

He stood on the threshold and stared back at her, an expression in his blue eyes she couldn't read. Finally, he shook his head. "All that soda has me wired. Thanks, anyway."

Shelley swallowed hard, nearly drowning in disappointment. Tonight must have been some kind of test—and she'd failed. Zach didn't like spending time with her, didn't want to sleep with her again. He hadn't called for three months, then thought maybe he should double-check his judgment, to be sure. One more dose of Shelley Hightower convinced him that he'd had enough. On to the next candidate.

Well, he didn't need to know how much that hurt. "I had a great time this evening. The Indigo was a real pleasure. Tell Jimmy thanks for the special treatment.'' She started to close the door.

''Shelley?''

She looked out into the dark, saw his face caught in the line of light from indoors and hardened her heart against his cocky grin. ''Yes?''

The chill in her voice banished that grin. He backed up a step. ''Sleep tight.''

''You, too.'' She shut the door before he'd even turned around, and locked it.

Leaning back against the panel, she let herself slide down to the floor. There, she drew up her knees and curled her shoulders and bowed her head, cradling her baby with all of herself.

''It's you and me together, kid,'' she whispered. ''And we're going to make it…on our own!''

CHAPTER FOUR

ZACH STOOD on the front porch and stared at the door to Shelley's house until the lights went off inside.

What the hell just happened?

He thought about ringing the bell, or pounding the damn door down. He thought about serenading under Shelley's window, assuming he could figure out which one belonged to her bedroom. He thought about sleeping on her doorstep and facing her over the morning paper.

In the end, he shoved his hands in his pockets and walked to the car. He carefully kept to the speed limit until he hit the interstate. Then he floored the gas. The Trans Am growled its way up to seventy, heading north.

After an hour of fast driving, he exited, got fuel and a soda, then started back to Denver. He reached the city limits without finding an answer to his question.

What the hell had happened?

All evening, he'd had the feeling he couldn't quite reach her. She'd been wary from the minute he walked into the house—except for the kiss. He'd known exactly where they were during that kiss.

And then, just as he was about to ask for another date, she froze him out.

"What did I do?" Zach stalked into his house and threw his keys on the kitchen counter. "What didn't I do?"

The only response was the blinking light on his answering machine. Darius the Perfect Persian strolled in, winked golden eyes and strolled out again.

"Glad to see you, too." Zach had adopted Claire's cat when she married. After two years, he and Dar had come to tolerate each other, and sometimes even sat on the couch at the same time. Not much of a replacement for Claire, but the best either of them could do, since Darius hated ranch life with a passion.

Pulling a carton of milk out of the refrigerator, Zach punched the message button on the machine as he took a swig.

"Zachary, it's Mom. Please call, no matter how late you get in."

She sounded well, but worried. Zach picked up the phone and hit the autodial number for his mother. Family problems would give him something to think about besides Shelley.

His mother's wide-awake "Hello" told him just how worried she was.

"Hi, Mom. It's Zach. What's wrong?"

"You sound strange. Are you okay?"

"I'm fine. Why did you call?"

"Your sister was nearly arrested tonight."

Zach choked on his milk. "Which sister?"

"Carol, of course."

"What happened?"

"She was caught shoplifting in a store at the mall."

"Damn. Did they book her?"

"Don't swear, Zachary. No, the officer let her off with a warning. But you have to talk to her."

"Mom—"

"You're the only one she listens to these days. Ever since your father died, nothing I say seems to matter."

He sighed quietly. "Okay, I'll talk to her. Is tomorrow soon enough?"

"Of course. I'll expect you for lunch after church."

"I'll be there."

"Sleep well, Zachary."

Yeah, right. "You, too, Mom."

Zach punched the phone's off button and set it back into the cradle. Finishing the last of the milk, he trashed the carton, flipped off the light and headed for the bedroom.

As predicted, sleep didn't come easily. He couldn't get his little sister out of his mind. She'd taken their dad's death hard—they all had. Zach had spent time with her for his own sake, as well as hers. He taught her to bat and pitch, shot hoops with her, took her and her best friend to Broncos games. She'd been busier since she started high school last September—more involved with friends and social events—so he'd seen less of her, which he'd considered progress for both of them.

Flopping over in bed, he groaned. "Guess that's another mistake I'll have to correct."

Like the mysterious goof with Shelley. Should he

call her again? Would she call him? Or was her brush-off tonight a not-so-subtle hint that she didn't want to see him anymore? He wasn't her type—she went for high-powered, high-profile, high-profit guys like her ex-husband.

"Damn her, anyway," he growled, bunching up the pillow. "I've got better things to do than chase after a woman who's not interested. Right, Dar, buddy?"

Zach turned his head and eyed the cat reclining in the blue wing chair, his usual throne. A circle of light from the street lamp outside spotlighted long white fur, an indolent pose, enigmatic eyes. As he watched, Darius lifted a paw, carefully cleaned the pads with a few elegant sweeps of his pink tongue, then lowered his head and closed his eyes. In another second, he was snoring.

"Gee, thanks, pal. You're a prince." Zach smoothed the pillow and tried to settle in again. "If that's what getting neutered does for you, maybe I should be talking to the vet!"

BECAUSE SHE USUALLY worked Sunday afternoons, Shelley made a point each week of calling her daughter by 8:00 a.m., before Allyson's father took her to church.

This morning, Allyson herself answered. "Hello?"

Shelley sighed with pleasure. Just a single word from her daughter soothed like summer rain. "Hi, baby. How are you?"

"I'm good. And guess what, Mommy? We have new kittens!"

"How many? What colors?" She didn't care what they talked about, as long as they kept in touch. Allyson updated details on her horse, Stormy, and his training progress, relayed every minute of the camping trip she'd taken with her dad and explained how her best friend from Cheyenne would be coming to visit for two whole weeks.

"And guess what else?" Her young voice reached its highest pitch. "We're going to have a baby!"

Shelley dropped the phone. *How could she know?*

When her cold hand had fumbled the phone back to her ear, she apologized and cleared her throat. "What did you say, Allyson, honey?"

"Claire's going to have a baby!"

"Oh. How—how wonderful." Shelley closed her eyes as the room around her dipped and swayed. "You and your dad must be excited."

"Yeah, and we're going to make a nursery here on the ranch and I'll get to teach her to ride and everything."

Despite the sick feeling in her stomach, Shelley had to smile. "You're sure the baby's a girl?"

"Well..." She sounded as if she'd never considered the alternative. "I hope so. A boy wouldn't be as much fun."

They talked a while longer, making some plans for the summer. "Grandmom's going to be there, isn't she?" Allyson asked.

"She wouldn't miss seeing you for the world. When she comes over this morning, I'll tell her what we're planning."

"Can we make ice cream like we did before?"

Pulled out of the doldrums, Shelley laughed. "I

know we can. You like Grandmom's ice cream, don't you?''

"It's good!" As they ended the conversation, Allyson said, "Daddy wants to say something, Mommy. I love you. Bye!"

"Bye, baby." She took a deep breath in preparation. Talking with her ex usually tied her in knots.

"Hi, Shelley." His voice had picked up the hint of a cowboy drawl during his years on the Wyoming range. "How are you?"

"Just fine, Dexter. I hear you have good news."

"Yeah." The pride in his voice reminded her of nine years ago, when she'd been carrying Allyson. "We're pretty happy."

"Congratulations." The perfect woman had accomplished the perfect task, perfectly. Unlike a certain unwed mother...

Dex didn't need to know that, at least, not yet. She wasn't ready to deal with his reaction. "Are we still on schedule for Allyson to come down in mid-July and spend the rest of the summer?"

"That's the plan. I'll call you when we leave, so you'll know what time to expect us."

"I'll wait to hear from you, Dexter. Give... Claire...my compliments."

"I will." He paused, and then said. "Are you sure you're doing all right?"

"Of course." Except for making an absolute mess of her life. "I'll let you go. Kiss Allyson for me."

"Sure. Goodbye, Shelley."

She pushed the button to disconnect without a reply. Then she buried her head in her arms on the kitchen counter and cried.

Minutes later, her mother came through the garage door into the kitchen. "Honey?" Gentle arms circled Shelley's shoulders from behind, drawing her into a soft embrace. A cool hand brushed back her hair. "Shelley, what's wrong?"

After a struggle, she managed to get the sobbing down to hiccups. "I—I just talked to Allyson."

Dorothy Owens was passionate about two things in life—her independence and her family. She tightened her hold. "Allyson's okay? She hasn't gotten hurt?"

"No. Oh, no." Shelley broke free, slid off the chair and went to get a paper towel to wipe her eyes and blow her nose. "No, everything is wonderful in Wyoming. Claire is pregnant."

Her mother's brown eyes widened. "I see. That's…"

"Yes, isn't it?" She took a shaking breath. "But here's the really funny part, Mom—I am, too."

"You are what?"

"Pregnant."

This pause lasted even longer, while surprise changed into shock. "I didn't know you were seeing anybody."

"I wasn't. I'm not." New tears spilled over, and she grabbed another paper towel. "He isn't interested."

"He must have been—" Dorothy took a deep breath and brushed the feathery silver bangs off her forehead. "Never mind that. You and I seem to have a talent for picking the wrong man."

"At least you were only stupid once. I make the same mistakes over and over again."

Her mother filled the teakettle and put it on the cooktop. "Have you seen a doctor?"

Shelley nodded.

"And what happens when the baby is born?"

Still sniffling, Shelley left the kitchen for her light-washed family room. The windows looked east toward the plains and the morning sun. "When the baby is born, I bring her or him home. With me."

"Do you think that's a good idea?"

"Oh, yes." She turned to face her mother. "That's one thing I am sure of. I want to be this baby's mom. I want to take the time to raise this little person like I never did with Allyson. I missed so much, going back to work, leaving her with au pairs and nannies. This time, I'm going to be the person who hears that first word, sees that first step."

Even from the kitchen, she could hear the maternal sigh. "Single parenting is tough. But you have the money to be comfortable, at least."

"That's right. I don't have to depend on anyone else for help. I can do this all by myself. In fact, I think I'll like it that way." She wouldn't lose control of her life—and her child—to a man this time.

Dorothy brought in a mug of tea. "So you've told the father and he wouldn't take responsibility?"

"Um, no." Shelley fiddled with the string on the blinds. "I—I haven't told him."

"Then how do you know—"

She let the string swing free. "Because we talked. Because he made things clear—no ties, no commitment, no family. And because I know he'd try to change if he knew, and then we'd all be unhappy. It'll be better this way."

The line between her mother's eyebrows conveyed doubt. "I don't think you're being fair. He's bound to find out, isn't he?"

"Not if I don't see him again." She'd figure out later how to avoid Zach forever.

"But what if you bump into him?"

"I'll tell him the baby is someone else's." An expression of horror crept over her mother's face. Shelley put up a hand. "I know, that's terrible to do. I've been through one custody battle, though, and I can't do it again. I can't take the risk that he'll drag me into court. I *want* this baby—he doesn't." She spread her fingers across her stomach. "And I'm going to keep it."

"But, Shelley...what are you going to tell your daughter?"

"Good question." She sighed, and the tears returned. "Sometime between now and July I'll have to figure that out."

HE SHOULD HAVE DECIDED what he was going to say before he arrived.

Zach dropped onto the couch in the family room of his mom's house. His sister sat at the opposite end, staring off into space.

"Hey," he said.

Carol didn't move, not even to brush the green-tinted bangs out of her eyes. She had his mother's straight, dark hair, their dad's small frame and height. The current lopsided cut and streaks of rebellious color didn't disguise her essential prettiness.

He tried again. "I hear there's been some trouble."

This time, she rolled her eyes.

"Stealing is a crime, you know."

She muttered a rude word. "I was gonna take it back. Nobody would keep such dumb stuff, anyway."

"Why'd you steal in the first place?"

"I wanted to." Her shrug dismissed the issue.

He'd talked to his mother and gotten a few more details. "What's this club you're into at school?"

"Just some friends." Carol shrugged.

"Girls? Guys? Both?"

"Girls."

"Name?"

She sighed. "Crooked Women."

"And that means...?"

"We look at life differently from the rest of you."

"And from this different perspective, taking property that doesn't belong to you is okay?"

"It was an initiation stunt, that's all!"

"Have you known these other girls a long time?"

"Some of them. Jen just moved into the school this year. She started CW."

"What about your best friend...Samantha, right? Is she in this group?"

She stared at him as if he spoke in Martian. "Sam moved away. To Florida. Before last Thanksgiving. Remember?"

Strikeout. He sat forward and propped his elbows on his knees. "So, you have more initiation stuff planned?"

Carol shrugged, but she picked nervously at the black polish on her fingernails, which gave him his answer.

"What are the goals of this Crooked crew?"

"Nothing. We just hang together, that's all. It's no big deal."

"I disagree, little sister. You're letting somebody else's screwed-up ideas ruin your life. Not to mention your mother's, and mine. That makes it a big deal."

Silence claimed the room. Sounds of the traditional Harmon Sunday ball game drifted in through the open window. Zach would have preferred to be out there pitching balls, instead of in here pitching discipline.

Carol brought him back to the moment. "So what am I supposed to do? Apologize?"

Zach shook his head. "We tried that last time, after the water balloons out the third-floor windows—didn't seem to make an impression. I'm assigning my own version of community service."

She looked at him in outrage. "What does that mean?"

"You're coming to ball practice with me to work with my batters. I've got some baby-sitting ideas, too. See you here tomorrow at five." Case closed. He stood and started for the door.

"And what if I'm somewhere else?"

He stopped with his hand on the knob and glanced over his shoulder. "You won't be. Otherwise, I can arrange for you to try out juvenile hall for a day or two. See how you like the alternative."

As the daughter and sister of cops, Carol would know she didn't want detention. He heard her tortured sigh as he shut the door, but she'd be here tomorrow. Zach knew he could trust her that far.

His mother caught up with him in the kitchen as

he took an apple out of the refrigerator. "Have you settled that girl, Zachary?" She'd been to the basement for a pan full of potatoes. Her face was flushed from climbing the steep stairs.

"Yes, Mom." Like he'd been settling things since he was twelve years old. "I'm gonna bring her to baseball practice, see if I can get more information out on this club nonsense."

"Good. I hardly know what to do with her anymore." She set to washing the potatoes. "We're having pot roast for dinner. You'll stay, won't you?"

His parents had eaten pot roast for dinner on Sunday every week for the forty years of their marriage. Now that his dad wasn't here to demand the same meal, maybe they could change the ritual. "How about we go out to dinner, instead? I'll take you to a decent Italian place I know."

Mary Harmon shook her head. "That is nice, Zachary, but Sunday is pot roast. Maybe another time?"

"Sure, Mom." He thought about staying, because he loved her. But he couldn't face pot roast. "I'm gonna catch up on paperwork before I go on duty, so I'll eat later. See you tomorrow." He gave her a kiss and a hug, then made his escape out the back door.

The ball game had ended. Most of the players sprawled in the backyard shade, drinking sodas and arguing points.

"That pitch was wide by a mile!" Grant—the tallest of the Harmon clan—took a swallow of beer. "Never thought a brother of mine would be so blind."

"Not blind. Accurate." Stefan lay on the grass, a sweating can against his forehead. "That pitch was a strike."

"Yeah, right. And Jess didn't drop the ball on the last out, either."

"I wouldn't have dropped it," Jessica said calmly, "if Michael hadn't knocked into me. Of all the dumb moves—"

Michael sat up. "If you had called the ball, I wouldn't have been there!"

Zach stood listening for a minute as the noise escalated. He'd been part of this scene his whole life—Sunday-morning Mass, lunch, sports and fights all afternoon, pot roast for dinner. But tonight the circle felt too tight.

"See you guys later," he called. "I've got work to do."

"See ya'!" "Be careful out there." "Call me!" The goodbyes followed him out to the Trans Am. Zach got into the car, punched up a jazz CD and increased the volume. He waved to all the neighbors as he drove down the street, but kept his windows up and didn't stop to talk.

He resolutely didn't think about spending the afternoon with Shelley, either. The case had closed on that situation, too.

AT THE PRECINCT station, he changed into his uniform and headed out on patrol. Life as a street coop wasn't as exciting as, say, vice or criminal investigations. but Zach figured there were people out here with problems—traffic accidents, temporarily misplaced kids, vandalism and harassment—who needed a cop's help. He liked providing that kind of assistance.

As he circled the park, a young couple playing on the swings caught his attention, just because they looked so happy together. With his window down, he could hear them laughing. They would make a great advertisement—"Denver is for lovers."

An hour later, he saw them again, this time on the street near some of the bars. Good times had given way to an argument. The young woman stood, arms crossed, back toward her boyfriend, with her chin tilted in defiance as he yelled at her from behind. Before Zach turned the corner, the guy threw his hands in the air and stalked into the nearest joint. The lady appeared not to care.

Zach circled the block and came back to the scene in less than ten minutes. There was no sign of the couple. Following his instinct, he parked on the opposite side of the street, crossed over to the dive he'd seen the man enter, and found himself in a cave filed with smoke and the fumes of beer.

"We don't need the cops," the bartender said, without preamble. "Ain't no trouble here."

"I can see that, Joey. I'm just checking things out."

"Yeah, sure."

"I thought there might have been an argument in here, the last hour or so. A cute lady, giving her man a hard time?"

"Do I keep track of the whole frigging world?"

Zach stared, and the bartender gave in. "Yeah, they were here."

"Did they buy drinks?"

"They came in a couple times. The guy bought maybe five beers all together. Drank 'em down like water. And then they left and I ain't seen them since. Happy?"

"Delirious. Have a good night." Zach returned to the almost empty street. Which way would she have gone to make her point?

He turned right and started walking, quietly. No one passed him, and the twilight came down without a sound. He'd almost decided to turn back when he heard a small, agonized sob.

She was huddled in the next alley, between up-ended garbage cans and plastic bags stuffed with trash. Zach crouched down in front of her. "Officer Harmon, Denver police, ma'am. Let me help you."

But she flinched and shrank back, putting a hand out to ward him off. "No," she whispered. "No more, please. No…"

Zach took her hand, seeing broken nails and a bruised wrist. "He's gone. I promise. Nobody's going to hurt you. Can you stand up?"

She didn't seem to hear. Zach pulled his radio off his belt and called for EMTs and backup. Then he tried again. "I won't hurt you. I promise. Do you hear me?"

Her head came up, and she focused on his face. For the first time, Zach realized how young she was. Too young for bars, barely old enough for high school. Her dark hair and eyes reminded him of Carol, and his stomach started to churn.

"He's gone?" she whispered.

"Yeah. You're safe. Can you stand up?"

The girl sighed. "I think so." When he helped her

to her feet, Zach got another blow beneath the belt. She was pregnant. Not much, but enough for him to be sure.

He moved her away from the garbage as the ambulance stopped beside them. In seconds the EMTs had her on a stretcher, where they could treat the split lip, the swelling along her jaw and above her eyes.

Once they had her stabilized, Zach stepped close. "Who hit you?" he asked quietly.

The girl only stared at him, her swollen lips pressed together.

"Do you know the person who did this?" She closed her eyes. "Please. We need his name so we can punish him for hurting you."

But she shook her head, and kept her eyes closed. Zach got a signal from the EMTs, who were ready to move, and he backed away. The ambulance pulled out in a flare of red and white light, leaving him standing in the street feeling sick.

"You see anybody?" Rafe Delgado, a cop who often shared shifts with Zach, came up beside him.

"Yeah, I saw the bastard. Six feet tall, dark hair in a ponytail. T-shirt and jeans, silver-toed boots. Urban cowboy type."

Rafe wrote the description down. "The boots should help. Her cooperation would be even better."

"Maybe her family will know." He wiped his face with a shaking hand.

"Maybe." Rafe clapped him on the shoulder. "We'll finish up here. If you see the guy again call me."

"If he's still alive."

His friend laughed. "If he's still alive."

Zach got back into his car, but the memory of that girl's battered face kept him motionless. Pregnant, no wedding ring, hanging out with a guy who beat her up when she made him mad. What kind of life was that? How did she get herself into such a lousy situation?

And what could he do to keep Carol from taking the same path?

CHAPTER FIVE

THE MIDDLE OF JULY arrived at last. Allyson was due any minute to spend the last six weeks of the summer with her mother.

Shelley had worked out the perfect plan for their talk. She wasn't showing much yet, but she didn't want to wait until her daughter noticed something. After Allyson had spent the afternoon in the pool, after they'd had a good dinner, they would sit down together and Shelley would explain the facts of life as they now stood.

In the meantime, she paced the house, straightening, dusting, rearranging knickknacks. She stood at the big front window for long minutes, as if staring at the street outside could make Dex's car, with Allyson inside, appear. Her stomach tightened like a screw and she tried to eat, but only felt worse. She changed clothes twice, hoping to look as slim as possible.

When the doorbell finally rang, she ran down the staircase, heart in her throat, to fling open the door. "Allyson? Baby, how are you?"

She bent down, and a pair of strong, slender arms circled her neck tight. Sweet-smelling black curls tickled her cheek and ear as Allyson's head burrowed into her shoulder. "Hi, Mommy! I'm here!"

"You are." Shelley hugged tighter. "Oh, you feel so good."

"You smell good, Mommy. Like always."

"Thanks, baby. Here, let me see you."

She let Allyson step back a bit. Short hair, shiny black like her dad's, and his direct gray gaze. Freckles on her nose—she'd been in the sun. A sturdy body, taller than Shelley remembered. "You keep growing!"

"Two inches this year," Allyson announced proudly. "I had to let my stirrups down."

"Wow." For the first time, Shelley became aware of the man and woman standing in the doorway. Her face heated as she straightened up. "Hello, Dexter. Claire. Sorry—I didn't see you for a minute. Come in."

"That's fine, Shelley. How are you?" Attorney Claire Cavanaugh Hightower stepped inside. She looked poised and graceful...and more pregnant than Shelley. But still elegant, with her glossy golden hair and dancer's poise. Her simple, expensive clothes made everyone else look over dressed.

"Just great, now that Allyson's here." Shelley ruffled her daughter's curls. "Would you like something to drink?"

Claire smiled and shook her head. "Thanks, but we both have meetings downtown. We'll just leave Allyson to get settled."

Dex had stayed on the threshold. "Allyson, come and help me get your gear out of the car."

"Yessir. Wait'll you see my new bathing suit, Mommy. It's really neato." She ran out and her father followed, leaving Shelley alone with the perfect woman.

"Why don't we sit down?" Shelley motioned Claire into the living room, where they both perched on the edge of white velvet armchairs. "Congratulations on your baby."

"Thank you." I have to admit I'm thrilled and scared to death, all at the same time."

"Scared?" The one who could do anything was scared?

"I haven't spent much time with babies. I'm not completely sure how to start."

Shelley shrugged. "Feed them, change them, hold them. Then as they grow, you just sort of figure out what to do next. Of course, I'm no expert."

"Allyson's a pretty special person. You've done a wonderful job." Claire's smile was friendly, her sleepy eyes kind.

Barely breathing, Shelley gazed at the woman across the room. This was as close to a truce as they'd ever come. She didn't know if she had the courage to accept the peace Claire offered.

"Dexter has a lot to do with who Allyson is," Shelley admitted. "He's a good dad."

"I'm counting on that." Claire turned her head as Dex and Allyson came back in the house. "Do you have everything?"

Allyson dumped her two suitcases and a gym bag on the floor. "Everything. Oh—except for the books in the back seat." She rushed out again.

"I'll get her to take these upstairs," Dex said.

Shelley followed Claire back into the entry hall. "Don't worry about it. We have all day." She got a sharp look from her ex-husband—no doubt he remembered the days when she'd been a fanatic about the house staying tidy.

Well, things changed.

Allyson came back inside with her armload of books. "I have to read all of these this summer, Mommy."

"We'd better get started, then."

Allyson's goodbyes to Dex and Claire lasted quite a while. "Take care of Stormy for me, Daddy."

"I will, Punkin'." He knelt to give her a hug.

She drew back. "And Britches and the kittens."

"Count on it."

"And tell Dr. Jeff I'll be back to see him before school starts, and he should tell Emily I'll play with her then."

"Yes, ma'am."

"Have a good time, sweetheart." Claire bent to deliver her own kiss, and Shelley watched with only a twinge of jealousy. They all loved their little girl—that's what mattered, right?

Allyson hugged her hard. "Mommy and I always have a good time. Are you gonna see Uncle Zach while you're here?"

"I think so."

"Tell him I said hi and he should come see me."

Dex glanced at Shelley. "Maybe you should check with your mom before you hand out invitations, Punkin'."

"Mommy always lets me have friends over. And she likes Uncle Zach. Don't you, Mommy?"

Shelley cleared her throat. "Of course. But he might be busy. We'll have to see how things go."

Finally, Dex and Claire left, waving from the windows of his Mercedes as they drove slowly down the street.

With a sigh, Allyson turned inside. Shelley shut the door. "Sad already? Do you want to go back to Wyoming?"

"No way," Allyson assured her. "I just wish we could all be together, instead of living so far apart."

"I know." She put her arms around her tall eight-year-old. "I wish we could have done that for you. But your dad is happy with Claire."

"Yep." Allyson put her head on Shelley's breast for a sweet moment. "Don't you need somebody, too, Mommy?"

"I've got *you*," Shelley said. "And…" she took a deep breath. Her careful plan flew out the window "…we need to have a talk."

In the kitchen, Shelley poured a glass of milk for Allyson and one for herself, then got down the box of bakery cookies she'd bought.

"You like milk, Mommy?"

"Sometimes." She sat beside her daughter at the counter.

"I like chocolate milk."

"I remember." *Here goes.* "Allyson, I know you're excited about Claire's baby."

"Uh-huh." She nodded, her mouth full of oat-meal-raisin crumbles.

"Well, I need to tell you that I'm going to have a baby, too."

Allyson swallowed. "Cool!" Then her face changed. "But Mommy—you're not married."

"No, I'm not."

"How can you have a baby if you're not married?"

Shelley dragged in another deep breath. "We've talked about how babies are made, right?" Allyson nodded. "Well, sometimes a man and a woman get...close enough...to make a baby without being married."

"Does that mean the baby won't have a daddy?"

"Not—not right now. People don't always stay together after they've made a baby. So...I'm going to be a mom by myself."

Allyson's eyes narrowed as she concentrated—a look Shelley had often seen on Dex's face. "That sounds like a hard thing to do."

"Well, I have you to help me, right? I know you're going to be a wonderful big sister."

"I won't be here all the time. Maybe Greta could come back?"

Greta was the last au pair Shelley hired before Allyson went to live with her father. "No, I'm going to stay home with this baby. At least for a while."

Allyson thought some more. "I still think there should be a daddy."

"There should be. And—and maybe there will be, someday. Just not now. Can you accept that?"

"Okay. Just tell me when you need help."

Shelley hugged her daughter again. "Count on it, baby. I love you."

"Love you, too, Mom. Can I go for a swim?"

That hadn't gone so badly, after all. "Let's see who gets her suit on first!"

WHEN THE PHONE RANG on a Friday night in late July, Zach thought twice about answering. He was quite happy in his solitude. Really.

On the other hand...

He caught the phone just before the answering machine picked up. "Harmon."

"Uncle Zach? It's me—Allyson."

"Hey, Ally Cat! How's my favorite person in the world?"

"I'm great. You know where I am?"

He settled back in his chair to play the game. "Uh...Timbuktu?"

"Nope."

"Iceland?"

Allyson giggled. "Nope."

"A little place in Wyoming called Flying Rock?"

"I'm right here!"

"Where? I don't see you."

"Not there, silly. At Mommy's house."

"That's right—Clarie told me." Before he thought about it, he said, "How's your mom?" And then winced.

"She's good." Allyson didn't notice undercurrents. "Can you come over?"

Zach sat up straight again. "Did your mom say I could?"

"Yep. When can you come?"

"Well..." Had Shelley agreed to this? Did she want to see him?

"Please?"

"Sure, Ally Cat. I'll be there. Can I talk to your mom a minute?"

"She had to work tonight. My grandmom's babysitting. Mom will be here tomorrow, though."

"I'll see her then. Thanks, Allyson."

"Okay, Uncle Zach."

He hung up the phone more enthusiastic than he'd been about anything besides baseball this summer. Allyson had been his friend since the first time they met, and he'd visited her—and Claire, of course—in Wyoming several times.

The Falcons won their game Saturday morning—a good omen, he decided. Maybe he would take Shelley and Allyson out for an early dinner. Nowhere fancy, just a fun place where the talk would be casual and easy. Shelley didn't want any pressure. Fine.

But Zach wanted another chance.

THE FOLLOWING AFTERNOON, the Hightower house looked friendlier than usual, with the garage door open and a girl's skates and helmet lying in the driveway. Shelley's white Mercedes sat inside the garage—an encouraging sight. She could have run away. Maybe this effort would turn out even better than he'd hoped.

He rang the doorbell and waited with his hands in his pockets. From within, he heard the sound of running feet and then a voice. "No, Allyson, don't open the door until I get there. I've told you—"

The blue door swung back. Allyson stood on the threshold, with her mother just behind her. Shelley pushed back her hair and looked up. At the sight of him, she started to smile—but then her face paled and her eyes widened with the proverbial seen-a-ghost stare.

"Uncle Zach!"

Zach cleared his throat. "Hi, Ally Cat. How are you, Shelley?"

She didn't answer.

Allyson took his hand and tugged. "Come in, Uncle Zach! Come in!"

With a sinking feeling in his gut, Zach stepped inside. "Hey, Allyson, I thought your mom knew I was coming. She looks pretty surprised."

"I—" Allyson ducked her curly black head. "I knew she'd be glad to see you, 'cause you're my friend. She told me I could have a friend over, and I chose you!"

Simple reasoning, hard to deconstruct. He turned toward the woman who'd retreated to stand by the staircase. "I'm sorry. I did think—"

His thought evaporated. He noted Shelley's hair, longer now than in June, a tumble of soft, white-gold curls. He noticed her tanned, shapely legs, with a drop of his heart remembering how the skin felt under his palms.

But the real news was between her head and her feet. Shelley was pregnant. Quite definitely expecting a baby.

Allyson was talking the way she always did, a mile a minute. Zach couldn't understand her words through the buzzing in his ears. Instinctively, he dropped his gaze to Shelley's left hand. She wore a ring on her third finger, a wide gold band.

There was a *husband?* Since June?

Another fact hit him. She'd been pregnant when he took her out to dinner that night. Maybe the reason she'd been hard to reach was right in front of his eyes. A wedding. And a baby.

Allyson pulled at his hand again. "Have you seen our pool, Uncle Zach? I can swim all the way from one end to the other. Want me to show you?"

"What's that?" He shook his head to clear it. "Sure. I'd like to see you swim."

"Your bathing suit is upstairs, Allyson." Shelley's voice sounded as if her throat had closed.

"Be right back!" Allyson took the stairs two at a time and disappeared at the top into a doorway on the right. The song she hummed floated down to the marble-floored entrance hall.

When Shelley walked toward the back of the house, Zach followed. She finally came to a stop at a window on the farthest wall of the family room from where he stood. He took two more steps forward, then halted. "Congratulations." His voice didn't sound any better than hers.

"Thanks." She glanced out the window—looking for an escape route?

Zach knew he only had a few minutes before Allyson came back. Somehow he had to understand this situation, with his brain as scrambled as eggs in a frying pan.

And he had no right even to ask the questions punching at him.

Were you seeing somebody when we spent the weekend together? Was that just a run-through for the wedding night? Where is this guy, anyway, and what makes him different from the other losers you picked? What about me?

He stared at the woman across the room. After watching his mother with four babies of her own that he could remember, he gauged that Shelley was about five months along.

"Wait a minute." His stomach went hollow as Zach started connecting with reality again. Five months, more or less—he'd bet an obstetrician's yearly wages on the timing. Counting backward, that was July, June, May, April…March.

The baby would have been conceived in March. Which meant—

"Shelley." His voice shook badly. She turned to face him.

He cleared his throat. "Look me in the eye and tell me that's not my baby you're carrying."

SHELLEY WANTED to scream at him. *What are you doing here? Why can't you leave me alone?*

But she gathered her breath and her thoughts, instead. The worst had happened, but if she could just persuade him…

"No, Zach. I'm sorry you were worried. This isn't your baby."

His eyes narrowed. "I don't believe you. When are you due?"

"November." She could be really small for six months.

He took one hand out of his pocket to run through his hair. "Can you fill me in, here? You're married now?"

Damn. She'd forgotten to take the make-believe ring off after work last night. "Yes. At the beginning of the month." She could only pray he wouldn't ask Allyson to verify that statement.

"Kinda sudden, wasn't it? I mean...you didn't mention a fiancé in June."

Here came the really hard part. "Actually, I've been seeing Mark for over a year. We'd broken up in February, when..." She couldn't find words to describe that weekend. "I was pretty down on him. But he called and we...worked things out...and...got married July first."

"I see." His fist went back into his pocket. Just looking at him was torture—summer sun had bronzed his face and lightened his hair, and his eyes shone bright blue in contrast. A knit shirt the color of butter showed off the tan on his arms. Strong arms, Shelley remembered. Strong and tight around her when they danced. And when they made love...

Allyson ran into the room. "C'mon, Uncle Zach. Watch me swim!"

He stared at Shelley as if he hadn't heard.

"Would you like a beer?" she asked, hoping to break that grim gaze.

"Sure." She practically heard a *snap!* as he turned his head and followed Allyson out to the pool. Slowly, carefully, she walked to a chair at the kitchen table and there, finally, relaxed her shaky knees.

What a nightmare! When Allyson said she'd planned a surprise, Shelley had never dreamed it would be Zach.

Had she convinced him? What would she do if he didn't believe her?

And how could she sit through the afternoon talking as if nothing had happened between them, as if none of this mattered at all?

Taking a deep breath, she stood up again. Somehow, she would. She had to, or all her careful plans would crumble. She'd made a career of submitting feelings to calculation. She could do what the moment demanded.

And fall apart later.

When she went outside again, Zach had pulled a chair to the edge of the pool. He sat there barefoot, cheering Allyson on. Shelley swallowed hard. The man had such nicely shaped feet.

She took him the beer. "Thanks," he said, looking up at her with a distance in his gaze she despised, yet needed. "You sit here and I'll get another chair." He stood and pulled over a second chair. They both sat down. "Ally Cat swims like a fish, doesn't she?"

"She's always loved the water. Or anything active and outdoors, really. Listen, Zach—"

He spoke at the same time. "Shelley, I want—"

They fell silent, but there was none of the usual laughter such situations produced. Zach found his voice first. "I really thought you knew I'd be coming over." He stared at the mug turning between his fingers. "I'm sorry I showed up and made things awkward for you."

She admired his generosity in taking the blame. "And I'm sorry my daughter played such a thoughtless trick on both of us. I'll talk to her about that later. She's so glad to see you, I hate to spoil her pleasure with a lecture."

"I'm okay, if you are. You don't need to yell at her on my account."

Like strangers, they were talking without actually looking at each other. Even his voice had changed. He sounded official—the cop she'd first met—instead of the man who'd made love to her during a wild weekend in March.

"She put us both in an embarrassing position, and I have a feeling she knew that ahead of time." Shelley watched the troublemaker swim the length of the pool underwater. "Allyson has a habit of wanting her own way and causing trouble if she doesn't get it. I'm scared to think about what happens when she gets to be a teenager."

Zach chuckled. "I can tell you that. My youngest sister is fourteen, and she's driving my mother crazy."

"Doing what?" She couldn't resist the urge to look at him. "I'd better be prepared."

"The latest stunt was getting her navel pierced. Without checking with any of us first."

"I'll bet that went over well."

"Yeah." He glanced over with a smile. "She's gotten involved with some kind of group at school organized around the principle of challenging parents at every opportunity. Carol was even picked up for shoplifting, back in…June." After a pause, he went on smoothly enough. "That didn't do much for my mom, the cop's widow, or my brother, and sister, the cops. Or me."

"I guess not. How does your mother handle stuff like this?"

He slouched down in his chair and took a long sip of beer. "Usually she calls me. Carol and I are pretty close, have been since I got out of the army when my dad died. So sometimes she's prepared to listen to me."

"Can't any of your other siblings help?"

"My brother Grant was diagnosed with leukemia when he was a kid. Mom was pretty busy with him. Dad worked as a cop, plus nightshift as a security guard. As the other kids came along, I sorta took charge. And, I guess, the habit stuck."

No wonder he didn't want children. He'd already raised a family. "So you're keeping tabs on your sister. How'd she get away to get the piercing done?"

He sighed. "She said she went to a movie. But my sister-in-law dropped her off without staying to watch and make sure Carol paid for a ticket and went inside. The little sneak waited until the coast was clear, then called her friends and ran around for two hours."

"That's scary."

He nodded, not looking at her. "Definitely scary."

Allyson came to a stop just below them and leaned on the edge of the pool. "I did ten whole laps, Mommy. Did you see me swim underwater?"

"I did. You're as good as a seal. You've got a drink over on the table."

"Thanks!" The splash of Allyson's turn as she headed for the ladder spattered Shelley from the waist down.

"Ack!" Shaking off her hands, she looked over to find Zach in the same shape. "I'm sorry—let me get you a towel."

"Don't worry about it." He was laughing, thank goodness. "Sun'll dry me in just a few minutes. But you're drenched. Maybe you…should…change."

His words slowed as he looked her over. Shelley glanced down and saw that she'd gotten wetter than she first realized. The light knit of her T-shirt dress now clung all too closely to her rounded stomach. She looked exactly what she was. Pregnant.

With *Mark's* baby. Remember Mark.

"That's probably a good idea," Shelley grabbed at the chance to escape. "I'll be right back."

And just in case, maybe she'd better spend the time figuring out where her imaginary husband was this afternoon, before she got hit with a question she obviously couldn't answer.

ZACH WATCHED Shelley hurry into the house as if she couldn't get away fast enough. Which made sense, since having him here had to remind her of that weekend...something her new *husband* wouldn't be happy to know about. Zach could sympathize— thinking of Shelley with another man didn't exactly brighten his day.

Fortunately, a distraction sat nearby. He joined her at the table. "Hey, Ally Cat—you're quite a swimmer."

"Thanks!" She had wrapped herself in a towel and sat at the table with a glass of lemonade. "Are you going to swim, too?"

"Didn't bring my suit. But you got me wet—does that count?"

She grinned. "Sorry. Did you know we're having a baby?"

For a second, the earth shifted underneath him, at least a five on the Richter scale. Which baby did she mean? "Are you excited?"

"Oh, yeah. It'll be cool to have somebody to play with."

He still wasn't sure who they were talking about. "I bet. What do you think the baby's name will be?"

"I like Matilda. But Daddy's not too sure about that."

Zach relaxed a little. That would mean Claire's baby. "What if it's a boy?"

"No way." She shook her head and spattered him with a few more drops of water. "I want a girl."

"Okay." He had an overwhelming urge to push the topic, to ask about Shelley's baby, about Shelley's husband. But he didn't intend to interrogate a child. "What are you doing to keep busy down here?"

As Allyson described a trip to the zoo in Colorado Springs, shopping, concerts, and more shopping, Shelley came out onto the deck in dry clothes. Her shorts and shirt in a crisp, lime green linen made her look almost as slim as ever, almost as slender as the nights he'd held her in his arms...

Wrong train of thought. "Sounds like you're having a great time this summer."

"Oh, yes." She sat down across the table from him and Allyson. "Next week we're going down to Phoenix for a few nights to visit my grandparents. After that, we might fly to San Diego. I haven't been to the coast in a long time."

"Cool!" Allyson bounced in her chair. "Can we go to Sea World?"

"I wouldn't miss it." Shelley leaned forward to ruffle wet black curls. "And the Wild Animal Park. And the zoo. You'll be sick of animals by the time you get home again."

"Not me. I'm gonna be a vet when I grow up. Dr. Jeff said I could work with him."

"Dr. Jeff is...?"

"The vet in Wyoming, Mommy. 'Member?"

"That's right."

For a second, the light in Shelley's face dimmed at the mention of Wyoming, and Zach got a glimpse of the hurt she still carried. For a reason he didn't want to think about, he came to the rescue with a change of subject. "That sounds like a great plan. Better keep your grades up."

"I made straight A's this year."

"Good job! What do you think fourth grade will be like?"

"Hard." They talked for a while about school and sports and Darius the Perfect Persian. When the drinks were finished, Allyson jumped up. "I'm going back in—watch me dive, Uncle Zach!"

Zach stood, too. "Before you get wet again, Ally Cat, I'd better say goodbye. I've got some work to do this afternoon."

Her lower lip stuck out. "Do you have to go? I wanted you to stay for supper. He can stay, can't he, Mommy?"

Shelley hesitated, and Zach knew he'd made the right choice. "Thanks, I'd like to. But if I don't get these reports done, I'll spend all week trying to catch up. Maybe another time." Not that there would be another time, with *Mark* in the picture.

"But you could stay a little while, couldn't you?"

"Allyson." Shelley silenced the little girl with a raised hand. "Arguing isn't polite and won't change his mind. Let's just say goodbye, okay?"

"Okay." Her woeful sigh could have melted a heart of granite.

Zach squeezed her shoulder. "Good girl. Look, I'm coaching a baseball team this summer. I'll bring you to a game, okay?"

"Cool!" She danced into the house ahead of him, with her mother following them. At the doorway, Zach stood back for Shelley to go first.

She started to pass him, then stopped and looked up. "You're really good with her. Thanks."

"My pleasure." They were close enough that he could touch her face, almost close enough for a kiss. But she was married, wasn't she? And pregnant. Off-limits. Right?

In the cavernous entrance hall, he gave Allyson a hug. "Take care of your mom, Ally Cat. I'll call you about the ball game." He stood up. "You're welcome to come, Shelley. We're hoping to reach the playoffs. I've got a really good team."

"Sounds like fun. I'll see if I can get free."

As Zach turned and opened the door, the devil he thought he'd conquered took hold of his will. He looked back over his shoulder. "I'm sorry I missed Mark. He can come to the game, too, by the way."

"Mark?" Allyson's clear voice echoed off the walls. "Who's Mark?"

CHAPTER SIX

As the silence intensified, even Allyson began to realize something was wrong. She looked from her mother to Zach and back again. "Mommy?"

Zach finally remembered how to breathe. "Shelley, I think we need to talk."

She had lost every bit of color in her face. "Not now."

"Yes. Now." Damned if he'd leave until this was straightened out.

On cue, Allyson piped up again. "Who's Mark?"

Since Shelley wasn't moving, Zach did. He crossed to put a hand on the girl's shoulder. "Nobody to worry about, Ally Cat. But your mom and I need to talk by ourselves. Can you watch TV or something?"

"I want to go back in the pool."

"Not right now, Allyson." Shelley's voice was dry and low. "You know you can't swim without someone there. Give me a few minutes, and then I'll go out with you. Meanwhile you can watch the movie we bought."

The girl looked from one adult to the other, and whatever she saw in their faces must have convinced her. Without another protest, she headed up the staircase. In moments, the opening music from *Peter Pan* drifted down into the hall.

Zach took a deep breath. "Where can we talk?"

Shelley didn't say anything. But she turned and led him through a hallway on the left side of the house, to a room at the very end. He stepped through the open door into a cool green space with blinds at the windows. A big desk sat in the center of the floor, its top covered with neat stacks of paper. The only chair was the one at the desk.

Behind him, the door shut. A switch clicked and overhead lights came on, dousing the shadows with an impersonal fluorescent glow.

When nothing else happened, Zach turned around. Shelley stood by the door, back against the wall, eyes wide, hands fisted at her sides. "What do you want?"

"There's no Mark, is there?"

"No."

"What about the ring?"

She shrugged. "I made up a husband and a wedding for the clients. Some of them are uncomfortable, with…"

"The fact that you're pregnant?"

"Yes."

"With my child."

"Yes."

"You weren't planning to tell me."

"No."

"Why the hell not?"

"I didn't think you'd want to know."

"You didn't—" She was right. This was just

about the last thing he'd ever wanted to hear. "We were careful!"

She sighed, then shrugged. "There's only one fail-proof method of birth control. Abstinence. And we didn't use that one."

Zach shoved his hands into his pockets and paced across to the window. The half-opened blind gave him a view of the pool and the smooth lawn beyond the deck. He watched heat waves shimmer over the concrete for a minute, trying to control the shakes in his knees. "Exactly what were you planning to do?"

"I am planning to have a baby."

Invisible hands squeezed his throat. "By your-self?"

"It's not a team sport."

He faced her. "Parenting should be."

She hadn't moved. "I've been a single parent. I grew up with a single parent. That works okay."

"Two parents work better."

"Maybe."

"Damn, Shelley. I had a right to know about this."

"I'm sorry." He'd never heard her voice so con-trolled, so flat. "But I understood your plans didn't include kids of your own."

"I don't shove my responsibilities onto someone else's plate!"

Her mouth twisted. "Neither do I. But we aren't your responsibility."

"Of course you are."

"No, what happened was...an accident. We should have walked away. But we didn't. Decisions have consequences."

"For both of us." Zach swallowed hard. "We have to get married, Shelley."

She stared at him for a few seconds. And then laughed, a low, regretful sound. "Thanks but no thanks. Now, if you're finished—"

"No, damm it, I'm not finished! You can't just throw me out."

"I'm not throwing you out. But I think we've said all there is to say."

"Wrong." He tried to gentle his voice. "Why won't you marry me?"

"Because I don't want to. Because I don't need to."

"Why don't you think about what the baby needs?"

Her dark eyes flashed. "Oh, and what's that? A father coerced into marriage? A family tied together by mistake?" She chopped at the air with the side of her hand. "Two people who have nothing in common but sex trying to act like parents?"

Zach gritted his teeth. "That's not the situation."

"Yes, that is the situation. And I'm not interested in being part of such a wreck. Again."

That put him solidly in the picture. She'd said herself, her first marriage had been a disaster. A thought struck him. "Does Allyson know?"

"About the baby, of course."

"About me?"

"No." One word. Wielded like a machete.

He waited to speak until he could trust his voice. "What did you tell her?"

"That I would do this by myself, with her to help."

Eyes closed, he wished for another beer. "Don't stall, Shelley."

"That the father wasn't interested."

"You lied." He opened his eyes to watch her face.

"Did I really?" She looked almost amused. "Do you want to be a dad?"

"Just because I didn't plan this—"

"Wouldn't you much rather just walk away?"

The same devil that prompted him to start this conversation now tempted him to do just what she suggested. Walk away. Forget Shelley. Forget there was a baby. She was willing to handle this alone. So let her.

Bile burned in his throat. "I can't do that. Whatever I want, the fact is a child of mine is coming into the world. I'm prepared to take on that obligation."

Shelley bent her head, and for a second he thought she might start to cry. That would be helpful—if he touched her, tried to comfort her, maybe they could salvage something out of this disaster.

But then she looked up. Her distant, hostile expression defeated his hopes. "I don't see how you can assume any *obligation* unless I choose to let you. And I don't."

The last of his patience evaporated. "I'm trying to help you, damn it!"

"The biggest help you can be, Zach, is to walk away."

He stared at her, trying to see past the mask. But there were no seams, no edges. If she wanted anything different from what she was saying—if she thought he had any rights at all in this situation—she wasn't about to let him know.

The control in her voice only made him furious. "Great. Just great." He pulled his hands out of his pockets, stalked to the door and flung it open. "I hope you don't come to regret this decision."

"Thanks for the concern."

Her sarcasm bit like a snake. He left without a goodbye, without even a call to Allyson. He shut the front door firmly behind him.

So much for second chances.

SHELLEY STAYED where she was until she heard the front door close. A distant roar assured her Zach had driven away.

Blinded by agony, she crossed to her desk and felt along the edge. When she reached the chair, she fell onto the seat and dropped her head on her arms.

Zach. His reaction had been justified…and unbearable. If she'd ever cherished the faintest spark of hope that somehow he might want their baby, want her, this afternoon had killed it.

We have to get married. Obligation. Responsibility.

He couldn't have made his feelings any clearer. He would take care of her and the baby because his sense of honor demanded he do so. His family and his church and society would expect that gesture.

But he didn't want the commitment. Didn't want the baby—or her. Maybe especially her.

We have to get married. When he'd actually said the words, she'd almost agreed, out of her own need.

But she'd seen his face. Zach couldn't hide the fact that he'd never planned for marriage, for children.

"No." She said it aloud, sitting up straight again, determined to get back on her feet. "No chance in hell. Get over the idea that there's a white knight waiting to rescue you. That's not the way life works, Shelley. You're a grown-up. Start acting like one."

ZACH SKIPPED the family lunch on Sunday. He couldn't face his mother with Shelley and the baby on his conscience.

He had a hard time facing himself in the mirror. So he opted not to shave, not to go out, not to get dressed beyond the gym shorts and T-shirt he slept in.

But he sat down at his desk about ten o'clock to call a lawyer. "Hi, Claire. How are you?"

"Wonderful, Zach. What about you?"

He was going to have to learn to lie better. "Not too bad. How's your summer?"

"Slower than usual. Dex worries about my driving so much now. I'm staying home more and working on some notes for a book. Tell me about the Falcons' season. Are you winning?"

"Going great. If we win the next two games, we'll be in the playoffs in August."

"Thanks to expert coaching."

"Yeah, sure." He picked up a paper clip, balanced it on the end of his thumb. "Listen, I wanted to ask you a semiprofessional question."

"Shoot."

He managed a chuckle. "Take a cop's advice—be real careful who you say that to these days."

She laughed. "Yessir. Now, what's your question?"

"In your experience, what are the chances of a single dad getting custody of his child?" That sounded like a casual question, didn't it?

"Better than a couple of years ago, when Dex went after custody of Allyson. But not really good, if the mother resists. Visitation is usually the most viable option. Is someone going through a messy divorce?"

"No—this couple hasn't been married." He pulled the paper clip into a straight wire.

"Boy, did the percentages just drop. You'd have to have some strong arguments before a judge would consider a custody petition. Even then, I'd be pessimistic. Visitation rights for unwed fathers are more common these days, though."

"That's what I thought." Zach concentrated on coiling the wire around the barrel of a pencil.

"Are you okay? Is everything all right down there?"

Once he would have confided in Claire. But today he couldn't. "Sure, Counselor." He tossed the ruined paper clip into the trash. "Everything's right as rain. Fill me in on this book of yours."

Zach listened, asked the right questions and promised to treat her to lunch the next time she came to Denver. Hanging up, he went into the kitchen confident that he'd handled the consultation pretty well. He'd given Claire no reason to think he was the dad involved.

And she'd given him no reason to hope that he

could use the court system to get more than occasional access to his baby.

He paused in the act of pouring coffee. Now that he knew there was a baby out there with his genes...what? What did he think? How did he feel?

Irritated, he decided while vacuuming the living room. Given that he and Shelley had used birth control, he thought the universe had played a dirty trick in letting this happen.

Resentful, when he pictured the lifestyle he'd built being destroyed. He *liked* living alone, dammit. He liked his house neat and his time free for what he chose to do. He did not want to be tied to nap schedules and the demands of hungry kids. He'd lost his childhood to those pressures. Why give up more years?

"So don't." The answer seemed to come from Darius as they both stretched out on the couch in the afternoon sunshine. "Shelley's taken the responsibility. She doesn't want you in the picture. Play by her rules. Forget the baby even exists."

Closing his eyes, Zach decided he might just take that advice. If he was going to be selfish, why not do the job right?

TWO WEEKS LATER, the Falcons made the playoffs. By the time Zach got to the field for the first game of the series, Jimmy had started the team on their warm-up.

"Sorry, man." Zach dropped the bag of bats and balls with a clunk. "Didn't even hear the alarm."

"No problem. They're halfway through their run around the field." Jimmy glanced at him once, then a second time, lifting his black shades for emphasis. "You look rotten."

"Had a late night."

"More than one, I'd say."

"Okay, a few late nights. And I changed shifts. Always throws me."

"That's what I like about you, Harmon." Jimmy clapped him on the shoulder as the first Falcon ran toward the dugout. "You have a talent for burning the candle at both ends without going up in smoke."

The players mobbed them and saved Zach the problem of a reply. "Hey, Coach!" "Let's go, Coach!" "Where ya' been?" "You're late!"

"Yeah, I blew it, guys. Sorry. But I'm ready now. Are you?"

He sent them onto the diamond to field his hits, though every contact of ball with bat magnified the invisible sledgehammer pounding on his head. When the umpire signaled to give the other players their practice time, the Falcons gathered in the dugout for his final words of inspiration.

Zach had never felt less inspiring. But he knew what to say. "This is just a game, guys. Goal number one—have fun. Goal number two—work to improve your personal best. Goal number three—win the game. Got it?"

They shouted the team chant in unison. "Soar, Falcons, soar!"

Just as his first batter stepped up to the plate, a voice came from the fence beside the dugout. "Uncle Zach! Uncle Zach!"

He summoned a grin and turned. "Hi, Ally Cat! Glad you could make it."

"Can I watch there with you?"

"Sorry…" He glanced toward the field as the ump called strike one. "Only team members in here for now. Get yourself a place high on the bleachers." By major force of will, he did not scan the crowd for whoever had brought Allyson to the game.

Whoever? Yeah, right.

His team groaned as a second strike was called. "I gotta go, Ally Cat. Later, okay?"

"Sure. Good luck."

Zach turned back to the field in time to see his first batter strike out. "That's okay, Kenny. You'll get 'em next time."

The second batter doubled. Then Cinda stepped up. Zach watched with half his brain, hoping for a good hit to put them on the board. With the other half, he wondered if Shelley had come.

Fourteen days had passed since that afternoon at Shelley's house. As Jimmy noticed, Zach had spent the time doing what he did best—living free, staying out late, getting up early for the day shift. After the first week, he'd kept his drinking to a minimum, because he couldn't work with a hangover. And the cab fares were eating him alive.

He'd dated six—no, seven—different women. A redhead, three blondes, three brunettes. None of them danced, but they liked the jazz at the Indigo, or the movie he suggested, or the experimental-theater productions. They were easy to be with, laughed at his jokes and signaled an interest in doing more with him than just laughing.

Somehow, though, he couldn't make himself accept their invitations. And he hadn't called any of them a second time.

He'd called Shelley's number instead, only to get the answering machine. Leaving a message about today's game, he hadn't really expected to get a call back. And he'd been right.

Which only proved that she was every bit as stubborn as he thought.

He brought his mind back to the ball game. Cinda took a mighty swing, but the second baseman was ready. She made first before the throw, and the other runner made third. One more hit, and they'd have a run on the board.

"Eye on the ball, Tim. Make him pitch to you!"

Short, stocky Tim planted his feet and cocked his bat. The pitcher stretched. Strike one.

Tim adjusted the batting helmet and set his stance again.

The crack of the bat surprised Zach. He watched with his mouth open as the ball sailed over the second baseman's head. Cinda rounded third and headed home. Two runs, guaranteed. The Falcon bench went crazy.

Tim's big hit proved to be a good-luck omen. The Falcons won six runs to two. Their next playoff game this afternoon was against an easier team and Zach felt pretty good about the chances of a championship.

Allyson caught up with him in the middle of the postgame celebration. "Congratulations, Uncle Zach! You won!"

He picked her up and twirled her around. "We did, didn't we? Did you enjoy the game?"

"Oh, yeah! I want to play baseball. Do you think I could?"

"Don't see why not, Ally Cat. You're a—"

He stopped as a woman rounded the corner of the bleachers. Shelley?

"I'm what? What, Uncle Zach?"

"A born athlete. That's what you are." No, not Shelley. This was an older woman—a little heavier than Shelley, and definitely not pregnant. Short white hair feathered around a face in which he recognized Shelley's dark eyes and pointed chin.

Hanging on to his hand, Allyson dragged him toward the woman. "I'm gonna play baseball, Grandmom. Can we go get a ball and a bat so I can start practicing?"

A warm smile met that request. "I think we probably have your mom's bat and ball at my house. Her glove, too."

"Cool!" Letting go of Zach, Allyson went to the bottom of the bleachers and started up, using the benches as stair steps.

"Careful, Allyson." The smile faded as Shelley's mother looked at Zach. "I'm Dorothy Owens. Allyson's grandmother."

"Zach Harmon, Ms. Owens." He shook her hand. "Glad to meet you."

"I've heard a lot about 'Uncle Zach.'" Her cool gaze sized him up, but he couldn't read her opinion. "Congratulations on your win."

"Thanks. I'm glad you two came to watch. I thought Allyson might still be in California."

"They got in yesterday and picked up your message," she told him. "I asked if I could bring Allyson—I enjoy a good game. You've got some strong players.''

He struggled for the right thing to say. He couldn't exactly ask about Shelley. ''The team's going for pizza—would you and Allyson like to come?''

''We'd better not, thanks.''

Allyson suddenly popped up from nowhere. ''Grandmom, let's go with them. It's lunchtime and I'm hungry.''

Dorothy Owens shook her head. ''I don't think so.''

''Please? Please, please, please?''

''If you wouldn't mind, I could bring Allyson home afterward. In fact, she could stay through the second game and be home for dinner. What do you think?''

''Grandmom, please?''

Shelley's mother glanced at Zach, then nodded. ''I guess that would be all right with your mom. But you have to promise not to wander off anywhere while Zach is busy with the game.''

''I promise.''

''A friend of mine is here.'' Zach kept his voice easy, though he felt like crowing. ''He'll keep an eye on her.''

''Great. I'll let Shelley know you'll be bringing Allyson home late this afternoon.''

''Count on it.'' He watched Dorothy Owens walk away, realizing that for the first time in two weeks he could genuinely smile.

''You look about a thousand percent better.''

Jimmy came up beside him. "You really wanted this win."

"I haven't won yet." Zach loaded bats and balls into the bag. Then he grinned at Jimmy. "But at least I'm back in the game!"

CHAPTER SEVEN

"YOU DID WHAT?" Shelley shifted the phone to her other ear and prayed she'd misunderstood her mother.

"I let Allyson stay at the game. Zach Harmon said he would bring her home late this afternoon."

"Mother!" Shelley covered her eyes with one shaking hand.

"I assumed that would be okay. Allyson talks about him all the time. I thought he was a friend of her stepmother's." She paused. "And yours. He's certainly a personable, good-looking young man."

"Well, yes, but—"

"Am I wrong?" Dorothy Owens's voice took on an edge of concern. "I'm still close to the ballpark. Should I go back to get her?"

"No...oh, no." She pulled her scattered thoughts together. "Zach will make sure Allyson's fine. He's a great guy."

"Hmm." Her mother let a few seconds go by. "And how do you react when the guy's not so great?"

Shelley laughed without humor. "Those are the ones I date."

Shortly after five, the Trans Am rumbled into the driveway. With dread fluttering in her throat, Shelley opened the front door. "Thanks for bringing her home, Zach." She eased Allyson back against her. "I know she enjoyed her afternoon."

Looking up, Allyson nodded. "Except the Falcons lost. Can I play on Zach's team next year?"

"That's...hard to say right now, baby."

"But it would be fun."

Shelley held on to her patience—barely. The man on the porch didn't say a word to help. "Next summer is a long way away, Allyson."

"But, Mommy—"

Zach broke in. "Shelley, can we talk outside a minute?"

That was not the help she wanted. "I don't—"

"Please."

Finally, she looked directly at him, seeing in his tired eyes a reserve she could blame only on herself. Whatever he had to say, she should at least listen.

And then he would go away. Wouldn't he? "Of course. Allyson, there's a snack on the kitchen counter. I'll be right here."

"Okay. Thanks, Uncle Zach. I had lots of fun at the ball game."

"You're welcome, Ally Cat. Be good."

Shelley stepped out and closed the door behind her, keeping her back against it. "I'm sorry you got knocked out of the playoffs."

He shrugged. "Kids need to learn to lose as well as win." Hands in his pockets, he leaned sideways on the column in the corner of the porch, diagonally as far away from her as possible.

He didn't say anything for so long, she got nervous. "Zach—"

"Shelley—" he started at the same time.

"Go ahead," they said together, and then fell silent, staring out over the lawn in opposite directions.

Zach cleared his throat. "What I wanted to say is plain and simple. I'm asking you again—will you marry me?"

At least he had the wording right this time. But nothing else had changed. "No, Zach."

"Why not?"

Shelley dragged in a deep breath. She would get out of this. She would make him leave her alone. "Did your parents love each other?"

He shrugged. "Sure."

"Why would you settle for anything less?"

"Shelley—"

She'd taken the afternoon to work out her reasoning, in case he forced a scene like this. "How successful could a marriage be, based on coercion?"

His mouth tightened, but he didn't answer.

"A bad marriage is bad for the child, not just the parents." No one could argue with that, not even Zach. "Sacrificing yourself won't do me or the baby any good. And vice versa."

He stood still for a long time, staring down at his shoes. Shelley watched the sun move over him, pulling glints of gold out of his hair, bringing a shine to his skin. She missed his grin and the laugh in those blue eyes, the kind, easy-going man she'd known in March.

"Well." Zach drew a deep breath. "You've got everything covered. I guess all I have to do is exit, stage left." Pushing off the column, he jolted down the steps to the walk.

"Thanks for trying." She said it softly. If he didn't hear, that would be even easier.

But he turned to face her, his hands still deep in the pockets of his shorts. "My pleasure. Be seeing you."

Weren't social conventions wonderful? "Of course. Take care."

She waited outside while he started the car and backed down the driveway. Neither of them waved as he passed the front of the house—she couldn't even be sure he saw her.

"Done." Shelley said the word aloud, for emphasis.

Trying to feel relieved, she opened the front door and stepped into the house, glancing at the mirror on the wall.

So if everything had gone just the way she wanted...why did she have mascara-streaked tears running over her cheeks?

WHEN IT CAME to escaping the Harmon family's watchful eye, cutting loose was as easy as melting ice cream in August. Mention the word *library* and nobody at home asked any more questions.

After her brother, Grant, dropped her off at the front door, Carol walked inside, straight past all the shelves, down the stairs and out the lower-level entrance. In the parking lot, Jen had pulled her new Mazda up to the curb. Ten seconds later, they were headed downtown. Freedom!

"Whew!" Jen blew out a plume of smoke. "Feels good, huh?"

In the back seat, Faith lit her own cigarette. "Extremely good," she agreed, passing the lighter and the pack to Carol.

Wishing she liked the taste better, Carol put a cigarette between her lips, clicked the flame to life and breathed in. An acid fog filled her mouth and lungs, but she managed not to cough. She blew out as soon as possible and handed the lighter back. "Thanks."

"Where we going?" Diane, in the front seat, scrubbed at her short bleached hair. "Somewhere crazy, I hope."

"Always crazy," Jen announced. "Crazy or Crooked, yes?"

Everybody else laughed, and Carol joined in. This was the life she wanted—limited only by *her* decisions, enjoyed with *her* friends, adding to *her* experience. Getting away from all the rules her family laid down was like crawling out from under a concrete slab. Finally, she could breathe!

But experience was a little hard to come by on a hot summer Saturday in Denver. They hung around City Park for a while, doing crazy stunts on the playground equipment...until a lady with two little boys chased them off. At Jen's suggestion they bypassed the museum and wandered into the zoo, where Diane threw pieces of popcorn into the monkey cages.

Carol almost protested—the signs clearly warned against feeding the animals. But that would make Jen mad. And it didn't really matter, did it?

The chimps hopped down to the floor, grabbing up the treats. Laughing, Jen and Faith threw handfuls of popcorn. Carol took a fist of kernels, but couldn't bring herself to toss them into the cage. She made sure her popcorn fell in the gutter outside the bars.

A deep voice broke through the racket of excited monkeys. "That's enough!"

She looked over her shoulder...and way, way up, into the face of a security guard.

He was young, and easy to look at—for the straight-line, short-haired type, anyway. But he wasn't in the mood to flirt. "Do you see the sign? No human food for the animals."

"Aw, man, we were just fooling around." Jen grinned at him. Carol had a feeling she was trying for sexy. "No harm done."

"We don't know that," the guard said. "But if you can't follow the rules, you won't be allowed to stay."

"I'm not leavin'." Diane folded her arms. "You can't make me."

The guard stared at her with contempt plain on his face. "Don't tempt me, little girl. I'd enjoy calling the police and letting them solve your attitude problems."

Carol closed her eyes. With her luck, Zach would show up. She wasn't sure exactly where his precinct officially stopped, but she knew he considered the whole downtown district his territory. Another incident like the shoplifting collar, and he'd condemn her to baby-sitting for life.

She tugged on Diane's shirttail. "Come on, let's leave. There's nothing fun here, anyway."

Jen started to protest. But, without moving a muscle, the guard managed to look even bigger and meaner than before. With a shrug, she turned toward the exit. Diane and Faith followed. Carol thankfully brought up the rear.

Back in the car, another round of cigarettes got started.

"Stupid pig." Jen threw the gear stick into reverse and backed up with a screech. "Like those monkeys don't eat popcorn every damn day."

"Forget it. Let's get to the real action." Diane practiced blowing smoke rings.

Carol buckled her seat belt. "What's the plan?" Jen or Diane always had a plan.

"You'll see." Jen glanced over her left shoulder, then threw her cigarette out the window. "I've been wanting to do this ever since I moved here."

She drove into the business district, which was pretty much deserted for the weekend. Tall buildings towered over them, creating shade that felt almost cool. Carol looked up at the windows, wondering what kind of work went on in all the offices above their heads. Did the people like their jobs? Did they like their *lives?*

The car stopped, and she looked down again. They had stopped on one side of an empty street. The only sound was the warm wind blowing bits of paper along the sidewalk.

"Okay," Faith said. "Now what?"

"Let's go." Jen got out and walked to the back of the Mazda. By the time Carol and the others came around, she had the trunk open and her supplies ready. "For you." She handed Diane a can of spray paint. "And you." Carol and Faith got paintbrushes. "And me." She held up another paint can. "Let's go."

Graffiti? On all this marble? Carol hung back, with

a picture of Zach in her head. He didn't get mad often, but when he did...

"Come on, Harmon!" Jen motioned as she started across the street, with Faith and Diane behind her.

Carol caught up as they stopped in front of a fancy, old-fashioned-looking building. "The Bull Pen," she read aloud. "What are we doing here?"

"We're gonna liven up the place." Jen pointed. "See those?"

"Those" were two life-size, black marble statues of cattle—bulls, Carol supposed—standing guard from the top of a pedestal on either side of the Bull Pen's door. "I don't get it."

"This is, like, one of the biggest, richest clubs in town." Diane snorted. "They don't let women join."

"How do you know?" Carol said. "And isn't that against the law?"

"My daddy's a member. They get around the law somehow. Probably bribes."

"So what are we doing here?" Carol asked.

Jen smiled. "Watch." She walked to the nearest bull. Her head reached to about his shoulder. Putting the spray can on the pedestal, she hoisted herself to sit beside the statue. Grinning now, she took the top off the can and shook it until the mixers inside rattled. Then she started spraying.

Carol gasped. Faith and Diane screamed, then ran to the other statue. In minutes, the bulls had gold zebra stripes, along with gold on the ends of their tales, their noses and their horns.

"Come on, Harmon! This is cool!"

No, this was crazy. Carol wavered, trying to de-

cide what to do. It wasn't as though they were hurting people, exactly...

She stepped forward, raising her brush, just as a
car squealed to a stop on their side of the street. The
door opened and a man exploded into the sunlight.
"What the hell do you think you're doing?"

"Run!" Jen yelled. She didn't have to say it twice.
Carol sprinted up the street, with Faith and Diane at
her back. Footsteps pounded the pavement behind
them. A glance to the rear showed Carol a fat man
in a suit, cursing and trying to catch up. She doubled
her speed, flung herself at the Mazda's door handle
and dived into the car.

"Hurry! Hurry!" Jen revved the engine and
started moving before Diane got the door closed.
"Let's get out of here!"

The car swerved and jerked through the empty
streets. Carol fought to buckle her seat belt.

Jen was half laughing, half swearing as she tried
to get out of the business district. The streets kept
going in the wrong direction. "Damn. I'm gonna turn
down one of these streets in a minute, no matter
which way it goes."

A siren sounded in the distance. "Go, girl," Diane
said. "They're after us."

"You got it." Jen glanced to her left, then turned
the wheel hard right at the next intersection.

"Slow down, Jen—" Carol glanced across the intersection at the traffic signs.

Faith screamed. "There's a car!"

"Oh my God." Diane turned around as if she
planned to scramble between the seats into the back.

Carol caught a glimpse of the car facing

them...then shut her eyes. Metal screeched and moaned. Guns exploded nearby—at least that what it sounded like. Something shoved her forward against Diane, against the seat belt, and into the headrest of the front seat. Somebody screamed again.

The last word she heard was one she would have gotten her mouth washed out for at home.

THE PETITE MEXICAN WOMAN spoke English—but her speed and accent made the words a blur. Still, Zach grasped the general idea.

"Yes, Mrs. Alvarado." He wrote down the details of the graffiti on her wall. "Yes, ma'am, I know you're tired of this. I know this is the third time this year."

Finishing the description, he pocketed his notebook. Mrs. Alvarado didn't pause for breath, even when he held out his card. "Yes, ma'am. We'll do everything we can. My pager number is there in the corner of the card. Anytime you see somebody out here you don't like the looks of, page me and I'll get here as fast as humanly possible. We'll see if we can't get these guys to clean up their mess."

His radio chirped, then blared. A traffic accident, right in the middle of his precinct. "I need to go, Mrs. Alvarado." Zach saluted her off the brim of his hat and backed down the walk.

Mrs. Alvarado followed, still talking. Her voice rang in his ears as he drove away.

Zach reached the location of the wreck in minutes. A head-on collision at the corner of a one-way street had left a sporty Japanese model looking like crumpled aluminum foil. Another police unit had arrived ahead of him, but the fire and ambulance sirens still hailed from a distance.

He picked his way through a field of glass around the nearest vehicle. Another officer leaned into an old Cadillac, checking the driver's pulse. Zach put his hand on the cop's shoulder. "You've got backup, Rafe. How about the other car?"

Rafe straightened up. "A bunch of teenagers. They're alive, but they're all hurt. And, Zach—" He put a hand on Zach's arm. "One of them is Carol."

Zach stared blankly for a second, while his insides froze. "You said…"

"Alive." Rafe nodded. "You stay with this guy, I'll go to the girls."

"No." Zach held up a hand. "No, I can do it. I'm okay."

But his stomach clenched as he saw the damage to the Mazda. Someone inside was sobbing. At the front passenger door he looked through the open window, seeing only exploded air bags.

He swallowed against nausea. "Everybody stay still. The police are here, and we'll take care of you. Just relax."

"Get me out of this thing!" The driver struggled with her air bag.

"As soon as we can, I promise." The back window on the passenger side had crazed but not collapsed. He carefully tried the door, and was surprised when it actually opened.

Carol stared out at him. Tears rolled down her face. "Zach?"

"Everything's going to be fine, sweetheart." He steadied his voice with a deep breath, reached out to touch her cheek. "I'll get you out in a few minutes. How's your friend?"

Another girl lay with her shoulders in Carol's lap, moving her head from side to side. "I don't know," Carol whispered. "I don't...know...what happened."

The ambulance and fire department arrived; in seconds the area swarmed with uniforms. Zach followed orders from the rescue squad, providing support and a shoulder where needed to get the girls out. All of them were in shock, bruised, battered. The driver of the Cadillac had suffered cuts from the glass. But because of air bags and the fact that the big car had been stationary when the Mazda turned the corner, the mess looked a hell of lot worse than it actually was.

Still, cleanup would take a while. Zach directed traffic around the site, helped set up barricades, controlled the crowd. Only as the ambulance with Carol inside was packing up did he ask Rafe to take his place.

The EMTs allowed him to crawl in next to the patient. He took her hand. "You're going to be fine."

"Thanks." Her lips quivered. "Mom..."

"I'll tell Mom. Don't worry. She's strong. And you'll be home again tomorrow, with her to fuss over you."

"Or at me."

Zach grinned. "That, too. I'll wait my turn until she's finished."

She closed her eyes. "Gee, thanks. Is Jen okay? Faith and Diane?"

"Sure. You guys can have a pajama party at the hospital tonight."

"We're ready to go, Sergeant." An EMT stood just outside the ambulance door.

"Right." Zach bent to give Carol a kiss. "I'll be right behind you."

She gave him a shaky smile. Satisfied, he backed out and jumped down. The ambulance pulled away, and the scene finally quieted down.

Which meant Zach now had time freedom to think about what might have happened here.

After he'd found a quiet alley and a trash can in which to lose his breakfast, he arranged a substitute for the rest of his shift and drove to his mother's house. She went white when he gave her the news, and swayed a little. But then, in seconds, she was bustling again, packing up clothes and a couple of books for Carol, getting herself neatened up with fresh lipstick and a spritz of cologne.

In spite of himself, Zach chuckled. Mary Harmon could face anything with lipstick and cologne.

Carol looked so pitiful when they reached her at the hospital that neither of them fussed at her. Jen's parents didn't bother to restrain themselves, and their voices could be heard in the hallway outside the girls' rooms.

Grant arrived an hour later and raged up and down the hall for a few minutes. But when he emerged from seeing their sister, the anger had died.

"What's going on with her?" he asked Zach. "She could have—"

Neither of them needed to say it. "Yeah." Zach rubbed a hand over his face. "She's headstrong and

independent and determined to do her own thing."
He thought of another woman with those same qual-
ities. "And I'm just about the last person these days
who knows how to deal with that."

CHAPTER EIGHT

BECAUSE DEX would surely recognize her pregnancy when he came to pick up Allyson at the end of August, Shelley called a few days ahead of time, to warn him.

The line hummed with a stunned silence. "Shelley," he said finally. "I don't know what to say."

"You don't have to say anything. Allyson will probably be talking about it, so I wanted to let you know."

"What are your plans?"

"My plan is to be a better mother this time."

"You're keeping the baby?"

"Yes, I am." She braced for his protest.

Another pause. "You aren't thinking about... marriage?"

"No." She wouldn't elaborate unless he forced her. And how could he do that, all the way from Wyoming?

"I...see." Dex cleared his throat. "Let me know if there's anything Claire and I can do."

"Thank you, but we'll be fine. What time should Allyson be ready to leave on Saturday?"

"Sometime midafternoon?"

So soon. "Okay. See you then."

"Sure."

She spent her last few days with Allyson playing in the pool, shopping and packing. "You've grown so much this year." Shelley folded a new pair of jeans. "I'll bet all of last winter's clothes are too small."

Allyson hung a velvet dress in the closet. "Now I can save those clothes for my little sister—she'll have things to wear when she grows up." Her face grew thoughtful, and she was quiet for a few minutes.

"Mommy?"

"Yes?"

"When am I coming back to see you?"

"Well..." Travel would be more difficult this autumn, Shelley realized for the first time. "I was thinking your dad might let you come down in October. And then there's Thanksgiving—you're due to be here this year."

"So I'll see you again before—" She hesitated, her expression uncertain. "Before your baby comes?"

"Sure you will. At Thanksgiving, we'll do our Christmas shopping together, like always." Shelley went to the closet and folded Allyson in a hug. "I'll always be your mom, you know."

"I know." Allyson's voice was muffled against her breast.

"Even though we don't live in the same house all the time. And even though there'll be another person here soon. I won't love you any less because I have a baby."

Allyson sniffed, but didn't say anything.

Shelley backed up to the armchair, sat down and

pulled her daughter into her lap. "I guess having two babies coming into your life at the same time is pretty scary, huh?"

Under her chin, Allyson nodded.

"Like you're being replaced?"

Her daughter shrugged.

Shelley hugged her closer. "That's not the case at all, baby. If there was never another baby for me, or for Dex and Claire, we would all be happy because we have you." She placed a kiss on those black curls. "You're the light in my life, Allyson. I didn't realize that until you went away. But I can't imagine being happy without you in the world."

Warm tears wet the front of her shirt.

Shelley thought a minute. "Did you know that Zach has ten brothers and sisters?"

"Uh-huh."

"That's a lot of children in one family. Who do you think his mom loves the most?"

Another sniff, but fewer tears. "I don't know."

"You know what? I bet she loves each of her children exactly the same. Zach and his brothers and sisters—they're all special, they're all precious. Just like you. If I had a hundred babies, you would still be my Allyson."

Her daughter gave a watery chuckle. "A hundred babies is a lot."

"You're right. I'm going to need all the help I can get with just one. Are you ready for that?"

Sitting up, Allyson managed a smile. "I'm going to get lots of practice, I guess."

Shelley blinked back tears of her own. "I guess

you are. And you'll be the best big sister two babies ever had.''

ZACH WAITED until Allyson had returned to Wyoming before putting his plans into action. Though he liked her daughter very much, he needed time alone with his future wife. He didn't want there to be any mistake about his intentions. The lady had to understand that they would get married for *her* sake. Not just the baby's.

Meanwhile, he kept tabs on his sister during the rest of the summer. He personally supervised the cleanup at the Bull Pen, scheduling the exercise on a Friday morning so the girls would face their task during the busiest time of the week. Their embarrassment was everything he'd wanted.

Finally, on a chilly Wednesday night in the second week of September, he rang Shelley's door bell with his free hand.

Inside the house, footsteps tapped across the marble floor of the entry hall. The lock and knob rattled slightly as Shelley peered at him through the glass sidelight. After a second, her face disappeared. Nothing else happened for a long minute.

Then the door swung back, and her silhouette filled in the doorway. ''Zach?''

''I thought you might be up for a killer Monopoly game and some Chinese.'' He held up a bag from the local take-out restaurant.

''I don't think—''

''You can't send me back to town after I drove all the way out here.'' He stepped forward and, before

Shelley could protest, was in the house with the door shut behind him.

"That's better." He made his way to the kitchen to set down the food. "We might need to zap a couple of these to warm them up."

"Zach, you're not staying."

"Why not?" When he turned to look at her, his concentration faltered a little at the sight of her rounded shape under a bright purple sweater. "I...uh...seem to remember that you're good at Monopoly. We said we'd have a match sometime. How about now?"

Her hand came to rest on her stomach. "I—I don't know."

"Well, why don't we eat while you find out?" Facing the kitchen again, he unloaded cartons of food. "I brought paper plates—no sense in making a mess to clean up. Can you get a couple of big spoons? Do you use chopsticks?"

Still, she didn't move. Zach made a show of checking the containers, all the while wondering if he'd end up out in the cold anyway.

Suddenly, she stalked behind him and around the counter into the kitchen. A drawer rattled as she jerked the handle, then slammed shut.

She dropped spoons on the counter. "You're insane."

"Nope. Just hungry." He ladled rice onto plates. "Spoons and forks, and we're ready. I've got napkins."

Shelley eyed him with distrust. "Do you want something to drink?"

"Water's good."

Filling two glasses from the refrigerator dispenser, she shook her head. "I can't decide what you're after."

"No strings, Shelley—just like before. Enjoy the food, the game. That's all."

She sighed, and set down the glasses beside their plates. "You are a strange man, Zach Harmon. I never realized how strange until now."

Zach just grinned.

TWO HOURS LATER, Shelley got up from the kitchen table to take a bathroom break. "Don't cheat and take some of my houses while I'm gone," she warned Zach.

He looked wounded. "I am an officer sworn to uphold the law. I never cheat."

"Of course not. I counted them, you know." She went upstairs to her bedroom to check her makeup and run a comb through her hair.

She'd struggled all evening with the surprise of seeing him. Why had he come? What did he want? Though she'd tried pretty hard, she couldn't break his good mood. He hadn't mentioned the baby or getting married or...or anything dangerous.

He hadn't touched her, either. Not even a brush of shoulders. Of course, he wasn't here for sex. If he wanted someone to go to bed with, he had his choice of lovely women all over Denver.

Get used to it. It'll happen one day soon. At the thought, Shelley closed her eyes, not willing to examine her reaction to the idea.

When she went downstairs, Zach had prepared

popcorn. "Something about unbridled greed makes me hungry."

She laughed reluctantly. "Did you leave my houses alone?"

"I'll never tell."

Her knuckles brushed his as they both reached into the bowl at the same time. Shelley jumped. Zach, she decided, didn't notice.

"Okay." She sat down at the table again. "I'm about to make your life miserable. Prepare to be bankrupt."

"Yeah, right." He straddled the chair across the board from her. "I haven't even started manipulating. We'll see who bankrupts who."

"Whom."

"Just roll the dice."

AT ELEVEN-THIRTY, Zach pushed back from the table. "Okay, okay. I'm down to fifty dollars. I could win it all back, but not tonight. Tonight, I'll let you have the game."

"Famous last words. I beat you fair and square."

He grinned at her. "I'd never contradict a lady."

To his pleasure, she grinned back. "Since when?"

As they put the game away, she insisted on sorting the money by denomination. "We can do that next time." Zach protested.

She stopped shuffling bills for a second, then went on smoothly. "You never know when next time will be."

Zach knew exactly when the next time would be, since this was only the first step in his plan. But he didn't see any reason to let her in on the secret.

He took the game box with him when they walked to the door. "I admit, you play tough. I got some bad breaks, of course. Still—"

"Somehow, that's not quite the way I remember it." She reached for the doorknob. "But thanks for coming. The food was good. I...enjoyed the evening."

"I'm glad." His strategy called for a simple, uncomplicated goodbye. Zach struggled with himself, wanting more. Shelley's drowsy gaze was downright sexy. Her mouth, once again wiped free of lipstick, invited him. He'd spent many long nights thinking about that weekend in March. Endured many a cold shower to calm down.

"So...take care of yourself." He stepped out into the cold and shivered. "Stay warm. Sleep well."

"You, too." Her sweet, sleepy smile followed him as he backed across the small porch. Zach forgot about the steps behind him until his heel came down on thin air.

"Damnation!" He stumbled down to the next step, off balance, arms flailing, barely keeping hold of the Monopoly box.

Shelley hurried toward him, hands outstretched. "Zach! Careful!"

One heel hit the sidewalk. Zach threw his upper body forward, fighting for control. His toe slipped over damp grass and he came down hard on his knees.

Shelley bent over, put a hand on his shoulder. "Are you okay?"

He couldn't look up right away. "Except for shattered kneecaps, I'm great."

"Are you really hurt?"

Zach lifted his head just as the wind blew Shelley's hair back from her face. Such a delicate face, lively and clever and mischievous, all at once. A strong woman with an elf's smile. He wanted...

No. "Not hurt at all. See?" He jumped to his feet, managing not to groan. "And I didn't spill the game, either."

She backed up onto the lower step, arms crossed just above her stomach. "You athletes are so coordinated."

"Agility R Us." He decided to watch where he was going as he went to the car. A second fall and he might not be able to get up. "'Night, Shelley."

"Goodbye, Zach. Thanks again."

"Anytime." He made sure she went into the house and closed the door before he drove off. And he got all the way out of her neighborhood before, half laughing, half crying, he pulled off to the side of the road to check out his bruised and bleeding knees.

THREE DAYS LATER, the school sent the Crooked Women home at noon for smoking in the bathroom.

Zach got the message when he came in from his shift at four. Fifteen minutes later, he walked into his mother's house, took the stairs two at a time and knocked on his sister's the door.

"Go away!"

"Not likely." He leaned against the door frame, easing the weight off his left leg. The trip up the steps hadn't done anything good for his battered knees. "Open up, Carol."

"I'm not talking to anybody!"

"So talk to the wall and tell me what's going on with your head." A long silence was the only reply. Zach sighed. "Didn't watching Dad die of lung cancer teach you anything?"

"I wasn't smoking! I was just standing there talking."

"Ever heard of secondhand smoke?" He waited, but she didn't answer. "Okay. I'm tired of yelling and I'm not going away. Can we talk face-to-face or do I have to break the door down? I can, you know. They taught us how in cop school."

After another long pause, the door opened a crack.

Taking that as an invitation, he stepped inside and sat on the chair under the light switch. "This scene is getting old, kid. Aren't you tired of it yet?"

His sister flopped on the bed and buried her face in the pillow. She wore jeans two sizes too big and an orange sweater at least one size too small, with two inches of bare skin in between. "I'm not accountable to you."

"No, you're not. Label me curious."

"Hah." She kept her face hidden. "You're on Mom's side."

Zach propped his elbows on his thighs and rubbed his throbbing kneecaps. "This is a family. We're all on the same side."

"As long as you fit the pattern. Step outside the line and everybody's on your back."

Zach bit back a smile. "Getting kicked out of school is more than just stepping outside the line."

"Spoken like a true good guy. Don't *you* ever get tired of it?" She turned a flushed face toward him. "Didn't you ever cut loose, do something reckless?"

His face heated as a certain weekend in March came to mind. "Sure. But you have to be prepared to take the consequences. After the last stunt, I would think you'd realize that."

"Smoking isn't so bad. Mom acts like I came home pregnant or something."

He cleared his throat. "What exactly are you trying to do, Carol? What do you want?"

"A chance to grow up! I've been ordered around since I was born." Shaking her head, she clutched her fingers in her hair and pulled. "Cops and good guys telling me what to do until I can't breathe without getting criticized. I want to make my own decisions."

"And what would those decisions be?"

She rolled to her back. "Something different, that's for sure."

Zach thought about that young girl he'd found in the alley. The cops had picked up her boyfriend, but she'd refused to press charges. "Different, how?"

"I want my own life. I want peace and quiet and something besides pot roast for Sunday dinner and fish on Friday."

"Understandable."

"Tell that to Mom." Carol folded her arms over her eyes. The sweater now rode the edge of her ribs. "She's expecting me to grow up and marry a nice Catholic boy and have eleven kids like she did."

"Be grateful. That means she's happy with her choices."

Her fists clenched. "I would rather die!"

He fought back a smile at the typical adolescent overstatement. "What do you want to do?"

"I want to go places, see things. Earn my own money. Build my own life, run it my way."

Zach leaned back and crossed his arms. "And breaking the rules—endangering your life and, incidentally, giving the rest of us prematurely gray hair—will accomplish this?"

"Oh...I don't know!" She sniffed, hiccuped and was silent.

Carol's goals weren't so far out. Her methods of achieving them—as the family kept trying to point out—were questionable at best.

But words alone hadn't—wouldn't—make the point. Zach needed a role model, somebody for Carol to look up to. Somebody like...

Shelley. Of course. She had the guts and the drive to succeed, and the style to make winning look easy. She lived exactly the kind of life Carol admired.

Not to mention that getting Shelley involved with his family would be a simply brilliant move. His brothers and sisters, and especially his mother, would draw her inside the circle and show her the advantages of family life. She couldn't help but like them, and she could use all the coddling they loved to dish out.

Zach nodded in satisfaction as he got to his feet. "What are you doing next weekend, little sister?" He gave her a light slap on the rear of those baggy jeans.

She lifted her head, fisting tears out of her eyes. "Why?"

"I'm taking over your Saturday. There's a lady I want you to meet."

CHAPTER NINE

SHELLEY'S SECRETARY answered the phone just as they were about to leave the office Friday night. "Somebody for you." She held out the receiver. "He says it's urgent."

"Who does?" After a day showing properties, Shelley wanted to get home and relax.

"Zach Harmon."

Two words, and her heart jumped into overdrive. Why would he call again? Saying goodbye got more difficult each time she saw him. She was afraid that some day, if this continued, she'd lose the strength to let him go.

She took the telephone reluctantly. "Zach? What's wrong?"

"I need your help."

His voice—smooth and warm and sexy—did nothing to slow her pulse. "What do you mean? Why?"

"Remember I told you about my sister Carol? About the trouble she's getting into these days?"

"I remember." From the doorway, the secretary gave her a questioning shrug. Shelley mouthed *See you Monday* and waved her out the door. "Navel piercing."

"Right." He gave a short laugh. "If only that were all. She and her friends were sent home from school today. The principal is threatening to suspend them all.''

Shelley eased her weight onto the reception desk. ''That sounds serious, but I don't see what I can do. Your family—''

''Is going ballistic. Nobody can get through to her. Not even yours truly. So I thought…''

He paused just a moment. ''I hoped maybe you could talk to Carol.''

''Me?'' Her racing heart skipped a beat. And another. ''Why?''

''Because you're a successful businesswoman, one who's managed to take control of her life.''

She basked for a second in the light of his praise, but then sobered. ''Not exactly.'' She glance down at her expanding figure. ''I doubt your family would consider a divorced single mother a good role model.''

''In a way, that's what makes you perfect.''

''Explain.'' Did the man ever think in a straight line?

''Carol could learn from you how to overcome challenges in order to succeed.''

Shelley was tempted. The idea that he thought of her as someone he wanted his sister to emulate stroked her ego like a soft hand over a cat's back. She hadn't felt valued that way in a long, long time. Certainly not by a man like this.

But she could not afford to get more involved with Zach. ''I think Claire Cavanaugh would be a better choice.''

''Claire's not in Denver.''

Of course, if she were, she'd still be in Zach's life.

And Shelley would never have asked him to take her to that stupid awards dinner, they wouldn't have spent the weekend together, and Shelley wouldn't be pregnant. The perfect woman could shoulder the blame for everything.

And the not-so-perfect one could do damage control. "I don't think so, Zach. It just doesn't make sense to me."

He didn't say anything for a long time. Finally, he sighed. "Any other ideas?"

She hated leaving him with no options. "You know…my mother's pretty easy to talk to."

"You think she'd have some suggestions?"

"Maybe. Or maybe she could talk to Carol. She's a great role model." One who wasn't in danger of liking Zach Harmon too much.

This silence was even longer. But his voice came back strong. "That's a thought. Can you give me her number?"

Shelley relayed the information. "I'll let her know you'll be getting in touch."

"Thanks. I appreciate the help."

"No problem, Zach. Take care."

"Sure. See you later." He hung up before she did.

SHELLEY CALLED her mother after dinner to explain. "I wanted to let you know you'd be hearing from Zach sometime soon."

"I'll try to help. He seems like a nice guy." She hesitated, then said "I…um…didn't realize you knew him so well."

How do you define the word "know"? Shelley

smothered a rueful laugh. "I was a little surprised, myself. Men don't usually ask for advice or help."

"He seemed very relaxed."

A good description, Shelley realized. "He's satisfied, I think, with himself and his place in the world. He doesn't have anything to prove."

"That's a lesson you could learn. You can be happy with what you are."

Shelley sighed at the inevitable maternal response. "I don't need a lecture, Mom."

"I just think you try too hard. You have many reasons to be proud of yourself and what you've accomplished."

"I know that."

"Evidently Zach does, too, or he wouldn't be asking for your help with his sister."

Time to change the subject. "Have a good weekend, Mom. I'll talk to you later."

Unsettled, even irritated, Shelley hung up the phone. Her mother liked Zach—no surprise there. There probably weren't too many people—especially women—who didn't.

Which was why she couldn't let him any further into her life. He was dangerous to her plans. And yet…didn't he deserve to know his child? Could she deny him the pleasure?

The answer had come from Zach himself. Even though he'd asked her to marry him, he didn't want a child. He didn't need a child.

Shelley did. She needed this baby to hold, to love, to care for. Second chances came along rarely in life, and she wouldn't mess this one up. She'd be a single parent, and she'd do as good a job as could be done by anyone, anywhere.

At least, she hoped so.

AFTER WAITING all weekend to hear from her mother, Shelley gave into her nerves and called again Monday night. "How'd it go?"

"How did what go?"

"Your meeting with Zach."

"We didn't get together after all."

"Why not?" And why did it make her nervous?

"Well, we discussed Carol over the phone. I gave him my opinion. And while I was flattered, I told him I thought you would be a better choice to talk to the girl, because you're younger, more up-to-date."

"Mother!"

"Teenagers don't like to listen to old fogies like me, you know."

"But—" Shelley drew a many-petaled daisy on the pad beside the phone. The first petal she labeled T. *Tell her.*

"I can't imagine why you'd object to helping Zach out."

D. *Don't tell her.*

"He's good-looking and genuinely nice." her mother continued.

"And I'm very pregnant."

"What does that have to do with anything? Are you swearing off men?"

Tell her. "Doesn't that seem like a good idea, considering my track record?"

"You've had bad luck, and you've made some bad

choices. That doesn't mean you're doomed to spend your life alone.''

"You have." *Don't.*

"For the simple reason that I loved your father and I've never met another man who could change the way I felt. If I had…well, I might have married him."

Tell her "How could you still love a man who deserted you and your baby?" On second thought, she wished she'd left that question unasked. She didn't want to hear her mother's answer…or her own.

"Your father never made me any promises. And I always knew he would leave when the time came. I chose to have his daughter in my life, and I've never regretted that decision."

"Do you know where he is?" Why ask now? What did any of this matter?

"I don't keep track. Every so often, I'll see his name somewhere. But I don't bother him. He'd come back if he wanted to, if he could."

"If he wanted to." Zach said he wanted to—but wouldn't the whole situation just be worse if they actually made promises?

Her mother couldn't answer a question Shelley wouldn't ask.

"He's the one who missed out," Dorothy said instead. "But enough of this digression. Are you going to help Zach with his sister?"

Last petal. *Don't.* Shelley flipped the pencil across the room. "I don't see what I can do."

"Talk to the girl, Shelley. Tell her about your

business, about high school and college. Let her into your life. You could be a big sister to her.''

Suspicion reared its head. "She already has sisters. Did Zach put you up to this?"

"Up to what? I've got to run, honey. Call me later this week. Bye."

Shelley stared for a full minute at the phone whining in her hand. She had the distinct impression she'd just been outsmarted.

That feeling increased on Tuesday night when she opened her door to the man outside. "Now what?"

Zach held up a shopping bag. "Just delivering your videos."

She didn't know whether to laugh or curse. "I didn't call for videos."

"Sure you did. I distinctly heard you ask for Hepburn and Tracy. So here I am."

"You're crazy."

"I brought ice cream." He held up another bag. "And butterscotch sauce."

The laugh escaped. "I give up. Come on in."

"I don't even have to mention the whipped cream?"

Shelley left him standing on the threshold. "It's chilly out there. Close the door."

She headed for the kitchen but heard him stop a few steps behind her. "What's this?"

Without even turning around, she knew what he'd found on the table by the stairs. Relaxing her hands, she kept her back to him and her voice light. "A printout of the sonogram I had done."

"This is the baby?"

"Yes."

Zach was quiet. Shelley turned around to see him holding the picture up to the light, his eyes intently focused.

"You can see arms and legs."

She nodded. "And a shadow of the face. Not very clear, though."

He studied the photo some more. "Do you—" Whatever the question was, he didn't finish it. Putting the picture down where he found it, he walked into the hallway. "Amazing what they can do with technology these days, isn't it?"

"A little scary, but definitely amazing. Now what about that ice cream?" If he could recover, so could she.

They watched two of the old movies from seats on opposite ends of the couch, bowls full of butterscotch sundae in hand. Zach got up as the last credits rolled. "Good stuff. Too bad they don't make many movies like that these days."

"There are still a few." Shelley put her hand over a yawn. "But they're outnumbered by the action-packed, blow-everything-to-bits contingent."

The tape started to rewind. When she risked a glance in his direction, Zach stood by the television, watching her with a question in his eyes.

Wide awake now, Shelley sat up straight. "What? What's wrong?"

He shook his head. "Nothing." When he came closer, she picked up their bowls and started toward the kitchen. Zach followed, but stopped on the other side of the counter. "Did you talk to your mom?"

"Yes." She rinsed the dishes and opened the dishwasher. "Sounds like I've been drafted to deal with your sister."

"Well...maybe. Though if you really don't want to, that's okay." He shrugged and headed back to the TV, ejected the tape and put it in the case. "I'd better get home. Tomorrow's shift starts early."

Before she could collect her objections, he'd gone into the front of the house. He would leave, taking no for an answer. Finally.

Except that she was chasing after him. "Zach? Zach? *Zach!*" She caught him at the front door as he shrugged into his leather jacket. "You are the most manipulative man I've ever met."

He turned, with a serious look on his face and a laugh in his eyes. "Really?"

She didn't bother to answer. "What do you want me to do?"

"Well..."

"Come on. Get it out. And then get out."

He grinned. "I had this idea that you could let Carol come to work with you one day."

Shelley crossed her arms above the baby. "Of course you did. I guess I'm supposed to act like a mentor, gain her confidence, point out the error of her ways?" As if she had any right to criticize someone else's mistakes.

"Nah. Just tell her about how you got started, give her a look at how successful you've become. She'll get the point without being hit over the head. 'Night!"

He left quickly, closing the door before she could come up with an answer. Shelley went into the living room and opened the curtains on the big picture window in time to see the Trans Am back out of the driveway. Zach gave her a wave as he roared away.

"I'm the one who should be hit over the head," she muttered, "for ever thinking I could escape untouched from a relationship with you!"

THE NEXT SATURDAY, Zach walked in on Carol at breakfast. "You've got thirty minutes, kid. Better get hopping."

She gazed at him with sleepy eyes. "Thirty minutes for what?"

"I'm taking you to meet a friend of mine, remember? You're going to work with her today."

She rolled her eyes. "Is this Take Your Sister to Work week?"

"This is the Come-with-me-or-spend-the-whole-day-cleaning-closets program." He sat down and grabbed a piece of her toast. "What do you think?"

"I think it's stupid."

"Well, if you like cleaning closets…"

"I suppose you want me to dress up."

He grinned. "You've always been a bright girl!"

She took fifty minutes, but the effect was worth the wait. She came down the stairs in a black suit jacket and black pants, wearing makeup only a little extreme around the eyes, a little too dark on the lips. Her hair had been tamed into a clip on her neck, and she'd washed the green out of her bangs. Though her fingernails were still black, Zach figured he could live with that.

"You look really nice." He got to his feet and folded the newspaper neatly, the way his dad had required. "Businesslike."

Carol scowled. "Thanks."

Their mother bustled into the room carrying a basket of laundry. "You're sure this person will take care of Carol?"

"I'm sure, Mom. She'll be back safe and sound before dinner. Relax." Zach kissed her cheek. "Why don't you make *this* person do her own laundry, like I did?"

He took the basket and ran it upstairs to the spare room, then came back to find his mother glaring at his sister. "You should have clean hands for work. Go take that stuff off your nails."

The teenager stuck out her lower lip. "My hands are clean. I'm not taking off the polish."

"Okay, okay." He stepped between them and gave each a gentle shove, pushing them apart. "Mom, the nail polish will pass. Carol, don't speak to your mother like that."

She looked down at the floor without comment. His mother hmmphed. "Of all my children, the youngest is the most troublesome. If her father knew…"

"If Dad knew, he'd still be here and maybe you'd have something to do besides pick on me!" Carol spat out the words, turned on her heel and stalked out of the house.

Zach looked at his mother. "Are you okay?"

Nodding, she waved him out the door. "After ten of you, I'm used to temper tantrums. We all miss your father. I hope she comes back in a better mood."

AFTER A SHORT RIDE, Zach parked on the curb at the front door to Shelley's office building. Carol stared up at the marble-faced tower with her mouth open. "Wow."

"Pretty nice, yes? Her office is on the second floor. Let's go."

She turned his way. "You don't have to come with me."

"I know, but I will anyway." He wanted to make sure Carol went where she was supposed to. And he wanted to see Shelley.

She was standing by the reception desk and looked up as they walked through the door. "There you are. I was wondering if I should send out the cavalry. Hi, Zach."

"Hi." Did the lady ever look less than great? His blood pumped faster at the sight of her. "Let me introduce my sister. Shelley Hightower, this is Carol Harmon."

Shelley put out her hand. "Hi, Carol. I'm glad to meet you." Her smile was friendlier than professional.

"Me, too." Carol had flushed a bright red. "I'm sorry I'm late."

"No problem. I'm just finishing up here. I'll be right with you."

Zach saluted Carol and executed an about-face. His sneakers squeaked on the marble floor.

"Zach, wait a minute."

He turned around again. Shelley had stepped forward, away from the desk. The book she held against her chest and the drape of her bright blue dress emphasized the increasing roundness of her figure. His mind flashed on to that sonogram picture—the little arms and legs, the barest impression of a nose and eyes and lips. A baby. *His* baby.

Zach took a deep breath. "What can I do for you?"

"I'll bring Carol home. What time should I have her back?"

"Mom's expecting her for dinner, if that's okay. If not, just call her and let her know when you'll be there."

"Sounds good." She changed her right hand for her left on the book she carried. The damn wedding ring winked at him.

"Great." He bit his tongue on everything else he wanted to say. "See you later, Carol."

Shelley lifted her eyebrows in surprise. Zach knew he was being too abrupt, but rudeness was preferable to losing his cool over a stupid ring. Maybe taking the stairs to the ground floor would help.

Not much, unfortunately. Behind the wheel of the Trans Am again, he sat for a minute, tapping out a drum riff on the steering wheel with all ten fingers and both palms. He had three hours before work. He'd thought about shooting some hoops in the meantime. But now…

Instead of heading home, he pulled into the parking lot of a small downtown jeweler.

"Zach, my friend!" The owner came around the end of the counter. "Great to see you. What can I do for you today? Pearls? I've got some beautiful earrings in pearls. A nice brooch for your mother— her birthday's soon, isn't it?"

"You're right, Louis. Just a few weeks. But that's

not what I'm here for today—or at least, not right now.''

"What, then?"

"Rings, Louis. I want to look at wedding rings."

CHAPTER TEN

HALFWAY THROUGH HIS Saturday night shift, Zach took an early dinner break and stopped in at the Indigo.

Jimmy looked up from polishing the bar. "Did I call the cops?"

Zach slipped onto a stool. "I keep tabs on the lowlifes in this area. That's my job. Can I have a sandwich?"

"Sure." Jimmy disappeared around the corner into the kitchen. "Roast beef and smoked cheddar," he said when he came back. "And fries."

"Sounds good." The place was empty, except for the two of them. Zach twirled the icy glass of soda Jimmy had poured, watching circles of water form on the shiny wood of the bar.

Eventually, Jimmy said, "How's it going?"

The truth or just…the usual? Zach opted for truth. "Pretty good. Town's been kinda quiet lately. Not that I'm asking for an exciting crime, you understand. I like my evenings free."

"You still seeing Shelley?"

"Yeah, some." He drew designs in the circles of moisture he'd created.

"How's that turning out?"

His wet fingertip traced a lopsided star on the bar. "Not as good as I hoped."

"I'm listening."

Zach realized he could use exactly what Jimmy offered—a friendly ear. "She's had some back luck. Her defenses are pretty strong."

"My impression of the lady tells me she's worth the extra effort."

"Sure. But there are complications."

Jimmy chuckled. "Aren't there always? Like what?"

"A baby." He put a square around the star.

"A—" The other man ran a hand over his hair. "That's a hell of a complication."

"Tell me about it. Then try convincing a gun-shy divorcée that you're Mr. Dependable."

"Anything I can do?"

After another long pause, Zach took the plunge. "Actually, I need a favor."

"You got it." Jimmy hung a stemmed highball glass in the overhead rack and picked up another one to polish. This time he didn't look Zach's way, which made things easier.

"I'd like you to keep this for me." Zach took the ring box out of his pocket and slid it down the bar. "That safe of yours is better than Fort Knox."

Jimmy finished polishing the glass before he picked up the box. "Sure thing. I'll be right back." His uneven footsteps echoed through the quiet room.

Even after he returned from the club office, bringing the roast-beef sandwich with him, Jimmy didn't ask questions. Zach knew he didn't have to volunteer an explanation. If he left it like this, his privacy would stay intact.

He'd almost made up his mind to say something, though, when his radio squawked against his hip. "All units, report of a disturbance, 322 Eighth Street."

Zach responded with his number. "On my way." He grabbed a last bite of his sandwich and slid to his feet. "Gotta go."

"Watch your back," Jimmy advised.

"Sure." But at the doorway, he looked over at the man who was closer, in many ways, than a brother to him. "If something happens to me..."

Jimmy kept polishing.

"Would you take that box to Shelley? The ring is hers, I just haven't gotten around to...giving it to her yet."

Shaking his head, Jimmy eyed an imaginary speck on the glass he held. "No problem. Won't be necessary, but...no problem."

"Thanks, man." Zach put on his cap and left the bar. Four minutes later he crouched behind the door of his car outside an empty warehouse, listening to gunshots and getting orders on breaking up a gang fight. Between saving his own skin and dealing with injured crazies, he didn't have time to worry about rings, or women, or babies.

That simplicity of thought and action was just one reason he really did like this job.

SHELLEY'S SATURDAY clients loved the first house she showed them. She suggested they view the others on her list, in case they saw an even better fit. But the couple remained convinced that they'd found their dream house on the first shot.

They all drove back to the office to write up the contract. Carol waited in the reception area while the financial details were discussed. Two hours later, the excited buyers left. Shelley saw them out, then turned around to face her charge, who was curled up in one of the armchairs, paging listlessly through a magazine.

"I'm sorry about this." She sat in the chair beside Zach's sister and put a hand on the girl's arm. "You've had a really boring afternoon."

Carol sighed. "That's okay. You've got neat magazines." She sounded completely disinterested.

Which was not what Zach intended. Shelley tried again. "I've put in a call to the owners of the house but they aren't at home, so we've got some time. Want a tour of the office?"

"Sure." Not exactly raging excitement, but it was a start.

The tour didn't help much. With most of the agents showing properties, the fax machine and phones did the work. Shelley showed off their Internet web page and the countrywide real-estate search function. Carol watched and listened politely, played around some by herself, but showed little true enthusiasm.

Desperately, Shelley racked her brain for something to interest a bored adolescent. All she could come up with was, "Shopping?"

Carol smiled, finally. "I like to shop."

Carrying her cell phone, she showed the girl some of her own favorite stores. At the boutique where

Shelley bought her cosmetics, Carol agreed to a makeover.

"I like that purple shadow." Shelley said, as they left the store. "Your eyes look huge."

"Yeah." Carol studied her reflection in a window. "Not bad."

Shelley checked in with her receptionist and her message machine. "They haven't called back. Let's look at clothes."

A few minutes later, the teenager surveyed herself in the mirror wearing a purple leather micro skirt. "I don't think I can sit down in this."

Shelley laughed. "Not many people can. And driving is a real challenge."

"You have a skirt this short?"

"A couple, actually. Whether I'll ever get into them again is the question." At the last minute, she wished she could call the words back. So far, they'd done a great job of pretending the baby didn't exist.

But now Carol came to stand in front of her. "You're so tiny, I bet you will. When will your baby be born?"

"The first of December, more or less."

"Have you picked out names?"

"A few."

Carol's questions continued. "Is your nursery all decorated?"

"I'm working on it." Which meant that she'd consulted a designer, but hadn't made any decisions.

"Is your husband excited? Do you want a boy or a girl?"

Shelley closed her eyes for a second. "Um… either. As long as it's—"

"Healthy." Zach's sister nodded. "That's what everyone says. But don't you have a preference, really?"

"Well...I already have a daughter. She lives with her father in Wyoming." Carol looked puzzled. "We're divorced," Shelley explained. At least now she'd told the truth—just not in the right order. And not all of it. "So a boy might be nice." A rambunctious little tiger with blue eyes and light brown hair and his dad's killer grin.

The saleswoman came over. "You look wonderful in that skirt, miss. Can I wrap it up for you?"

Carol rolled her eyes. "My mother would die. My brothers would lock me in my room for a year. I don't think so." She vanished into the dressing room.

Shelley checked her messages again and found one from the sellers of the house, who would be home until seven. She stood up as Carol reappeared. "I'm afraid I have to go present the contract."

The girl's face fell. But then she smiled. "It's been neat shopping with you. You go to some really great stores."

Shelley stopped herself just in time from suggesting they might do this again. If she didn't intend to see Zach anymore, she couldn't see his sister, either. No matter how much she enjoyed the company.

In the car, Carol gave directions for getting to her house. After a short silence, she said, "So you don't...get to see your daughter much?"

"Not as much as I'd like." Shelley turned carefully, keeping her eyes on the road. "She'll be down to visit in a couple of weeks. And we get time together at Christmas."

"You must miss her."

"I do."

"I miss my dad." The confession was soft, a little muffled.

"I know." Oh, how she knew.

"I was just a little kid, but..."

Shelley sighed. "Little kids need their dads."

"Yeah."

"You remember him, though. You've got good times to look back on. I...I never knew mine."

"I guess that's true." Tears choked Carol's voice.

"And you know that he loved you. If he'd been given a choice, he wouldn't have left. He would have stayed with your mother and his children." Shelley blinked hard against her own desire to cry.

"Yeah." Carol took a deep breath. "I do know that."

The rest of the drive passed in silence. Once they reached her street, the girl pointed out a house about halfway down the block. "That's it."

Shelley pulled the car into the driveway. "I apologize again for the way today has turned out. I hope you don't feel like your whole Saturday was a waste."

"Oh, no. I loved the shopping!" Carol caught herself with a hand over her mouth. "I mean—the business stuff was neat, too."

"No, it wasn't. It was totally boring. I'm glad things got better, though."

The front door of the house opened and a woman stepped to the edge of the porch. Slim and small, she looked young in the fading light.

"That's my mom." Carol opened the car door.

"Thanks, Shelley." She waved, then walked briskly up to the house. The woman on the porch said something, and Carol shook her head. Shelley started to put the car into Reverse, but when Carol's mother came down the steps, Shelley braked and lowered the window.

"Miss...Mrs. Hightower. Thank you for taking such good care of my daughter." Her eyes were blue and sharp, like Zach's.

Shelley shook the offered hand. "My pleasure, Mrs. Harmon. Carol was a good sport today."

"Will you come in for a cup of tea?"

"I'd love to, but—"

"Come on in. A cup of tea won't take long." Zach's mother turned around and crossed to the front door, leaving Shelley very little choice but to follow.

And so she stepped into Zach's family home.

The living room was slightly worn but tidy and neat, just like the woman who brought her tea and cookies. Mrs. Harmon looked only a little older in the light, more like Carol's sister than her mother. "When is your little one due?" the woman asked.

"December."

The blue eyes softened. "My twins Stefan and Jessica were born in December. The fifteenth. We had a very merry Christmas that year."

Shelley smiled. "I imagine I'll be trying to catch up on my sleep at Christmas."

"Just take the baby to bed with you, nurse it to sleep and then go back to sleep yourself."

"That's a good idea." She'd thought about nursing. Allyson had been fed with bottles, so Shelley could get back to work as soon as possible. "But what if I roll over on the baby?"

Mrs. Harmon smiled and shook her head. "Eleven children, and I never rolled over on one of them."

Experience was hard to argue against. "Thanks for the suggestion, then. And now I really do need to go. I have some work to do."

Carol joined her mother at the door. "Thanks again, Shelley."

"You're welcome, Carol. It was good to meet you, Mrs. Harmon."

"Take care of yourself. Eat plenty of vegetables!"

"I will." Shelley went down the steps, smiling at the motherly advice.

As she hurried along the walk, a police car pulled up at the curb. Zach unfolded from the vehicle to lean his arms on the top of the door. "Well, hello. You're even earlier than I thought you'd be. How'd the day go?"

After a second of shock, Shelley found her voice. But she didn't move any closer. "I don't think the business stuff was too interesting, but Carol and I did some shopping and that was fun." She started toward the Mercedes again. "I'm on my way to present a contract. Have a good evening."

Again she made it into the car and got her seat belt on before someone—Zach this time—appeared in the window, motioning for her to roll down the glass. Shelley cranked the engine and pressed the button.

He put an elbow on the windowsill, bringing their faces close. "Thanks for taking her on. I really appreciate your help."

"I'm not sure I did much good—things didn't go the way I planned and she spent a lot of the afternoon bored out of her mind."

"But she saw you working, and that was the whole idea. Can I take you to dinner?"

The breath stopped in her throat. "I...I told you. I'm going to present a contract. I could be working until midnight."

"Even better—I'm going back to work for another three hours, myself. We could share a midnight snack."

He wore what Allyson called his "cop costume," though in the twilight, Shelley could only see the dark shirt, with the glint of gold on his chest and shoulders. She suddenly understood the appeal of a man in uniform.

Or maybe it was just Zach.

With a rueful laugh, she shook her head. There was no *maybe* about it. "Thanks, Zach. But...no, thanks." She put the car in Reverse. He stepped back without a word.

Then, reluctantly, she escaped temptation one more time.

CHAPTER ELEVEN

THREE WEEKS AFTER Carol's day with Shelley, Zach caught the ring of the phone as he stepped out of the shower Friday afternoon. "Harmon."

"Hi, Zach." Claire Hightower sounded tired.

"Hello there, Counselor. How are you?"

"Wonderful and worn out. I'd introduce you to the new arrival but he is, mercifully, asleep."

"You had your baby! A he?"

"We got home just this morning. Jackson Walker Hightower was born on Tuesday at 3 a.m. He's beautiful."

"Your kid couldn't be anything else." He sat down on the bed. "How'd it go?"

"Pretty well. Compared to, say, climbing Everest."

Zach grinned. "So I hear. Is the little guy sleeping okay?" A boy. Claire had a son. Weird concept.

"Of course." She sighed. "Jack sleeps peacefully from ten in the morning until five in the afternoon, naps from nine until eleven in the evening, then wakes up to play."

"No problem, right? Just turn your whole life upside down, you'll be fine."

"Ah, but he's worth it. Simply watching him sleep

is a pleasure. Even hearing him cry makes me smile.''

"You've fallen in love. But I don't suppose your husband minds.'' And neither relationship bothered him, Zach realized with surprise.

Claire laughed. "Dex hasn't gone out to the barn in three days. That has to be a record.''

They talked about the baby and traded stories about mutual friends in Denver, until a croak of sorts interrupted.

"I think you're being paged.'' Zach couldn't help a laugh of his own as the croaking escalated to a full-throated cry.

"Definitely. Take care, Zach. I'll call soon.''

"Congratulations, Claire. Give Dex my best.''

He set the phone down and pondered, still wearing just his towel. Claire had officially become a mom. A real baby lived with her now. Everything had changed.

As for the other pregnant woman in his life—nothing had changed. He'd never considered himself a quitter, but after almost three months of trying to convince Shelley to marry him, Zach had started to wonder if he was wasting his time. He'd backed off on his surprise visits in the last couple of weeks, and he hadn't seen Shelley at all for seven days—maybe eight. He filled his time with extra shifts for friends at work, endless rounds of basketball and new books by some of his favorite authors.

Still, whenever he let his mind wander, she took control. Like right now—why wasn't he thinking about Claire and her new baby? Or thinking about getting dressed—at least he could do that while he brooded over his conspicuous lack of success with the mother of his child.

Fifteen minutes later, he was on his way to pick up Carol for the Women's Work Fair. Their sister Rachel would give a department demonstration on women in law enforcement at tonight's session and he'd promised her an audience of two, at least.

Just as important, Carol had expressed interest when she received a notice about the Fair at school, and he wanted to take advantage of that. A recent lull in the activities of Crooked Women led him to hope that particular phase of adolescence had passed. The extra credit Carol would get with her history teacher confirmed this trip as a deal too good to miss.

A respectable crowd filled the convention center. Mostly women, of course. Several of the men Zach passed appeared to act primarily as baby-sitters— they pushed strollers, carried knapsacks front and back and hoisted toddlers on their shoulders. Sometimes all three at once.

Modern fatherhood apparently called for an even heavier time commitment than Zach had realized. Was he ready for that?

Carol tugged on his jacket sleeve. "What time does Rachel's talk start?" Her nails were purple tonight, and she'd streaked her hair with yellow.

Still, he welcomed the distraction. "Eight. We've got about an hour to browse."

They cruised the rows of booths—weavers and crafters and musicians tucked in side by side with lawyers, engineers and architects, all of them female. Local hospitals provided information on women in health care—nurses, doctors, administrators, therapists and lab workers, just to name a few.

"This is pretty wild," Carol commented. "I never thought about a lot of these jobs."

"There's a world of interesting work out there. You can choose a career that appeals to you and then focus on achieving it without rejecting everything else."

Carol stuck her tongue out at him. "You're always on my case."

Zach shrugged. "I'd rather be *on* your case this way, instead of *working* your *case* when I'm on duty."

His sister rolled her eyes. "Why me? Why did I have to get born into a family of cops?"

"Maybe because you're so hard to handle?"

She gave him a wicked grin. "Or maybe so you could bother me all the time and keep yourself out of trouble?" Without giving him time to answer, she turned away and blended into the crowd.

Zach followed, trying to keep her in his sights, with that last comment bouncing in his brain. *Keep yourself out of trouble…* If that was the plan, he reflected, the strategy had failed. With Shelley and the baby and their current situation, he could hardly be in more trouble.

Muttering a rude word, he stopped at the end of an aisle, realizing he'd lost Carol in the crush. The flow of people buffeted him like a rock in a river as he stood still, deciding how to proceed. The best bet would be to park himself at the exit. She'd come through there sooner or later…

As he stepped forward, a man with a little boy on

his shoulders passed by. The kid had tears on his cheeks, as if he'd recently thrown a tantrum, but he was laughing now, playing with his dad's Stetson.

Zach chuckled…and at the same time got hit in the chest with a shoulder. He reached out to steady his assailant…and found himself holding the very woman he'd been thinking about.

SHELLEY HAD BEEN listening to a child cry for what seemed an eternity. Finally she saw a tall man in a cowboy hat cut through the crowd to arrive at the booth across the aisle. Over the noise, she couldn't hear what he said. But she saw the little boy's mother smile in relief as the man swept her son high onto his shoulder.

The boy laughed and gripped the cowboy hat. "Dada go!" he squealed, as the tall man bore him away.

Shelley dropped back against her chair. Just a typical outing with a two year old. Not for the first time, she wondered if she was really up to the job. There would be no one to turn to—except her mother, who had her own job and lived across town. No instant relief, no privacy. Nobody else to wake up in the middle of the night. Nobody close by to share worries with, or the joys.

How in the world was she going to manage all alone? What was she thinking?

Almost blindly, she stood and moved to the end of the table, then stepped out of the booth. Someone bumped her on the left, someone else on the right. Shelley sidestepped, turned toward the nearest exit, and bumped into someone else. A pair of hands gripped her arms. A familiar cologne tantalized her. And then a voice—Zach's drowsy lion voice—sounded in her ear.

"Hello there, lady. Haven't seen you for awhile. How's it going?"

DAMN, she looked good.

Zach allowed himself the luxury of staring. Shelley wore a suit in bronzed green that set off sparks of light in her hair. Her face was full and soft.

But her eyes were terrified.

He tightened his grip. "What's wrong? Are you okay?"

She put a hand to her head, effectively blocking his view of her face. "Of course I'm…fine. It's just a little crowded in here, that's all."

"More than a little. Why don't we go outside for a few minutes?"

Her shoulders straightened and she looked him in the eye. "Maybe because it's below freezing?"

Zach approved of her spirit. "Details, details. We won't stay long."

"I don't know…"

But he wouldn't let her get away, at least not right now. He made way for both of them through the press of people and steered Shelley to a quiet corner of the lobby, where two folding chairs waited, as if by design.

"Sit." He pushed her gently into the chair. "Can I get you something to eat or drink?"

"No, thanks." She looked around and sighed. "You were right—this is much less congested. Just being out of the craziness helps."

Zach straddled the other chair and rested his arms across the back, enjoying the chance to look at her. "What are you doing here?"

"The company has a booth." She cocked her head. "I could ask you the same question."

Was that a sign of interest? "My sister, Rachel, is speaking about women in law enforcement in a few minutes. And Carol wanted to come. She's here somewhere—I lost her in the crowd."

A surprised smile crossed Shelley's face. "Things are going better, then? Not so much trouble?"

"Not so much." Her pleasure pleased him, although he didn't know quite where to take the conversation. The subjects they really needed to talk about were off limits. "How's Ally Cat? Wasn't she coming down soon?"

"I talked with her on Tuesday. She called to say—" her hands twisted together in her lap "—to say that Claire and Dexter's baby was born. We decided this wasn't the time for her to leave home."

"I guess not." The hurt in her eyes twisted his heart. "Claire's on top of the world."

"Dexter sounded pretty proud of himself when I spoke to him."

They could only go one place from here. "Shelley, I—"

"There you are!" Carol strode toward them across the polished floor. "I looked around and you had disappeared."

Zach fought back impatience. "You're the one who disappeared."

His sister barely noticed him. "Hi, Shelley! I saw your booth—picked up lots of brochures." She held up her gift bag full of papers. "I figured I could give some to friends at school."

"Great idea, Carol. I'm glad you came." Shelley stood up, not quite as easily as she had even ten days ago. "I'd better get back to the booth, myself." She glanced at Zach, and he could have sworn her cheeks flushed.

He got to his feet. "Are you working here all weekend?"

"Pretty much. It's a good place to make contacts for sales." She backed away. "Thanks for the breather. You two have a good time." Turning around, she retreated quickly into the madhouse.

Zach stared after her, thinking fast. She hadn't seemed so resistant this time. Not so determined to push him away. Maybe...

SATURDAY NIGHT, Zach arrived at the fair about eight o'clock—an hour before it closed. He wandered the aisles, careful to stay away from Shelley's booth. If she saw him too early, she might take off running.

As the mob thinned toward closing time, he homed in on his quarry. She was straightening stacks of paper, talking with another woman he recognized as her receptionist from the office.

Shelley looked up as he came closer. Her eyes widened. "Zach?"

"Hi. How'd today go?" Brilliant opening.

"Great. Just great." She stared at him, a puzzled line between her eyebrows. "What are you doing here again? Was Carol that enthusiastic?"

"No. I came by myself." Even to his own ears he

sounded half-conscious. Why was he having so much trouble making conversation these days?

The receptionist stepped forward. "That looks like everything. Are we ready to go?"

Zach nearly swore. If Shelley had given someone else a ride, that would be the end of his plans. He could handle an extra car. An extra person just would not work.

"Sure." Shelley sat down in a chair, reached under the table and stood up again with her purse. She looked at Zach. "Mindy drove us over from the office this morning. I left my car in the garage."

The tension in Zach's gut let go. "I could give you a ride. If Mindy doesn't mind."

"That's okay—" Shelley started.

"Sounds good," the receptionist said at the same time. She grinned at Zach and he winked back at her. "Your car has to be closer than mine—they make the exhibitors park a million miles away. Is it still snowing?"

"Wasn't when I came in. And there's not much accumulation." He made a mental note to send flowers to the front desk Monday morning.

Mindy nodded. "You don't need to walk that far in the cold, Shelley." She put a hand on the other woman's shoulder, then slipped out of the booth. "I could bring the car around, but this way, I can go straight home—if you don't mind."

Shelley looked from her receptionist to Zach and back again. "That's true. Thanks for all your help—enjoy your Sunday."

"See you Monday." Before her boss could say a word, she'd vanished into the crowd.

Zach watched her disappear, then turned back to find Shelley looking at him with raised eyebrows. "Real finesse."

He grinned. "Pretty good, wasn't it?"

No smile in reply, just a puzzled frown. "But why?"

"Because we need to talk. Because I haven't seen you in a while. Just...because." A bank of lights somewhere in the hall cut off. "We'd better get out or we'll be stuck in the dark all night."

She gave him a suspicious glance, but picked up her coat. "I guess I don't have a choice."

"You always have a choice, Shelley." He took the coat from her hands and opened it so she could put her arms in. "I'll call you a cab and pay for it myself if that's what you want."

She froze for a second, then moved all the way into the coat and let him put it over her shoulders. As always, being this close to her took his breath away.

"Never mind," she said. "I appreciate the ride, Zach."

"Anytime." Her soft smile drew one from him. He put a hand in the small of her back and gently urged her toward the door. "Have you had dinner?"

"N-no."

"Neither have I."

Under his palm, he felt her take a long breath. "Why don't we go somewhere and get something to eat?"

Zach gave a silent cheer. "Sounds like a plan. What kind of food are you in the mood for?"

"Chinese?"

"You got it."

His favorite Asian restaurant featured white tablecloths, low lighting and excellent food. After they ordered, the server took the menus away and brought a pot of green tea, which Shelley poured for both of them. And then she looked over at Zach.

"Well," she said softly. "I certainly didn't expect the night to end like this."

"Pretty amazing," he agreed. And then, gently, "How are you feeling these days?"

"Good. Tired. Clumsy."

Zach shook his head. "Not clumsy."

Shelley laughed. "You haven't seen me trying to get off the couch."

"No, I haven't." Disappointment must have come through in his voice, because she sobered, and toyed with her fork. With a sense of fatalism, Zach took the jump. "Shelley, this isn't working."

She avoided his gaze. "You could have taken me to my car."

"That's not what I'm talking about. And you know it."

Her shoulders moved with a sigh. "I know."

Taking another risk, he reached for her hand. When she didn't resist, he pulled in a needed breath. "I really want to be a part of your life."

Shelley sighed again, but this time she looked up, and her eyes were gentle. "I know."

"Can we work that out?"

The server came to their table with bowls of soup. When she'd left again, Shelley said, "We can try."

Relief exploded inside him like fireworks. Zach squeezed her fingers and sat back.

"Good answer." He grinned. "Now let's eat!"

CHAPTER TWELVE

THE EVENING had to end, but Shelley didn't want to say goodbye. She'd missed Zach these last weeks, missed his unpredictable visits, his grin, his kindness, like a warm blanket around her. Being with him made life simpler, encouraged her to think she might be able to manage, after all.

But they couldn't spend the night in a garage. Time to make a break. "This has been lovely." She put her hand on the door latch.

His fingers closed around her wrist. "Shelley."

She looked back at him. Shadows shaped his face. His eyes sparked blue in the darkness. Her gaze fell to his mouth and desire curled in her chest as she remembered the taste of his kisses. She had to concentrate to understand what he was saying.

"I tried to…lure…you into some kind of relationship before. I thought if I showed you we could get along—" He cleared his throat. "I guess that wasn't a good idea. So now I'm saying it plainly. I want to see you, know how you're doing, what you're doing. Just give me a chance, okay? I know we can work this out for all of us, if we're careful and patient."

"I'll try, Zach. That's the best I can do." She opened the door and got out of the car. "Thanks for dinner."

"You're welcome." He stared at his hands on the steering wheel for a few seconds, then looked her way. "Can I come over some night this week? I'll bring food."

She would have liked to feel less enthusiastic at the prospect. "Okay. Call me."

"I will." He flashed a grin. "Sleep well, Shelley—after you get home, that is."

She laughed and shut the door. Zach waited while she unlocked the Mercedes, got herself settled and started the engine. Then he followed her out of the parking garage and all the way to the interstate out of town. With a tap on the horn, he took the southbound exit as she turned north.

Questions assailed her during the drive. He'd said he lived southeast of the city. What kind of house? she wondered. Was he neat or messy? Did he like antiques or modern furniture?

So much they didn't know about each other, even though they'd shared their bodies and created a child. Would time together before the baby was born change anything? Was she being weak, simply giving in to her own wish to be with Zach? Was she leading him on, creating a situation both of them would regret? Or was *he* the one leading *her* on?

She'd argued herself into a headache by the time she got home. The house was quiet and dim, a bit too chilly. She turned up the heat and climbed the stairs, thinking about her aching legs and back, her tired, swollen feet. A little pampering right now would feel so good...someone to bring her a drink and massage her shoulders, maybe run a bath and talk to her while she soaked. Someone to hold her in bed, his hand rubbing her belly as the baby bumped and punched.

No. Not just someone. Zach.

Mechanically, Shelley hung up her suit, put her shoes in their cubbyhole and her lingerie in the hamper, then donned the oversize T-shirt she'd taken to sleeping in. Without a drink, without a massage, without Zach's body curved around hers, she huddled under the covers, alone and miserable but so tired that sleep had claimed her before she could shed more than a few hot tears.

ENCOURAGED BY Shelley's acceptance of his plans, Zach suggested they get together on Friday night, for a movie, maybe.

He came up with an even better idea on the drive to her house that evening. "How about the Indigo, instead?" He thought she'd enjoyed Jimmy's club. Success was always worth repeating.

But even before he'd closed the front door, Shelley shook her head. "I don't think so, Zach."

"You don't like jazz?"

"Actually, I do. I bought a couple of CDs recently."

Another point scored. "Jimmy's got a good group lined up this weekend. And a better cook. The roads are clear and dry. What other reason could there be not to go?"

She glanced down at her stomach, and he followed her thought. "You look great." And she did. Every time he saw her, she only got more beautiful.

"I look like a candidate for the Macy's Thanksgiving Day parade."

"Nah." Zach pretended to study her closely. Her red sweater and black leggings practically begged for a pointed cap trimmed in white fur. "Now, there is some resemblance to a certain jolly old elf." He grinned at her. "All you need is the reindeer."

"You jerk." She turned her back. He heard a tell-tale sniff.

Damn. What a time to get clumsy with women! Zach closed his hands over her shoulders. "Shelley, I'm teasing. I've never seen you that you didn't look like a million dollars. You're as gorgeous right now as you've always been, and sexy as hell."

"You're just a smooth talker." She shook her head, and the scent of spiced lemon drifted over him. "I'll bet you say that to all the expectant mothers of your acquaintance."

Smiling, he slid his hands down her arms to her elbows and back again. "As a matter of fact, I don't."

The red sweater left her neck bare. Zach took a risk and eased his palms inward across her shoulders, underneath that shining hair. He cupped the sides of her neck with his fingers and pressed his thumbs firmly into the muscles along her spine.

Shelley gave a soft gasp. "That's so good. My neck has been stiff for weeks."

"You work too hard," he murmured. "Let your chin drop."

She did as he asked, at the same time as Zach took a step forward. Their bodies came into contact, her straight, narrow back pressing into his chest. Her breathing slowed, the tension seeped out of her body as he continued to rub her neck. After another couple of minutes, she practically purred with contentment.

Zach took a deep breath of his own. He enjoyed making Shelley feel good. And he could do so much more...with his hands roaming, down over her breasts and along her swollen stomach, shaping her hips and the curve of her bottom...with his mouth wandering, over her head, along the side of her neck, across the sensitive palm of her elegant hand...with his arms folding, pulling her back, tucking her tight against him and recovering that rhythm they'd found so many months ago.

All of which would do wonders for him, too. He had wanted Shelley the first time he saw her.

But sex wasn't part of the picture. Not now, not until she realized there was much more between them than just the physical needs they could satisfy.

So he moved away from Shelley's warmth. He took his hands from the bare and vulnerable nape of her neck. His body shivered with tension.

"Are you sure about a night out?" His voice wasn't as steady as he'd hoped.

"I'm sure." Her voice wasn't any better. "How would you explain why you'd brought me? Jimmy wouldn't understand."

"Oh, Jimmy already knows."

"What?" She whipped around, faster than a woman in her condition should move. "He knows what?"

"That we're...um..." Involved? Connected? "That you and I—" The hole he was digging got deeper.

She stared at him with a chill in her eyes. "Explain exactly what you told him."

"That I'm interested in you."

"That I'm pregnant?"

"Well...yeah."

"That you're the father?"

Lust wouldn't be a problem anymore. Zach had a feeling getting out alive might be. "I, uh, told him that part, too."

BREATHING FAST, Shelley struggled to stay calm. How could he do this? How could he put his hands on her, give her such pleasure, when he'd betrayed her so thoroughly?

"Who else have you told? Your mother? Carol?"

"Nobody. But Jimmy's my best friend."

Some comfort. "And who has he told? All the guys he hangs out with?"

"No. He wouldn't do that."

She paced around the entry hall, torn between shame and fury. "I was trying to keep things as quiet as possible, Zach. The whole city does not need to know about...this." Her knees wobbled and her hands had started to shake. She wondered if she could handle this argument sitting down.

Zach pushed his fists into the pockets of his jeans. "I understand that. But it's pretty hard to hide a pregnancy."

"I covered that aspect of the situation."

The tilt of his head was skeptical. "Oh, sure—with a lousy ring and a fake husband. Great solution."

If it weren't so unbelievable, she'd have thought

he was jealous. "What's wrong with the ring and the husband?"

"They're a lie, Shelley! A lie that cheats me out of what I'm asking for—a wife and our baby."

She stared at him, at the hurt and… and…loss?…on his face. What in the world was he saying? "You'd *rather* be—" She cleared her throat. "Married?"

"Hell, yes!" He stood silent for a few seconds, his stare caught somewhere between laughter and…tears? "What else have I been telling you for the last three months?"

The room went black for a second, then started to spin. Shelley grabbed the banister to stay on her feet. Fighting Zach—fighting herself—suddenly seemed impossible. "Well, okay, then. Let's get married!"

Zach gazed at her, and she almost laughed at the shock on his face. His eyebrows drew together. "What did you say?"

"I said we should get married." Repeating the words was even scarier than blurting them out the first time. She would have liked to disappear into the floor. Maybe she'd misread him…

Zach looked down at his shoes, and then into her face again. "Okay. This weekend?" His calm only tripled her fear. "We can go to Las Vegas."

Her stomach dropped as reality crashed in. She put up a hand. "Wait—don't we need to think about this a little more?"

"No, we don't. We need to get married first, and the rest of the situation will fall into place."

"Your family…my mother…" The room had

stopped spinning, but only the banister kept her standing up.

"They'll have to adjust." He stepped close and took her hands with his. "I'm going home to make plane reservations. I'll have to check that it's okay for you to fly. You're going to go to bed, get a good night's sleep, and pack in the morning. We'll spend the night there. I'll let you know what time to be ready." The blue of his eyes was as deep, as hypnotic, as she'd ever seen it. "Clear?"

She couldn't muster the strength to argue. The situation had gone beyond her control, and she didn't know how to retrieve it. "Clear."

"Good." He leaned forward and touched his mouth to her forehead. "Sleep well. Lock the door behind me. I'll talk to you in the morning."

"Okay." She stood where she was, watched him walk to the door and open it, then step through, closing the panel behind him. After a few seconds, the door reopened.

Zach put his head in. "Lock the door, Shelley."

"Right." She did as he said, and then leaned back against the panel, heart pounding, throat tight. Was this another mistake? Had she just ruined the rest of her life...and Zach's...and the baby's?

The good night's sleep Zach ordered her to get resisted every effort she made. She pictured him in her house. Swimming in the pool, reading in the family room, playing with a baby on the living-room floor. She saw his clothes in her closet, his shoes by the bed. His scent filled her bathroom, and she imagined his face in the mirror, steamy after a shower they'd taken together. She would dry beads of water from his smooth, tan back, leaning close every now and then to lick a drop or two, and then more, until he turned to take hold and bring her up against him for a wild and wicked kiss...

But Zach hadn't mentioned sex. She knew he would fulfill his commitment to his child, because he was that kind of man. She would be selfish and...and silly...to expect anything more.

Not the kind of thoughts that made for a restful night.

ZACH CALLED at ten Saturday morning. "How'd you sleep?"

"Just fine," she lied. "How about you?"

"Great. Our flight leaves at two. I'll pick you up about noon, okay?"

"Why don't I just drive to the airport and meet you? That's an extra hour of driving you won't have to do."

He was quiet for a moment. "Okay, sure. I could use the time. I'll meet you at the ticket desk at one?"

"See you there." Her hand was shaking as she set the phone down. She'd never been this nervous in her life. If only someone could tell her she was doing the right thing...

Shelley picked up the phone again and dialed her mother's number. "Hi, Mom."

"Good morning! How are you?"

Terrified. "Pretty good. How was your week?"

"Busy, the way I like it. What's going on?"

"I thought I'd better let you know..." Deep breath. "I'll be leaving town today."

"Oh? Anywhere special?"

"Um...Las Vegas."

Her mother chuckled. "I'm picturing you at the slots. Are you going to gamble away your fortune?"

Might as well take the plunge. "No. I'm going to...get married."

After a long silence, Dorothy said, "To whom?"

Shelley squeezed her eyes shut. "Zach Harmon."

"Why?" The one word carried a whole world of shock and confusion.

Her hands shook so badly she needed both of them to hold the phone. "Because...because Zach's the father. Of my baby."

Dorothy's voice, when she finally spoke, was cool. "No wonder you were so upset back in July, when I let him bring Allyson home from the ball game. I gather you changed your mind about telling him?" Hurt tinted the question.

"He found out before I could. I'm sorry I didn't tell you. I really did think we would all be better off apart, even after he knew. But Zach keeps pushing, and I can't keep fighting." Herself, as well as him.

"Well." Dorothy sighed. "I'm glad he's willing to assume the responsibility. This is probably for the best. You could use some help, and a chance to be taken care of. Do you want me to come with you?"

"I don't think so, if that's okay."

"You'll be getting married with none of your family there?"

"We're only doing this for the baby, Mom. It's not exactly a celebration."

"Well, be sure to take something old, new, borrowed and blue." The reserve in her voice diminished the encouraging spirit of the advice.

"I will. And I'll call when we get back."

"I'll be waiting. Good luck, honey." Her voice softened on the last word, at least.

"Thanks. Love you."

Shelley set down the phone and went up to her bedroom to choose a wedding outfit. The options were limited, because she hadn't bought a whole closet of maternity clothes. She finally settled on a soft angora sweater in winter white, with a pair of wool slacks in the same color. Those covered the new part. A gold necklace and earrings that were her first luxury jewelry filled in for something old, and a scarf with shades of gold and blue and red finished up the rest. Right?

"No…" Shelley sighed. "Something borrowed." This family would need all the good luck it could get.

She went down the hall into Allyson's room. Its emptiness reminded her of all she'd lost. Both her mother and her little girl should be there to share this wedding. If indeed, there should be a wedding at all.

"Oh, stop it!" Shelley opened the top drawer of Allyson's chest and took out her christening bonnet, fashioned from a delicate linen-and-lace handkerchief. She would take this cap to her wedding. In that way, Allyson could come, too.

As she folded the tiny square into her purse, the ring she wore caught her eye. The make-believe wedding ring.

Should she keep it in her pocket for Zach to give back? He wouldn't have time to buy a ring, even if he had the inclination. Should there even be a ring to symbolize such a…a…counterfeit marriage?

Zach had called *this* ring a lie. So she took it off. Ring or no ring, there would be a wedding. And then…?

The baby punched at her. ''I know, I know,'' she told it. ''You think this is a good idea, too.''

Shelley folded her arms around her belly. ''So it's just me,'' she whispered to the little person inside. ''I'm the only one who can't believe this will ever, ever work.''

CHAPTER THIRTEEN

ZACH WAS on his way out the door when the phone rang. He stopped in his tracks and waited to hear the message, in case there was an emergency he needed to handle. Otherwise, he wasn't talking to anybody until he and Shelley returned...from their wedding.

The answering machine clicked on. "Zachary, this is your mother. Please come to lunch Sunday. I need to talk with you about Carol. Take care of yourself."

He dropped his head back against the door frame. His mother would like to know that he was getting married. She would want to meet the woman first. She would expect to help with wedding plans and reception food and all that jazz, just as she had for his brothers and his sister.

Instead, he was sneaking Shelley off to Vegas for a quickie ceremony by a justice of the peace. No priest, no family, no friends. His mother would be devastated.

But if he didn't take advantage of Shelley's offer right away, there might not be a wedding at all.

Zach straightened up and started moving again. So that was the answer. There would be a wedding. Tonight. He and Shelley would come back to Denver tomorrow as husband and wife and take up their lives together, for better or worse.

He wasn't sure, yet, which outcome was more likely. He'd spent a sleepless night going over the decision, remembering the conversation, discussing with Darius the changes in store.

Did Shelley even like cats?

And would she be comfortable in his place? He'd rolled out of bed before 6:00 a.m. to neaten things up, trying to see his house through her eyes. Nothing here resembled the grandeur of her home, of course. But there were three bedrooms and a kitchen he'd remodeled with concern for efficiency and convenience. She might feel a little cramped at first. They'd both have to compromise.

That possibility seemed easier, less threatening, when he glanced toward the door at the airport and saw her coming his way. She looked fantastic, all in white and gold, with a colorful scarf around her shoulders and her hair shining in the afternoon sun.

But her eyes, meeting his, were wide with apprehension.

Zach grinned and took the suitcase out of her hand. "Right on time. Let's check in, then get something to drink."

She didn't say much during the check-in, didn't say anything at all as she sipped hot chocolate in the airport coffee shop. Because the lack of conversation was getting on his nerves, Zach reached over and twined his fingers in hers. So cold. "Shelley?"

She gazed at their joined hands, then looked up. "Yes?"

"It's going to be okay. *We're* going to be okay. I promise."

Her fingers trembled in his. "I hope so."

"I know so. Try to relax."

"I am." She sighed quietly.

He'd booked first-class seats, wanting Shelley to be as comfortable as possible. "The flight isn't very long," he told her as they buckled in. "We'll be on the ground almost before they have a chance to serve drinks."

She didn't answer. The plane taxied away from the terminal and down the runway, then took off with a leap of power. Shelley only spoke after they heard the flaps go up and the wings had leveled.

"I told my mother that you're the baby's father." She didn't look at him as she said it. "She wasn't exactly thrilled."

"I'm sorry—I hoped she'd like me a little."

"She does like you. She's just worried about what we're doing. And she's right. I can't help wondering…"

"If we're making a mistake?"

Eyes closed, she nodded.

Zach watched her face from the side. He had a feeling that the whole deal rested on this one conversation. If he blew his chance, everything would fall apart.

He took her hand again. How could she have gotten even colder? "I know this is scary. And if you want to call it off, right here, right now, you can. I won't force you to marry me. I can only say that I'll do my best to take care of you and the baby, to make all of us comfortable and safe."

With the tips of his fingers, he touched her cheek, turning her face toward him. The motion disturbed the tears in her eyes. They fell onto her skin like a slow rain and burned his heart like acid. "Shelley, I believe we can be happy. Won't you trust me? I really want to make this work."

Her lips trembled, her gaze clung to his. "I always trusted you, Zach. I'm the one who never…who can't…" She turned her face away and slipped her fingers out of his to wipe her cheeks.

"Something to drink?" The flight attendant stopped beside their seats. "Peanuts?"

Shelley shook her head. Zach shook his. They rode the rest of the way to Vegas in their separate silences.

THEY DIDN'T WAIT LONG at the wedding chapel—October wasn't the most popular month to get married in Vegas. Zach had called ahead to set up an appointment, make a reservation, whatever the hell getting married this way was called.

Crazy probably came closest.

"Do you, Zachary Briggs Harmon, take this woman to be your lawful wedded wife? To have and to hold from this day forward? To honor and cherish, in sickness and in health, until death you do part?"

Quite a commitment. Not that he'd thought otherwise. But the words sounded so…final. Zach took a deep breath. "I do."

After a long hesitation, Shelley answered her own version of that question. "I do."

The J.P. nodded. "Do you have a ring?"

"No," Shelley said.

"Sure," Zach said at the same time. He slipped the band he'd bought out of his pocket and reached across for Shelley's left hand.

Her fingers clutched at his, and he looked up into her distressed brown eyes. "I—I don't…"

He put a fingertip on her lips. "No problem," he whispered. "With this ring, I thee wed," he said loudly, repeating after the judge. "And thereto I plight thee my troth."

"With the power vested in me by the state of Nevada," the J.P. declared, "I now pronounce you man and wife. You may kiss the bride!"

Zach looked at the pale face of the woman he'd just married. Emotions stormed through her eyes, too many and too fast for him to read. But anxiety edged them all.

He managed a small grin to cover his own nerves. Cupping her head with his hands, he leaned closer. "Just shut your eyes. I promise this won't hurt a bit."

Shelley did as he asked. Zach touched his mouth to hers with all the gentleness he could command.

Despite his intentions, a current ran through the kiss, a thread of passion he hadn't created, couldn't control. Shelley's palm came to rest on his shoulder. Her lips softened, then parted, under his.

All at once Zach was lost, as lost as he'd been the first time he'd kissed her. Then…now…reality disappeared beyond the searing need this woman could excite. He slipped his hands down her back, pulled her as close as he could and took the kiss fathoms deeper.

Beside them, the judge cleared his throat.

Disoriented, Zach lifted his head to look around. Shelley stepped back, breaking the connection they'd shared. He felt the loss as if he'd walked into a blizzard without his clothes. "Um...okay. What now?"

The legal formalities took another few minutes. Finally, they stepped out of the chapel into a cool desert twilight. Zach put a hand at the small of Shelley's back. "How about dinner?"

She glanced at him, and then away. "If you're hungry."

"I'm always hungry. And I just happen to have reservations." He waved down a cab and opened Shelley's door, gave the driver an address, then settled back against the seat.

"Have you been to Vegas before?"

She shrugged. "A couple of times."

"Did you win?" Maybe if he could distract her from what they'd just done, the situation would get easier.

"I don't have much of a head for cards. And I don't have the patience for a slot machine."

"Yet you're always gambling with real estate." Not to mention gambling on marriage. For the second time.

"That's different." She looked at him with a return of the fighting spirit he'd been missing. "I have control over a real-estate deal. The way things turn out depends to a great extent on how well I do my job. I don't have any control over the cards or the slot machine. Winning there is just luck."

"I've been a cop too long not to believe in good luck. And bad."

Shelley shook her head. "I'd rather make my own."

The cab slowed, then stopped at the end of a line

of cars edging toward the front door of Vegas's newest and ritziest hotel casino. "Gonna be a while," the driver said over his shoulder.

Zach leaned forward to peer through the windshield. A thick collage of sequins and loud shirts and cowboy hats milled around the door to the lobby, under a haze of smoke floating like high fog in the lights. Folks who had opted to walk passed the cab on either side, some of them following less than a straight line, all of them loud.

Somewhere up ahead, a bottle crashed and shouts broke out. The crowd stirred, separated, re-formed. Camera flashes sputtered, a spotlight danced across the sky and a million smaller bulbs flickered on the windows of the hotel. Money-fueled chaos.

"Is this crazy, or what?" When Shelley didn't answer, Zach turned to look her. He couldn't help a smile. Sometime in the last few minutes she'd fallen asleep, with her head tilted against the window and her hands clasped loosely over her stomach. The diamonds in the ring he'd put on her finger pulsed with their own life, nearly as brilliant as the hotel lights.

As they got closer to the entrance, music filtered into the mix, though the crowd noise defied any attempt to recognize an actual tune. Voices called, argued, complained. At least two babies cried in counterpoint. A dog barked. Shelley didn't even stir—she must be completely exhausted. Maybe she hadn't slept any better than he had last night.

At last, their cab reached the front door. Zach got out, turned, then stood staring at the commotion before him. This was the least romantic place he'd ever seen. Were he and Shelley going to spend their wedding night *here?* Was this the place to begin a new life?

As their driver walked behind him to open the trunk, Zach made a snap decision. "Is there somewhere else to stay in this town? Quieter, less crowded?"

The cabby shrugged. "This is Vegas, man. Who wants quiet?"

"I do." He pulled a bill out of his wallet. "Fifty bucks plus fare if you take us to a nice place where we can have dinner and a room without a neon view."

The trunk slammed shut. "I can do that."

In less than twenty minutes, the cab turned into the driveway of a house on the edge of town, where desert reclaimed the land and mountains hunched like black dragons against a sky sprayed with stars. "This is a B&B," the driver said. "Good food, nice rooms. I called on the way over—they got exactly one left."

"Thanks." He handed over two fifties, to cover the fare and the tip. While the driver took the bags up to the front door, Zach leaned into the cab and put his hand on Shelley's arm. "Wake up, lady. Dinner's waiting."

She turned her head slightly, then settled back into her nap.

"Shelley, wake up." He shook her lightly. "Somebody cast a spell?" Her breathing stayed even, her eyes closed.

Zach chuckled, then braced his weight with one hand on the seat near Shelley's shoulder and a knee near her hip. With the other hand, he tilted her face toward him. And paused.

My wife. A dynamo with cornsilk hair and a pouting mouth. An expectant mother, with the swell of a baby beneath her small breasts. A woman who used words as weapons but could be hurt by them, as well. A sturdy spirit, reluctant to depend on anyone else. Especially not the man she'd married.

"I'm going to change that," Zach promised in a low voice. Then he pressed a kiss against those soft, red lips.

THE KISS WAS LIKE a dream...or came out of her dreams, Shelley wasn't sure which. She warmed to the touch, turned into the taste and pressure of a firm mouth over hers. Patience and caring and concern poured into her through the kiss, filling the cold places inside with light and heat. So much heat. She wanted even more. She put up a hand, touched the curve of an ear, the arch of a jaw, the corner of a man's lips.

She opened her eyes, focused. And drew back, blushing. "I'm awake now. Sorry."

Zach traced the pad of his thumb across her mouth. He was smiling. "Don't be sorry. That was incredible."

Shelley looked away, feeling for her purse. "Where are we? What happened?"

His fingers drifted across her chin and away. "A bed and breakfast. I decided we didn't belong in a mob scene."

"Oh." The silence around them was a welcome change, though she wasn't sure she had a handle on anything very solid right now. She caught sight of the cabdriver coming up behind Zach. "I guess we should go in."

"Let me help you." Zach held out his hand. Shelley allowed him to steady her as she got out of the car, but drew her arm back as quickly as possible. She didn't know how to begin finding her balance when it came to this man. Her husband.

Inside the inn, a man approached them out of a hallway on the other side of the polished black marble floor. "Good evening. The cabdriver said you'd like to stay the night?"

Zach's hand settled on Shelley's shoulder. "If you have a room."

"Certainly, Mr...?"

"Harmon. Zach and Shelley Harmon." The two men shook hands.

But Shelley listened to those words—*Zach and Shelley Harmon*—echo through her mind. They seemed to bounce off the walls of her skull, moving faster and faster, until her head started spinning. She put a hand out for stability against the motion, and shut her eyes.

A hand closed over hers. "Shelley, are you okay?"

"I—I need to sit down."

"Sure." She kept her eyes closed as she was led a few steps and gently pushed into a chair, then leaned back gratefully. The whirling slowed a little.

The innkeeper's voice came from high above her. "I can call a doctor or an ambulance. They'll be here in minutes."

"That's a good idea." Zach seemed much closer. Both his palms cupped hers.

"No. I'm okay. Really." Shelley opened her eyes to find Zach's face level with her own as he knelt by her chair. His gaze was a combination of fierceness and worry. "It's been a long day."

"I know." He squeezed her hands. "Why don't we let a doctor check you out, just to be sure?"

She pulled her hands away from his. "I think what I need most is just to lie down."

"Right this way." The innkeeper headed down a long hallway. Zach stood, but before he could touch her again, Shelley labored to her feet on her own and followed their guide. Carrying their bags, Zach followed her.

A huge circular window at the end of the hall showed them the city in the distance, a fairyland of light and color. Beside that window, the man ahead of her unlocked a door and stepped inside. "I hope you'll be comfortable." A lamp turned on as Shelley entered, and then another.

She turned in time to see Zach pocket the room key. The innkeeper looked around, and then smiled as he backed toward the door. "Dinner is served until nine. Would you like to join us?"

When Zach glanced her way, Shelley nodded. "Food would be a good idea."

"Excellent. I'll prepare your table."

Their meal was more than quiet. Shelley ate because she knew she should, though she didn't really taste anything. Other guests sat at the tables around them, their faces lit by candlelight, their voices a smooth hum under classical music and the clink of dinnerware. She and Zach were the only ones not talking.

They left the dining room after dessert, arrived back at the end of the hallway without a word. Zach opened the door, then closed it behind him.

Now it was just the two of them. Shelley walked to the window. Her husband—*her husband*—came up behind her and took hold of her shoulders. "Feel better?"

She nodded. The quiet around them had weight, exerted pressure. Breathing normally had become a challenge.

"You didn't get to finish your nap. Why don't you lie down?"

Shelley glanced at the one bed, then moved beyond his reach. "That's...that's a good idea." She slipped off her shoes and sat on the gray-and-silver-striped spread. But lying down was impossible. She couldn't relax with Zach standing there watching her.

"Or better yet..." He glanced toward the door, then put his hands in his pockets again. "You get changed, really comfortable, and crawl under the covers. You must be beat." When she hesitated, his face closed and his mouth tightened. "If you don't mind, I thought I'd go back to the lounge for a drink."

Relief and despair swept through her in equal measure. "No, I don't mind at all. I—I'll be here when you get back."

"Sure." Zach paused, watching her, then pivoted quickly and let himself out. The door closed with a firm thud.

Alone. On her wedding night. Shelley put her head

in her hands. Even she and Dex had done better than this. What was Zach thinking? Were those wonderful kisses at the wedding…that glorious sense of rightness she'd felt waking up in the cab…only pretend?

Sleep was the only obvious solution to this disaster. If she slept, she wouldn't hurt so much. *Change clothes,* she ordered herself. *Crawl into bed. Escape.*

Just as she stood up, Zach stalked back into the room. The door slammed shut. ''I'm not going anywhere. Not until we get things settled.''

Now she couldn't breathe at all. ''What are you talking about? Settle what?''

''This,'' he said, rounding the bed. Before she understood what he intended, before she could move, he plunged his fingers into her hair and took her mouth in a desperate, devastating kiss.

CHAPTER FOURTEEN

INSTANT SECOND THOUGHTS...

Zach drew back almost immediately. "Shelley, I'm sorry." He pressed his mouth against her forehead. "I'm sorry."

"It's okay." Her small hands curled around his wrists. "You don't have to apologize. I understand."

"I didn't mean—"

"I know. Really. I don't expect anything else."

"You should have time to..." Zach let his words die away as the echoes of what they'd been saying *at* each other caught up to him. He lifted his head to look down at the woman he held, her flushed face, her evasive eyes. "You don't expect anything else? Than what, exactly?"

Shelley released his wrists and tried to step away, but he didn't budge, which kept her between his body and the side of the bed. "I—I—" She took a deep breath, staring at his tie. "We've done this for...for the baby. We don't have to pretend there's anything more."

"Anything more." Pain flashed through him like a headache, followed quickly by a laugh. "That's good. I don't like pretending."

"Well, then—"

"Shelley, I'm not pretending if I touch you...like

this." He rubbed his knuckles over the angle of her jaw, to the point of her chin, savoring soft skin and her very personal perfume. "Or this." With his other hand, he pushed the hair back from her face, letting his fingertips drift across the sensitive shell of her ear.

"Zach..." She looked up at him, anxiety and hope gathering in her gaze, along with desire.

"And you can believe me when I tell you you're beautiful." Using both hands, he lifted the gold chain she wore over her head, let it puddle gently on the table beside them. "That I've never looked at you without wanting you." He kissed her temples, her closed eyelids, her cheekbones, her chin. Just being this close to her set up an earthquake inside of him. "That there hasn't been a night in the last seven months when I didn't wake up thinking about you."

Shelley's lips trembled as he kissed her again, and again. He swept his hands down her back, pulling her close. The fit was different, with a baby between them. But the sigh she gave, as her arms circled his shoulders, was the one he remembered.

"Zach..." He tasted his name on her breath. His belly tightened as her hands slipped inside his shirt and she responded with all the passion he'd prayed for, all the intensity he remembered. Relieved beyond words, Zach made love to his wife through the dark desert night.

Sometime during those hours, a wall inside him cracked, then crumbled. A surge of emotions—desperate needs he'd never let himself think about—poured into his soul. He couldn't sort them out or understand their message, except that somehow the woman sleeping in his arms was the key to them all.

Satisfied with the moment, content with his conclusion, Zach tightened his arms around his wife and allowed himself to drop into sleep.

SHELLEY OPENED her eyes. After a few seconds, the scene framed by the window began to make sense— the desert, washed with lavender morning light.

She was in Las Vegas. Married to Zach Harmon. *Really* married.

She tried to move and realized Zach still held her close against his side, her head pillowed on his shoulder. At the same instant the baby kicked, with enough strength to make her gasp.

Zach's sleepy voice said, "Was that what I think it was?"

Her stomach was pressed close into his ribs. "Um, yes." Shelley scooted away as he loosened his arm.

But he turned onto his side facing her, his head propped on one hand. "Pretty strong, for a baby. Can I feel?"

She gazed at him, wondering. He looked so relaxed, so satisfied. As if this were the most normal marriage in the world. "If you want to."

His left hand slipped under the sheet, then under the camisole she wore to spread over her skin. Details of their night flashed through Shelley's head, making her blush. Making her want to start all over again. Making her aware that she was practically naked.

The baby obliged its dad with another powerful punch. "Cool." Zach looked up again. "I haven't felt that since before Carol was born. Suddenly you know there's a person inside there.''

"A very active person,'' Shelley said, wondering where this conversation would lead. Zach hadn't lifted his hand. The baby continued with morning stretches, and Zach lay there, his eyes focused inward as their baby moved. She couldn't tell what he was thinking. She only knew that after another minute of his skin against hers, she would give in to her need for him, let herself reach for his smooth chest and supple shoulders. They were married, after all, and she wanted him.

No, it was more than that, she realized suddenly. A shaft of light from the window struck his face, and by its radiance she saw the truth. Simply, purely...painfully...she loved Zach Harmon as she'd never loved anyone else.

The baby chose that moment to dance a jig on her full bladder. "Excuse me,'' Shelley murmured, sliding awkwardly to the side of the bed. Sitting up took time, and her face warmed as she thought of Zach watching her, then grew even hotter. All she wore was the camisole. She couldn't possibly parade across the room in a short piece of flimsy material that didn't reach her hips.

But when she looked over her shoulder, Zach had grabbed her pillow and pulled it over his face. "Wake me about noon,'' he mumbled.

How, in just a few seconds, could she come to love him even more? "What time is our flight?''

"Nine-thirty.''

She ached to touch him. To forget about going home. "Noon might be a little late.''

"Okay. Eleven forty-five." The noisy snores he faked followed her into the bathroom and left her chuckling.

She took her time in the shower, with her hair, getting dressed.

When she finally came out, he had fallen asleep for real. "Zach, it's eight o'clock." She shook his shoulder, cherishing the warm skin under her hand. "You need to wake up."

"Mmm. Yeah." He breathed deeply and rolled over. His heavy lids lifted. Her heart skittered when he smiled.

"You look good," he growled. "All the way down to the skin." With a huge stretch, he threw the sheets, blanket and coverlet to the foot of the bed, then followed them with a quick, athletic move that set him on his feet. She got a great view of his excellent backside just before he disappeared into the bathroom.

Shelley sank onto the bed, put her palm in the hollow of the pillow where Zach had buried his head, then closed her eyes. This seemed to be her fate, marriage to a handsome, sexy, incredibly compelling man who didn't—couldn't possibly—love her.

Without love, her marriage to Dex had ended in rage and recriminations on both sides. Only now, after six years, were those wounds beginning to heal.

She wasn't sure she would ever recover from Zach. As long as they stayed together, she would have to bear the knowledge he'd only married her out of duty. She didn't think he would leave her. His sense of honor was too strong.

But what would happen if—when—he found a

woman he could truly love? How would Shelley let him go? How could she allow him to stay?

Why hadn't she just gone home alone that night in March?

Zach came out of the bathroom, whistling. "Perfect timing. We've got an hour to get to the airport. We can get some breakfast there. Are you ready?"

"Sure." She gathered up her belongings in a sort of numbness, only half hearing his cheerful commentary.

"We'll be back at Stapleton by eleven. We've got the two cars, so I guess I'll go home and you can go to your place, pack up some clothes and stuff and come back down. But wait…" She looked up, caught his grin as he turned suddenly to face her. "You don't know where my house is, do you?"

Shelley concentrated on his question. "No…no, I don't. I guess I'll drive home and you can go to your place, get a few clothes and then come up."

The grin faded. He was quiet for a minute, playing with the zipper pull on his shaving kit. "I thought you would come to live in my house."

"Oh." She caught her breath. "But I have more room."

"You're a long way out of the city. I need to be close to my mom and the job."

"I work downtown, too, remember? The drive is easy, even in bad weather." Except for blizzards, of course.

Zach kept his gaze on the zipper on his bag. "Okay, to be honest…" He looked up, his eyes somber. "I'm not crazy about the idea of living in a house Dex Hightower built."

Because of Claire? Shelley took a deep breath against a surge of panic. "We don't have to do that forever. We can start out at my house, then find a place closer to town that we choose together." She tried a smile. "How's that?"

No smile came back. "Why not start out in my house?"

"Because it's too small."

He cast an exasperated glance at the ceiling. "Thousands of people live their whole lives in a house that size. I'm in a good neighborhood for kids—and we're doing what's best for the child, right?"

"My neighborhood is good for kids. We have one of the best public schools in the area. Not to mention a low crime rate and lower pollution than the city." Shelley noticed she was breathing as if she'd run the bases twice, and tried to calm down. "I worked hard for what I have now. I'm not happy about giving up my life."

Zach sliced through her objection with the side of his hand. "I'm giving up my life, too, Shelley. Getting married was not part of my plans."

"Yes, I know." And wasn't that the real point? She just hadn't expected things to fall apart so soon. "I tried very hard to keep from changing those plans. It's not my fault you wouldn't listen."

"You're the one who wouldn't listen!" With a quick turn, he paced to the door and back again. "If you'd said yes a couple of months ago, we could have gotten married at home, with our friends and family around, and taken our time to decide on where to live." He shook his head. "God only knows how I'm going to tell my family about this."

As she should have expected—he was ashamed of what they'd done.

Every feeling inside of her shut down. "Don't tell them anything." Shelley jerked the zipper on her own bag closed. "This has clearly been a mistake from beginning to end. You got what you wanted— we're married. Your child has a dad. And we can work out some kind of custody arrangement. I know really good lawyers." The laugh she attempted sounded like a sob. "This way, I live in my house, you live in your house, and your family never even needs to know what happened. See you later."

She tried to brush by him, but he caught her arm with a strength she couldn't fight. "Shelley, you know that won't work. Don't walk out of here. We'll get this settled."

"As far as I'm concerned, it is settled." Looking up, she focused on preserving her pride. "I won't even expect you to be faithful, since it's not a real marriage. Just think, Zach. You can have all the women you want, without strings, because you're already married!"

His eyes went gray with anger. "That's a stupid idea."

"Well, give yourself some time. Maybe it'll grow on you." She looked pointedly down at his hand on her arm, until he released her. "Goodbye. Please don't call me anymore." The click of the door closing behind her seemed very, very final.

The same cab they'd used last night arrived within minutes of the manager's call. When the driver got into the front seat, he looked over his shoulder. "We waiting for the mister?"

"No." Shelley risked a glance up at the house. Zach stood in the doorway, still as a column. Her vision blurred with tears. "No. Please, just leave. Now."

"Whatever you say."

WORKING WITH about half his brain, Zach got to the airport in time to stand in line to get a new ticket for a later flight. At the departure gate, he leaned against a wall of the crowded lounge, wondering what in the world he was going to do when he got back to Denver.

The passengers for first class boarded, and he moved into the line for the tourist seats. The flight attendants smiled as he stepped onto the plane. He tried for one of his own, then turned the corner into the aisle...and looked straight into Shelley's wide eyes. She sat on the first row of first class.

He thought she might faint, she turned so white. Her jaw dropped a little. Zach stared at her, speechless, while sentence fragments pitched through his brain. He couldn't choose the right one to start with.

"Hey, buddy, we flying standing up, here?" Someone behind Zach gave a push. "Let's move it!"

He stumbled forward, leaving first class behind, and dropped into his seat over the wing like a sack of dirty laundry.

Shelley had obviously wanted to avoid the flight she thought he would take, and they'd ended up on the same plane after all. Call it coincidence. Or call it torture.

But *she'd* booked a first-class seat. *She* wanted to live in her big house, not his little one. Was this all about money? Had she backed off from marrying him all along because he didn't earn enough? And had she realized this morning that such a drastic drop in her standard of living was too much to pay for great sex?

To make his trip completely miserable, the loud-mouth from the front of the plane sat between Zach and the window. He complained about the cabin temperature, the bumpy flight, the lack of food, the slowness of the attendants. Zach ground his teeth and wondered if a murder on this plane would be tried in Nevada or Colorado.

About twenty minutes from Denver, they flew into a cloud bank. The cabin darkened. Above hushed conversations, the captain warned of turbulence and asked them to fasten seat belts.

Almost before the request ended, the plane started falling. Straight down.

"Jesus!" Loudmouth smashed into the seat in front of him, then into the overhead bin. He hadn't buckled his seat belt.

Screams, shouts, and cries for help echoed off the walls. The plane continued to drop. Purses flew through the air, scattering checkbooks, combs, and pens. A laptop computer crashed into Zach's cheek, then moved on. He covered his head with his arms and prayed that Shelley had buckled her seat belt. Even so...

With a sudden thud, the fall stopped. Everything up in the air came down, including the man next to

Zach. Loudmouth clambered for his seat, swearing and yelling, adding profanities to the general chaos.

An attendant staggered down the aisle, and Zach caught her arm. "I'm a cop. Is there anything I can do to help?"

She brushed her hair back with a shaking hand. "I haven't found any serious injuries yet. I think we're okay. But you're bleeding!"

He put a hand to the ache over his cheekbone, came away with a red smear. "Compliments of IBM," he said. "I'll live." But he held her back when she would have moved on. "I know somebody up in first class. I'd like to go check on her."

The attendant shook her head. "Please don't move around. We've got enough people out of place."

"But—" He half rose from his seat. "I need to know—"

"Everyone in first class is fine. I promise." She pushed him down with a firm hand on his shoulder and a straightening of her shoulders that conveyed authority. "You must stay seated."

In a romance movie, Zach thought, the hero would get up to make sure his heroine was okay. Along the way, he might save a life or two. Or avoid death himself when his seat suddenly fell through the floor.

But—in real life—he would only be distracting the professionals from their job. Zach had coped with interfering civilians more often than he wanted to remember. They usually did more harm than good.

So he would stay here, as he'd been told. Wait...and worry. Agonize. What if Shelley wasn't okay? What if she'd been hit by debris, or had started labor? He wanted to know, wanted to hold her. Like any average guy, let alone a hero, he needed to be sure the woman he loved was safe...

Zach listened to his own thoughts. He closed his eyes, playing the words back to his mind's ear. "...any average guy...be sure...the woman he *loved*..."

Then he started praying. "Holy Jesus," he whispered. "What am I going to do now?"

CHAPTER FIFTEEN

THE FLIGHT ATTENDANTS refused to allow Shelley to walk off the plane. They got her a wheelchair and pushed her out ahead of all the passengers, straight into the arms of a waiting ambulance crew.

Before the last attendant could leave, though, Shelley caught her hand. "Can you get a message to a passenger on the plane for me?"

"I don't think—"

"Please." Shelley realized her grip had tightened and deliberately loosened her fingers. "Please, it's very important."

The attendant managed a shaken smile. "Okay. Sure."

"Thanks." Shelley took out the first piece of paper she came to in her purse and felt for a pen. "This will just take a second."

She wrote on the blank side.

Zach,
I'm okay, I'll let you know you if anything's wrong. Don't worry. Don't call.

Shelley.

Folding the paper in quarters, blank side out, she wrote his name and handed the note to the attendant.

"I really do appreciate this. So will he."

"No problem." The attendant turned away, then looked back around. "Is this the really great-looking guy in coach? The one with blue eyes and shoulders to dream about?"

That description fit Zach to a fault. "Sounds right."

"He asked me about somebody in first class—for a second, I thought we'd have to restrain him to keep him in his seat. Was that you?"

She'd known he would worry. "Probably."

"Wow. I'd like to have a man that fine checking on me." She walked away, shaking her head.

Shelley closed her eyes. The note should reassure Zach. It was the best thing she could do.

A cool hand covered hers. "Ma'am, are you all right?"

She opened her eyes again to see the face of a stranger, an EMT. "I think so."

"Let's get you to the hospital and check that out, just to be sure."

"Whatever you say." The misery would come along wherever she went.

HER MOTHER BROUGHT clean clothes to the hospital and kept her company through the anxious afternoon of tests. "Your Uncle Thomas and I picked up your car at the airport and drove it to your house." She studied Shelley for a minute. "But are you sure you're ready to leave?"

Shelley slipped into her shoes. "All I need, Mom,

is my own bed and a few hours of uninterrupted sleep. The baby's fine. I'm fine. Let's go.''

After a wheelchair ride to the front door, she sank gratefully into the seat of her mother's Cadillac. ''I hate hospitals.''

''I know.''

''They make you feel so helpless.''

''And you hate feeling helpless.''

Shelley sat up straight and smoothed her hair. ''Definitely. I want to take care of a situation myself. Hospitals don't let you do that. I get very upset.''

Her mother smiled ruefully. ''I noticed. What did you do when you couldn't stop the plane from falling?''

Just the thought set her heart to pounding. ''I grabbed my purse and covered my head and prayed. That was all I could do.'' That, and worry about Zach.

''Sometimes we have to allow other people to take care of the situation because we simply can't manage by ourselves.''

That remark sounded far from casual. ''What's your point?''

''Well...'' Dorothy accelerated onto the interstate. ''Maybe you have a problem letting Zach assume responsibility for you and your baby.''

''Why would you think that?'' Her heart picked up speed.

''You said it just a minute ago—you like to take care of yourself, in business and everything else. Staying in your own space would give you control of the situation—control you don't think you'd have at his house.''

Face hot, eyes stinging, Shelley seethed for a few seconds. "I do not need to be psychoanalyzed, Mother. Do me a favor and keep your insights to yourself."

"I'm just making observations."

"Well, don't." She turned back to the window and closed her eyes, hoping to signal complete lack of interest in further conversation.

By the time they'd reached her house, though, Shelley regretted her tantrum. She put a hand on her mother's arm as the car stopped. "Mom. I'm sorry I snapped at you."

With a smile, her mother patted her cheek. "This isn't an easy situation, honey. You're allowed some orneriness."

"Thanks." She didn't deserve such understanding. "Can you stay for dinner?"

"Of course."

Alone again that evening, Shelley tried to nap, as she'd promised she would. But the bedroom was too cold. She curled up in a blanket on the family-room couch, but the quiet bothered her. She turned on the television, but the noise only irritated without entertaining and she turned it off again.

Wandering through the house, she straightened a picture here and there, adjusted the set of a vase…and caught a flash of light from Zach's lovely ring, still on her finger.

I'm married. Again.

In two days, so much had changed. She'd married Zach and made love with him on their wedding night, committing herself to him in ways he would never know.

And yet...nothing had changed. She was here, in her house, alone. Anticipating the birth of their baby, alone.

Which—she assured herself—suited her just fine. If she depended on no one, if she controlled the situation, then she couldn't blame anyone else for her mistakes. And she wouldn't count on anyone else for her happiness.

Assuming she could be happy now, without Zach.

Did she have a choice? She'd engineered an argument that made the situation between them impossible. He was a forgiving man, but even Zach wouldn't be able to forget the things she'd said.

And she'd asked him not to call. Not to get in touch. He would respect that request out of courtesy. Maybe out of hurt. So she wouldn't see him again...unless she made the first move.

Shelley nearly chuckled. *There you go—in control again.* She remembered a saying she'd seen somewhere: When all else fails, do what your mother told you to. Her mom was right more often than not. Would *Shelley* ever reach that all-knowing status? Would she stumble through the rest of her life making stupid mistakes?

When it came to Zach and the baby and the marriage, she didn't know how to fix the mistakes she'd already made. As for the choices ahead...

Shelley admitted, with a sigh, that she didn't even know where to start.

ZACH PROMISED the EMTs he'd get the cut on his cheek examined right away if they'd let him loose. But by the time he reached the terminal exit, Shelley's ambulance had disappeared into a gray day and wind-whipped snow showers.

He pulled the note she'd written out of his pocket. The handwriting was a little shaky. But the flight attendant had assured him she was fine. Could he believe that?

What option did he have?

As he stared into space, thinking in circles, the devil wind that had taken control of the plane struck again, jerking the note from his hands to send it scooting along the walk. Zach dived after it, chasing some twenty feet before he got his foot on the paper.

The sheet unfolded as he picked it up. Turning the page over, he saw for the first time what stationery Shelley had used.

Their marriage certificate. She'd written *Don't call* on the back of the proof of their wedding.

THE ANSWERING-MACHINE light blinked its demand as he walked into the house. Darius curled around his ankles in a demonstration of affection the Persian rarely permitted his perfect self.

"Hey, buddy." He bent down to stroke the cat from head to tail. And then, because he was tired and confused, he sat on the kitchen floor and leaned back against the wall. Darius came into his lap, put his paws on Zach's shoulders and licked his chin.

"Thanks. Me, too." He picked up the cat and made a cradle of his arms. Darius curled up obligingly and relaxed. Zach did the same.

The phone woke them both. Darius jumped down with a snarl and a scrape of his back claws on Zach's hand. Wincing at the pain and the noise, Zach reached over his head and fumbled the phone down from the countertop. "Harmon."

"Zachary? It's your mother."

Damn. "Hi, Mom."

"Where have you been for two days? I left several messages."

"I'm sorry. I was...out of town." *Getting married.*

"A vacation? You could use one. Did you have a good time?"

Until about eight-thirty this morning, I was at the top of the world. "Sure. What's going on?"

"It's Carol again."

He had a headache suddenly. "More trouble?"

"No, oh, no. She's been much better these last few weeks. We talk without arguing...sometimes."

Zach rubbed his eyes, his temples, the back of his neck. "That's about all you can hope for with a teenager."

"But she's getting phone calls."

"From a boy?"

"The person I've talked to is a girl. Carol stopped answering the phone and asks me to tell anyone who calls that she is not here. I'm worried about her."

"With good reason." He took a deep breath. "I'll come over later this afternoon to talk to her. Maybe she'll tell me what's going on."

"I'll expect you for dinner. Thanks, Zachary."

"Anytime, Mom." He clicked the off button, reminding himself it was good to be needed. He hadn't exactly been thinking about his little sister the past couple of weeks—or the rest of his family, for that matter. He loved them all, though they crowded him too close, too often.

Luckily, his new wife refused to make any demands at all.

A brisk knock on the door scattered his thoughts. Zach got to his feet and turned the knob. "Hey, Jimmy."

His friend grinned. "I hope I'm not interrupting— just wanted to drop off your key. Not that the cat deigned to notice me while I was here."

"Come on in."

"Thanks, but three's a crowd, especially on a honeymoon."

"Yeah, well, this is as far from a honeymoon as you could get. Darius and I are here by ourselves. Come in."

Jimmy stepped inside the door. "Something wrong?"

"You could say so."

"So wrong she had to beat you up? Looks like she has a great right."

Zach touched the bandage. "Not quite. The plane hit an air pocket on the way back this morning. Somebody's laptop went flying."

"Casualties?"

"Don't think so." He ran a hand over his face and head, still trying to wake up. "They took Shelley off in an ambulance, but she left me a note saying she was okay."

His friend's sharp eyes narrowed. "A note?"

"On our wedding certificate. See for yourself." He dragged the paper out of his pocket and tossed it on the counter.

Jimmy spread his hand out to flatten the sheet and read the few words, then flipped the page over to see the certificate. "So you did get married."

"Yeah. Things didn't fall apart until this morning."

"What happened?"

Zach shrugged. "Hell if I know. One minute we're talking about where we're gonna live, the next she stomps out the door and leaves on her own. She flew back first class. I stayed in coach."

"What did you argue about?"

"I wanted her to live here. She wanted to stay at her place. From there...I don't even remember. But things got ugly."

"Hmm." Jimmy opened the refrigerator. "Can I have a beer?"

"Only if I get one, too."

Jimmy tossed him a can, then hitched himself up to sit on the counter. "So, you did the right thing. You married her. Your kid has a dad. You can sue for visitation, even custody. What's the problem if you never see her again?"

Zach sputtered his first swig of brew. "I *want* to see her again, dammit."

"Why?"

He wiped his chin. "Because I have to."

"Why?"

This time he swallowed. "Because I love her, you jerk."

"Must have been some wedding night."

Zach smiled unwillingly. "Definitely. But that's not when it happened. This summer...maybe even back in March." He hadn't wanted to let her go that weekend. Not his usual style. "I only realized how I felt this morning."

Jimmy looked smug. "Funny—I knew back in June."

"You could have said something."

"I like my teeth where they are."

"You've got a point." Zach rubbed his hands through his hair. "So what do I do now? She said not to call."

"I guess you don't call."

"Just let her go? Without a fight?" A hidden hand tightened around his windpipe and twisted, wringing out panic. "I can't do that!"

Jimmy laughed. "For a week or so, you probably can. Give her some time, son. The lady hasn't had things easy this year."

"Or for the ten years before that. She's had some tough breaks."

"All the more reason to be cautious."

Zach nodded. "But she's so stubborn—I'm not sure I'll ever get her to see that I'm not interested in running her life. I just think we'd have a good time sharing—our space, our lives, our…baby."

Jimmy took a long drink. "Have you told her that?"

"No chance."

"Well, I'd give her a little space to breathe. Then make the argument."

Zach rolled his eyes. "You, of course, are such an expert in women."

"Of course."

"So why don't you have one of your own?"

Jimmy lifted his beer in a toast. "Only a wide

experience with many different ladies provides this kind of knowledge."

"You are so full of it."

"So they say. Want to play some ball this afternoon?"

"Well..." He'd told his mom he would be there for dinner. But he could have a few minutes to himself, right? Jimmy didn't play ball with any of the other guys—didn't want to force them into making allowances for his bad leg. "Yeah—I've got time for a few hoops before I go correct somebody else's mistakes."

"Now that I've solved yours, you mean?" Jimmy eased off the counter. "What would society do without us?"

"Disintegrate, probably. Sweep off the driveway while I change."

GOING THROUGH her backpack for the third time, Carol ignored the phone's ring. Where had she put those history notes? The teacher had said stuff they couldn't find in the book, but would see on the test. If she didn't have the notes, she might as well not take the test at all.

The phone rang again, and again she refused to answer. Somebody from CW would be on the other end, and she wasn't talking to Jen or Diane or any of them.

"Carol?" Her mother called up from the basement. "Carol, can you answer? I'm hoping Zachary will call."

Another ring. And another.

"Carol, please answer the phone!"

With a sigh, she picked up the receiver. "Harmon residence."

"It's about time, Harmon." Jen's husky voice sent a shiver down Carol's spine. "You've been avoiding me."

"I told you. I'm not playing anymore. Find somebody else."

"Okay, okay. We just thought you'd like to get your history notes back. The ones for the test tomorrow?"

Carol cursed. "You stole them?"

"Borrowed, Harmon. Just borrowed."

"Damn you, Jen."

"I bet you say that to all your friends. If you want the notes, come now. Usual place. Otherwise, we're thinking about lighting a fire."

Carol hung up without a word. There was a good chance they'd burn the notes even before she showed up at Faith's house. But she had to try. Maybe she could make her point in person. After everything that had happened this fall, she'd had enough of their stupid group. She just wanted to be left alone.

Grabbing her coat, she went to the basement door. "Back in a few minutes, Mom," she shouted.

Then, with a deep breath, she started toward the showdown of her life.

WHEN HE ARRIVED at his mom's house, Zach found her practically hysterical. "She's gone, Zachary! I don't even know where to look!"

He got her to sit down on the couch. "Carol's gone? When did she leave?"

"I—I'm not sure. I went down to the cellar about

three-thirty to get the potatoes for the pot roast, like I always do. The phone rang, and Carol answered. And then she said she was leaving. Before I could get up the stairs, I heard the door slam.''

"Okay, Mom. Okay." This was what happened when you took time out for yourself. "That's just a couple of hours ago. She's probably meeting with the club. Any idea where?''

"Carol would never say.''

"Yeah." Zach squeezed her hand. "I'm gonna look around the neighborhood. You stay calm and stay here.''

"I'll finish the pot roast.''

"Good idea. We'll all eat when Carol and I come in.''

He stepped out into the cold, pulling on his gloves.

HIS JOB REQUIRED him to stay calm under the worst circumstances. But Zach had started to worry seriously by the time he'd walked around the third side of the high-school campus without a sign of Carol or her friends. He didn't like the feel of the situation. A teenage girl simply didn't stay off the phone, except in matters of life or death. Without even talking to his sister, he'd known she was in trouble. He shouldn't have put off their talk to play ball with Jimmy...

"Zach!" Carol's cry echoed off the school wall.

He looked up and saw her running—no, make that limping—toward him. They met at the corner, both of them on their knees in the frosty grass.

Zach turned her face to the streetlight and stared

at the purple bruises over her skin. "Damn, Carol. What'd she do to you?"

"We had a fight." She grinned proudly. "Jen looks worse, believe me."

"Yeah?" He thumbed a smear of blood off her cheek.

"What's wrong with your leg?"

"She tried to break my knee. Twisted it pretty hard. My hands hurt worse."

She'd left her gloves somewhere. Her bare knuckles were scraped raw, her palms bruised. "I'd say they do. Didn't anybody ever tell you that violence doesn't settle things?"

"Sure. I didn't go over there to fight. I planned just to tell them to get lost, then get out. But Jen jumped on me first, and I had to defend myself, right?"

"I guess so. Nobody else interfered?"

"Faith's parents weren't home. And I think the rest of CW is as tired of her as I am."

"So what turned the tide? How'd you win?"

Carol struggled to stand up. "This big brother of mine, he made me spend a perfectly good Sunday afternoon one week learning self-defense moves."

Grinning, Zach got to his feet. "What a jerk."

"Yeah. He showed me some holds and some releases and some moves that just might make somebody think twice about holding on."

"And?" They turned to walk toward the house.

"And I used them. All of them. Twice. Until, finally, I remembered the first thing he taught me."

"What's that?"

"A stomp across the arch. Jen was fighting barefoot. I left my boots on." Carol stopped and crossed her bad leg over the other knee to show him the three-inch heels. "I never heard anybody scream so loud. I might have broken her foot. She quit trying a minute after that."

Zach patted her back. "Well, I guess you did what you had to do. But your mother is going to faint when she sees that black eye."

"Black eye? Do I really have one?" She grabbed his hand and started running. "C'mon! I want to see!"

Zach ran after her, feeling lighter and stronger than he had just an hour ago. His little sister was back. Now he could concentrate on the other woman in his life.

That would be his wife.

CHAPTER SIXTEEN

ON THEIR TWO-WEEK anniversary, after no contact with her new husband at all, Shelley gave up...or, maybe, gave in. She needed Zach—his advice, his ideas, his jokes. His lovemaking.

Before she could argue herself out of the idea, she picked up the phone and dialed his number. After two rings, the machine answered. "Sorry I missed you. Leave your message at the tone."

Not likely. The only thing worse than not hearing from him would be leaving a message he didn't return.

She tried again the next day, Sunday. Monday night. Early Tuesday morning, with no luck. Was he screening his calls? Had he left town?

After another long, silent night and a miserable drive into work Wednesday morning, she felt desperate enough to call Zach's station. "Is Officer Zach Harmon available?" Her voice trembled, but she got the words out.

"Just a minute." The phone buzzed on hold, and she had the dubious pleasure of waiting, sick to her stomach with the anticipation that Zach would pick up the phone.

She got a warning click and took a deep breath. Then, "Lieutenant Daley here. Can I help you?"

Shelley couldn't answer. She didn't even understand for a few seconds that this was not Zach.

The same strange voice said, "Hello? Anybody there?"

Reality clicked into place. "I was—I was holding for Zach Harmon."

"Sergeant Harmon is on leave. Did you need to make a report?"

"N-No." On leave? Where? How long? All questions she couldn't ask. "Do you know when Sergeant Harmon will get back?"

"Sorry, I can't say."

"Is there somewhere I can reach him?"

"Who are you?"

"Shelley...um, Shelley Hightower. A friend." Loosely defined, however you looked at it.

"I suggest you call his family, Ms. Hightower. They'll be able to help you."

His evasion suddenly struck her as ominous. She squeezed her eyes shut. "Is something wrong? Can you tell me what happened?"

"I'm sorry, I can't give you any more details than were in today's paper, ma'am. Have a good—"

"Wait!" Shelley pulled her wits together. "I haven't seen the paper yet. I've been trying to reach Zach for days. Couldn't you please help me?"

The lieutenant cleared his throat. "He went out yesterday with a team and a warrant to pick up a problem dog in one of his neighborhoods. The owner barricaded himself and the dog in the house. Then he started shooting. Zach and a couple of other men were hit."

Shelley pressed her fingers against her mouth and

waited for the room to stop spinning. "Is he—is he okay?"

But whatever momentary kindness prompted the lieutenant to share the story had worn off. "I really can't tell you any more than that, ma'am."

"Is he still alive?" The baby kicked once, and was still. Her terror must have flooded every cell in both their bodies.

The man on the phone sighed. "Last I heard. Who did you say this is?"

Shelley hung up without answering and sat for endless moments, just letting the world reshape itself around the knowledge that Zach was hurt. Seriously—why else would the police refuse to talk? Had she lost him forever? Had she gone from make-believe wife to counterfeit widow? Without a chance to make amends?

She punched the intercom button. "Mindy, do we have today's paper?"

"Right here."

"Could you bring it in to me, please?"

The story shared the front page with politics and a Middle East war. The headline read, Dog Fight Wounds Police. Details were few, except that the man inside the house had killed himself and the dog before the police stopped him. The injured policemen were not named. But—thank God!—the hospital they'd been taken to was.

She grabbed her car keys and purse. "Cancel the rest of my day," she told Mindy as she rushed by the reception table. "The rest of the week. I don't know when I'll be back."

Mindy started around the desk. "What's wrong? Where—"

Shelley left the office without replying, and drove with barely a third of her mind on traffic. The paper was hours behind. Zach could have died early this morning.

No. She tightened her hands on the wheel. That would not happen. She would get the chance to apologize. Zach would hold his baby, know and—she hoped—love his child. Even if he didn't want to see its mom again, he would be the dad he intended to be.

All the hospital parking lots had filled up hours ago. She ended up at a meter on a side street, stuffing coins into the slot with numb fingers. The wind ripped through her, and she realized she'd forgotten her coat. A three-block walk in the freezing rain lay ahead.

She got strange looks as she finally stepped into the hospital lobby. The woman at the information desk stared at her in dismay. "Are you okay?"

"Yes. Yes." Shelley pushed back her damp, cold hair. "How can I find out what room somebody is in?"

"What service are they on?"

"I don't know." She fought down her hysteria. "He's one of the policemen who was hurt yesterday."

"Ah. Surgery, probably." She consulted a list. "One's in SICU— the intensive care unit. The other two are in the general ward."

"Zach Harmon. That's his name. Where is he?"

"General ward. Room 1438."

"Thanks." That meant he was okay, didn't it? Though still beating fast, her heart dropped back to its normal place in her chest. Shelley turned toward the elevator.

But the woman caught her hand. "Why don't you sit down first, have something warm to drink? You look half-frozen."

And wait another minute to see him? "No, no, thank you. I really need—"

"Now, honey, I'm going on my break." The woman stood up and came out from behind the desk to put her arm around Shelley's shoulders. "I'll walk you down to the cafeteria myself. You have to take care of you and that baby."

"No!" She pulled herself out of the woman's hold and backed away. "No, really. I'm sorry, and you're very nice, but I have to see him. Now." A door opened behind her, people streamed around her, and then she stepped backward and let the doors close her in.

"What floor?" someone asked.

"Fourteen." She combed her fingers through her hair again, then clasped her hands to keep them from shaking. She probably did look demented.

Two people had to step out of the elevator at the fourteenth floor because she was too big to squeeze past them. The doors closed as she stared at the directional signs on the wall. Frustration and anxiety settled into her stomach, making her sick. Why didn't the map make sense?

Once she understood them, the arrows sent her down another long hallway, around three corners and through a set of doors. As she approached the central desk, Shelley didn't know how much more delay she could handle without screaming.

A nurse looked up. "Yes?"

"Do you have Zach Harmon on this ward?"

"Yes." The nurse stared expectantly.

Shelley tightened her hands against each other. "Is he…going to be all right?"

"And you are…?"

"I'm his wife." She put a hand on her stomach. "And this is his child. Now will you please tell me what's going on?"

The nurse stood up. "I'm sorry, Mrs. Harmon. We didn't know—weren't expecting—"

On a deep breath, Shelley recovered her control. "Could I see him?"

"Certainly." The nurse led her down the hallway to the left. Five rooms along, she stopped and gestured. Holding herself together with her clenched fists and nothing else, Shelley stepped closer to the partially open door. From the sounds inside, a mid-morning cocktail party was in full swing.

She pushed the door farther in and stared at the crowd of people, all of them talking at the same time. If there was a hospital bed in their midst, she couldn't see it.

Then one of the women turned. "Shelley!" Carol shoved her way through the mob. "How are you? Did you hear about Zach?"

"Yes…I did." The crowd parted as Carol drew her forward. Shelley's throat tightened as the end of a bed came into sight. She registered blanket-draped feet and knees. And then hands, Zach's hands, lying crossed at his waist with tubes taped to the backs.

All the noise faded as she let her gaze rise higher, past his bandaged chest. His blue eyes, heavy-lidded yet wide with surprise, were not really focused. His face, thinner than she remembered, showed lines at the corners of his mouth and between his eyebrows.

She could barely hear his rough, faint voice. "Shelley?"

Stepping closer, she rested the tips of her fingers on the bed. Otherwise, she might just fall down. "Hi."

On Zach's other side, someone got out of a chair. "Hello again, Mrs. Hightower."

"How are you, Mrs. Harmon?" Shelley managed a smile. "Looks like your son has gotten himself into some trouble, here." Tears gathered at the back of her eyes. She only hoped she could keep them there.

"Not the first time he's been hurt on the job. But we could have lost him on this one. The bullet went underneath his arm where the vest didn't cover. We're lucky nothing vital was hit."

"Very lucky." She made herself look back into Zach's face. "How long will you be here?"

His mother answered. "The doctors say he can leave at the end of the week. And we were just deciding how to manage his care. My house has no bedroom on the main floor, which would make it hard for him, but—"

"Mine does." A taller version of Zach, with hazel eyes, spoke up. "I think that's the best solution—he can come to our house to stay and we'll take care of him."

"I don't think so, Grant," Zach said in a voice so quiet Shelley didn't think anyone else heard.

"We've got a guest room." A woman who looked just like Zach's mother spoke up. "On the main floor."

A big man shook his head. "And twins you spend a full day taking care of, Marian, plus a baby on the way."

"I'll just go to my place," Zach put in quietly.

The arguments escalated. His family—Shelley had gathered that much, though she couldn't put a name to most faces—stood round his bed debating who would take him home. She glanced at Zach, saw that his eyes had closed. He looked even more exhausted, more drawn, than when she'd come in a few minutes ago.

She raised her hand. "Excuse me?" The noise level climbed. "Excuse me?" No effect. As a last resort, she put two fingers in her mouth and blew a single sharp blast.

Silence reigned. Zach opened his eyes. Shelley took one long look at him, and then turned to the rest. "You're all very caring, and I know Zach appreciates your concern."

A little murmuring, a little shuffling, a couple of smiles.

"But you're driving him crazy."

A collective gasp.

She held her ground. "I think he should go home to his own house."

Mrs. Harmon stood up again. "But who will take care of him?"

Shelley swallowed hard. "I will."

More murmuring. Zach's mother smiled. "That's nice of you, Mrs. Hightower. But Zachary has his family. Besides, you're expecting. And what would your husband say?''

Good question. Shelley thought about handing the platform to Zach, letting him make the announcement and take the reaction. But even if he were well, that would be unfair.

And so she looked straight into his mother's face. ''Zach is my husband,'' she said very distinctly. ''We were married three weekends ago in Las Vegas.''

CAROL HEARD the words...but they didn't make sense. Zach, married? To Shelley? And he hadn't bothered to tell his family?

Grant echoed her thoughts. ''You didn't think we might want to know beforehand?''

Zach looked him in the eye. ''I had my reasons for doing it this way.''

What? What reason could there be for keeping them all in the dark? Wasn't family supposed to know about stuff like this?

Their mom looked across Zach to Shelley. ''But what about Mr. Hightower?''

''I'm sorry—I thought you knew.'' Shelley's voice was a little shaky. ''I was divorced from him six years ago.''

But...Carol remembered asking about her husband the day they went shopping. Had Shelley said something she missed?

Mom wasn't finished. ''And yet you are carrying his child?''

''No,'' Zach said. ''The baby is mine.''

Carol closed her eyes, then opened them quickly

to avoid the scene she could see in her mind. Zach and Shelley had...done it. Without being married. And there was a baby.

So much for the damn rules!

The pain inside her exploded. "That's it?" Hands on her hips, she glared at Zach. And his *wife*. "That's all you're going to say? We're just supposed to take this like nothing happened?"

Shellcy put a hand on her arm. "Carol—"

Carol shook her off without looking. "I'm not talking to you."

"That's enough—" Zach's warning was clear.

"Yeah, because she's such great stuff, right? Gee, you really had us going, didn't you? Miss Executive, Miss Does-It-For-Herself." She blinked back tears. "And yet she can't even tell the simple truth."

Zach sat up. "This is none of your business, Carol."

"You made that real clear, big brother. Your life is your concern. Well, guess what? My life is my concern, too. And I'm telling you right now—butt out. Leave me alone. I'm not interested in anything you have to say."

She reached the door before anybody stopped her and flung it open so hard it hit the wall. "Have a nice life, the three of you."

In the quiet hallway, the click of her boot heels echoed like a drumroll. Nobody came after her, but she wasn't surprised. Every man and woman for themselves, right?

So why cry about any of them? Carol didn't know. But her tears started on the elevator. They didn't stop for a long, long time.

ZACH GAVE IN TO the pain in his chest and dropped back against his pillow. "Don't let Carol leave alone," he managed.

"I'll go after her." His next-to-youngest sister, Elena, slipped out.

His mother stood up. "This is…a surprise. It'll take time for us to adjust."

She walked around the bed to Shelley, put her hands on the slim shoulders and bestowed a light kiss. "Welcome to the family." Looking older and wearier than when she'd arrived, she left the room. The rest of the crowd filed out after her, with similar bewildered farewells.

Shelley walked to the window and Zach took the chance offered by her silence to study his wife. Windblown hair, red cheeks and a smear of mascara under each eye—not Shelley's usual style. She wore a black sweater with a bright red scarf, but the silk drooped in a way he didn't think she'd planned. Her hand was almost blue against the white curtain she pulled back. She'd put her purse and keys down by his feet. Something important was missing.

"Don't you have a coat? Gloves?" He tried to sit up again and cursed at his body's reaction. "How did you get here?"

She shook her head. "I drove. I'm fine."

"Where's your coat?"

"That's not important." Her glare warned him to back off.

Zach ignored the glare. "Then the weather must have warmed up a lot since yesterday."

She tilted her head impatiently. "We can pretend it did."

"I think we're through pretending."

"I agree." She turned to face him, but didn't meet his eyes. "We should go into this knowing where we stand."

"What did you have in mind?"

After a moment, she shrugged. "We're married, and soon the baby will be here. We'll be a family, and we'll all get along fine. We've got as much as most people have. I'm sorry I've taken so long to see that."

Not exactly an avowal of undying devotion. But maybe he wasn't making the right connections. "So...you're saying I don't have to tell you I love you?"

Her laugh had an edge. "No. I'd rather you didn't."

"Clear enough." She was warning him off, plain and simple. The sharp ache in his gut rivaled the pain in his chest. He concentrated on practicalities. "Where should we live?"

"I meant what I said. We'll go to your house when you get out of here. You'll be more comfortable there."

"And exactly how do you benefit from this arrangement?"

"Don't think this is all for your sake." She turned to him with a semiprofessional smile. "I get somebody to wake up in the middle of the night to change diapers. A baby-sitter when I want to go shopping. I'd say there are a lot of advantages for me."

"Well, great." Zach closed his eyes. Suddenly, he felt too tired to try anymore. Maybe, if he'd been stronger...maybe, if he could just hold her...

But not today. Today he'd take what he'd been given and be satisfied. He'd have a lifetime to change her mind. He didn't have to start this minute.

"Zach?" Her voice was closer, right next to him.

"Mmm.?"

"I'm going to let you get some rest. I'll be back this afternoon."

"Fine," he mumbled. Darkness had begun to creep over the edges of reality. "Wear a coat."

"I will."

He thought she'd left the room. But then, just before his brain shut down, he felt her lips on his cheek. Zach slid into unconsciousness with a satisfied smile on his face, if not in his heart.

SHELLEY WASN'T SURPRISED to find Zach's family—most of them, anyway—waiting for her at the end of the hall.

"We need to talk," the taller version of Zach said. Grant, that was his name. "There's an empty room down this way."

Mrs. Harmon waited there. The rest of the family grouped around her as she stared at Shelley. "You're married to Zachary?"

"Yes, ma'am."

"Why?"

"Because this is his baby and we both want to raise it."

"There's no love between you?"

"I—" How could she answer that? Shelley cleared her throat. "We like each other very much."

"Obviously," said one of the brothers—Stefan or Josef, she couldn't remember which.

Nobody corrected the rude remark. Shelley decided to ignore it. "We didn't plan this. But we're going to take care of our child. And I will try to make them both happy..." She stopped because she was close to tears—and perilously close to admitting the truth.

She needn't have bothered. Mrs. Harmon walked slowly across the room and stood in front of Shelley, her blue eyes serious and perceptive.

And then she smiled, laying a cool hand along Shelley's cheek. "You do love him," she said softly. "That's good. Everything will work out."

Turning to her family, she beckoned them forward. "Zachary has his wife to take care of him. The rest of us will be in the way."

With that comment, Zach's family left Shelley alone in the waiting room, at the beginning of a life she hadn't expected and wasn't at all sure she would ever deserve.

CHAPTER SEVENTEEN

SHELLEY PULLED the Mercedes into Zach's driveway early on Saturday afternoon, coasted to a stop and gazed at his bungalow. Under six inches of snow, she couldn't tell much about the landscaping, but the overall impression was neat and tidy. She wasn't surprised. Zach was an organized thinker.

She used the key he'd given her, opened the front door and put her suitcase down inside. From the top of a small table just to her left, a gorgeous white cat with gold eyes and a regal snubbed nose eyed her with a combination of suspicion and belligerence.

"Well, well." Shelley closed the door against a cold wind. "You must be Darius." She held out her hand, but the cat didn't move. The gold eyes didn't blink.

As she took a step farther into the house, a warning signal from deep in the cat's throat advised retreat. Trust Zach to have a guard-cat. Keeping an eye on her adversary, she stepped backward through the doorway into the living room. "He should have sent you to handle that dog. Then maybe he wouldn't have gotten hurt."

The warning sound escalated and the Persian hopped down from its table perch to come after her, tail straight up, fur raised.

She glanced around and found the closest place to sit. Perched on the edge of the brown leather couch, she rested her palms on her knees. "I come in peace, you know."

Darius set up sentry duty between the couch and a doorway to the rest of the house, tail whipping on the floor with barely restrained rage.

Waiting out probation, Shelley studied Zach's space. Expecting sleek, contemporary furniture—or else secondhand bachelor stuff—she was surprised at the old-world, settled feel of the room. The house seemed sunny and warm, even on a snowy November afternoon. A carved Jacobean chair and warm wood tables complemented the old Indian carpet on the floor. A sound system took up most of one wall— the man obviously enjoyed music.

"Something the baby would have missed, with just me," she murmured. Why had she believed she could do everything all alone?

She looked back at the cat. "One of us is going to have to give, friend. I think it should be you." Standing, she took a step toward her guard. Back arched, eyes wild, the Persian hissed.

At the same time, the front door slammed open. Almost before Shelley could turn around, Darius gave a warning yowl, bypassed her with two long leaps across the couch and raced to the door.

"Hello? Anybody here?" Jimmy Falcon surveyed them both from the doorway. "Whew, I'm glad it's you, Shelley. For a second I thought I'd be confronting some dangerous perp in here." He closed the door, then turned around with a grin. "Maybe I am?"

Her heartbeat slowed. She managed a smile. "Not me. But Darius might be contemplating murder."

Jimmy looked down at the cat hissing at him from the tabletop. "You're just pretending, Darius. I know you're hungry. Let's show Shelley how to tame you." He nodded toward the back of the house. "The way to this guy's heart is definitely through his stomach."

In the kitchen, Jimmy opened a can of cat food while Darius sang for his supper. "Sorry I scared you when I came in. I picked up a key from Zach's mom right after he got hurt, so the cat would get fed. He's coming home this afternoon, right?"

Shelley nodded. "The doctors would rather wait until Monday, but Zach talked them into today."

"That's good. He'll do better in his own house. Between the nurses and his family, he sounded pretty crazed last night."

She looked over at Jimmy. "You talked to him?"

"Yeah, I've called him every day. I don't do the hospital scene anymore...unless I'm unconscious." He gave her his self-mocking grin. "Zach knows that—so he managed not to get hurt too badly."

She grinned back. "What a pal."

Darius cleaned his plate, and Jimmy gave Shelley several "dessert" snacks to feed him. The cat didn't become her slave, but at least the warning siren switched off.

"I'm glad you stopped by," she said as Jimmy pulled on his coat. "Darius had me stalemated on the couch."

"I'm not surprised. This guy doesn't like strangers. He barely tolerates Zach, some days. But feed him a couple of those snacks every day and eventually he'll let you have the run of the place.''

"I'll remember.''

They walked to the door. Jimmy turned with his hand on the knob. His dark eyes were serious, for once. "You and Zach are getting off to a kinda rocky start.''

She felt her face heat up. "I know.''

"Give yourself—and him—some time. Things will work out. Trust me.'' He flashed a smile and left.

While Darius cleaned himself after dinner, Shelley explored the rest of the house. The only bathroom was about the size of her linen closet. Zach had left his razor and shaving cream out on the last morning he'd been home. She blinked back tears at the sight of such personal tools. He was lucky to be coming home at all.

His bedroom wasn't a giant cavern, like hers, but large enough for the furniture—a four-poster bed, a big dresser and a chest, plus a simple table and a blue armchair by the window. Books were stacked on the table, hardcovers and paperbacks, romances and history books and magazines with official-sounding titles—*Law Enforcement Weekly* and *Public Service Journal*.

A historical romance lay open, spine up, on top of the stack of magazines. Well-thumbed pages told her he'd read this one more than once. Shelley focused on the words, saw that he'd stopped in the middle of a love scene. She read the page, drawn immediately into the mood and tone of the writing. Was the author that good? Or could her own heated reaction have something to do with standing in Zach's bedroom, beside his bed, with his personality all around her and the memory of sleeping in his arms beating inside her heart?

Trying to shake off the daydreams, she stripped the bed and remade it with clean white sheets under the blue blanket and soft red spread. She drew the drapes against the afternoon glare and turned on the lamps. The room glowed like an old painting.

And that brought back the dreams. Yes, she could picture Zach here. Picture herself in his bed, warm and drowsy, being wakened by his hands moving on her skin, and his mouth seducing hers, whispering love words in her ear. The baby moved strongly as her whole body tightened at the thought.

And then she blew out the breath she'd been holding. She shouldn't expect so much. They might get back the physical intimacy—their wedding night had been beyond wonderful. But emotionally...

Would Zach learn to love her? Shelley could only hope Jimmy Falcon's prediction came true.

ZACH SUBMITTED to the wheelchair ride out of the hospital with his jaw clenched. "I hate this part," he muttered to the nurse.

"Then you should stay out of the line of fire," she retorted. "A bullet-proof vest only goes so far, you know."

At least Shelley had brought him clothes, so he didn't have to leave in a robe and gown. At least Shelley was taking him home—home to his own house. And staying there with him.

But not, he realized when they arrived and he shuffled slowly down the hall toward his bedroom, *with* him. Her suitcase sat in the guest room. Pretty definite message there.

She came up behind him as he pondered the arrangement. ''You ought to lie down. The doctors said bed rest for at least a week.''

''Doctors talk too much. I want to sit in a chair. In the living room.'' He turned, and they were face-to-face, separated only by the swell of her stomach. He couldn't resist the chance to brush his fingertips along her cheek. ''Thanks for bringing me home. For being here.''

''I'm glad to help.'' She ducked away without meeting his eyes. ''If you're going to sit, do it before you fall down.''

Disappointment rocked him. ''Good idea.''

He claimed the armchair in the living room, put his legs on the ottoman and groaned. ''Feels good. I'll just stay here for the next couple of weeks.'' Darius jumped into his lap and made himself at home for a nap. ''Jimmy said he'd taught you how to tame this wild beast.''

Shelley perched on the edge of the couch. ''Food always works with males.'' She looked around the room, glanced his way, then around again. ''Um, would you like something to eat?''

He grinned. Was this progress? ''Don't think so. Do you like cats?''

She shrugged. ''I've never had one. Or a dog, either. I guess I'm a blank slate for pets.''

Two points for their side. But his head was beginning to ache. He let his eyes close. ''Not to say the doctors are right or anything, but I think I'll flake out for a few minutes.''

''Sounds like a good idea.'' Her footsteps echoed as she left the room.

Zach listened to the sounds of Shelley unpacking—gentle sounds that seemed to echo through the house. He'd hadn't allowed a woman into his space before. Definitely not for more than a night or two.

How long would Shelley stay? Did she see the relationship as permanent—and permanently bloodless? Had she decided that married life, minus love and passion, suited her just fine?

What would be the best way to change her mind?

The first mind he needed to change, though, was Carol's. ''I guess I have to deal with my sister,'' he told his wife that night as they ate Chinese takeout. ''I'll do it tomorrow when we go to lunch at Mom's.''

Across the table, Shelley looked up with panic in her eyes. ''Oh—I don't know...''

''It's really casual. We just sit around and talk.''

''But—'' She looked at her plate, then set her fork carefully on one edge. ''I don't suppose this is something I can avoid, is it?''

Zach shrugged, then remembered why he shouldn't. ''Ow... Sure you can. I'll tell them you had to work.''

Shelley rubbed her temples. ''No. I owe Carol an explanation.''

''She owes you an apology, as far as I'm concerned. She was way out of line.''

''She was upset.'' Standing, she picked up her plate. ''Are you finished?''

End of discussion, he gathered. "Let me help."

Shelley shook her head. "You shouldn't work that hard. I'll take care of it." Because she didn't want him too close?

Zach put his hands in the air. "Okay. You win. I think I'll turn in."

He took his time walking down the hall, hoping she would call him back. She didn't.

Darius scooted into the bedroom ahead of him, and Zach slammed the door behind them both.

Not exactly how he'd planned to spend his first night at home with his new wife.

THEY MET AGAIN the next morning with serious faces and not much to say. Shelley flipped pancakes and fried bacon. Zach didn't usually eat breakfast before his mother's Sunday lunch, but he ate this one and then retreated into the newspaper.

Not that he could concentrate on reading—he heard every move Shelley made as she straightened the kitchen, went to her room, showered and dressed. Like a masochist, he punished himself with images of what she was doing and how she must look.

She came into the living room about eleven-thirty. "What time do we need to go to your mother's house?"

"More or less now." He folded the sports section, added it to the neat stack by the chair, then looked up at her. "I can go by myself."

Her hair gleamed as she shook her head. "No, you can't. The doctors said no driving."

She tempted him almost beyond endurance, this

gorgeous wife of his, wearing a red plaid flannel shirt and slim black pants.

Zach fought for concentration. "So drop me off."

Her left hand, with his ring on it, moved protectively to her stomach. "We're married, Zach. We might as well act like it."

Frustration got the better of him. "You're making that a tough assignment."

She moved away. "I'm sorry. I'm trying."

Like a dog with a ham bone, he couldn't let go. "Trying to do what?"

Shelley turned to stare at him. "Why are you so determined to fight with me?"

"Because otherwise you won't talk at all."

"I—" She looked down at his face. Judging by the shadows under her eyes, she hadn't slept any better than he had. "Let's just go, okay? I'm ready whenever you are."

Zach sighed and slowly pushed himself out of the chair. "Great. Let's roll."

They arrived at his mom's house to find the whole crowd already in attendance. His mother opened the door. "Zachary, how are you?" She reached up for her usual kiss. But before he could answer the question, she'd turned to Shelley. "Come in, Shelley. Let Grant take your coat. Would you like something to drink before lunch? Please, sit down. Do you need a pillow for your back?"

Zach was left staring after them. "Close your mouth," Grant said as he walked by on his way to the closet. "You know how Mom loves the prospect of more grandkids."

"Yeah, I know." Would that work to his advantage with Shelley?

Stefan and Josef made room for him on the sofa in the living room. "I can't get over this." Stefan shook his head. "You're just about the last of us I expected to see changing diapers."

"Life's full of surprises." Though Shelley appeared to be talking to his mother, Zach hadn't missed the glance she cast his way at Stefan's comment.

"Can I have your address book? Can't remember if it's brown or black."

"No way."

"You won't be needing it anymore."

"Shut up, Stef."

He had a feeling the damage had already been done. His mother was still talking babies. Shelley kept her poise, surrounded by all of his sisters and sisters-in-law, but the expression she wore looked frozen...no, closed.

And then he realized that one of his siblings was missing. He nudged Josef. "Where's Carol?"

"Her room. Mom sent her upstairs when she refused to apologize to you and Shelley."

At Shelley's wince, Zach decided to stop asking questions. Each one only made the situation worse.

Lunch was the usual madhouse, with kids and parents of all ages talking at the same time. Somehow Zach got placed toward the end of the long table, away from Shelley. In trying to keep track of what was going on with her, he wasn't listening much to his twin nephews seated on either side of him.

Grant stood up to give thanks. He said the usual

rote prayer they'd all learned from church, and then added, "Thanks for the new additions to our family. Help us to love one another." The gesture actually seemed to thaw Shelley out some. By the time everybody was served, she'd even smiled once or twice.

Zach finally caught up with her as they cleared the table. "Are you surviving?"

"I'm okay. Your mother's very sweet."

"Unless you don't clean your room."

"She'd have to be organized, with so many to take care of."

"I've stood in this line for many, many hours. I remember before we had a dishwasher. Then we did the washing by hand."

Shelley nodded. "My mom got a dishwasher the year I went into senior high. Of course, we didn't dirty this many dishes in three days." They reached the sink. "Let me do yours."

"Sorry. That's against the rules. You insult my honor as a Harmon to even suggest such a travesty."

She looked up at him. "Is that why you got mad and slammed the door last night? Because I wouldn't let you clean up the table?"

He could lie. Or not. "Only partly."

"Ah." She rinsed her dishes and stepped to the side to load them. "I didn't think it would be that simple."

"Nothing about our relationship is simple, Shelley." Zach moved so that when she straightened up, they were close together. "Doesn't mean it can't work."

"You're blocking traffic," Rachel called. "No loitering around the dishwasher."

Shelley blushed and went back into the dining room. Zach followed, but she managed to avoid him during the rest of the cleanup operation.

The cold weather vetoed any kind of outdoor game, so the guys settled in to watch football. Rachel and Shelley joined them, while his mom and his sister, Marian, and Grant's wife, Joya, talked in the kitchen. The kids flopped in front of the upstairs TV with a parent-approved video. Typical Sunday at the Harmons'. Zach finally started to relax.

On his way back from the kitchen with a bowl of popcorn, he caught the telltale squeak of a stair and looked up to see Carol halfway down. She tried to back up, to disappear.

"Nope. Sorry. Can't run away." He came around to the foot of the steps. "We're gonna have to talk sometime."

"We don't have anything to talk about."

"You owe Shelley an apology."

She snorted.

"You were rude, Carol. She's my wife."

"Oh, yeah. How could I forget?" She snapped her fingers. "Maybe because I never got told about it in the first place?"

"Okay, that was a mistake. I'm sorry. But Shelley and I have had some trouble working things out. I couldn't say anything until the situation was settled."

"Maybe you should have settled things before you made a baby. Or is that only a 'do as I say' kind of standard?"

"No, it's not. Taking responsibility is part of being an adult."

"So how old will you be when you grow up?"

"Get over it, Carol. You like Shelley and you know it. Let's just move on from here."

"I liked her a lot better before I knew she was a slut."

The word took a second or two to register. With a curse of his own, Zach charged up four steps before the pain caught him. "You little—" He stumbled, but kept going.

"Zach, stop!"

He looked around to see Shelley at the bottom of the stairs. No need to ask if she'd heard—her face was as white as her sweater. "Give me a minute here, Shelley. We'll be ready to go shortly." *Soon as I wash my sister's mouth out with soap...*

"Come down, Zach."

"In a minute." He leaned back against the wall. Funny, how much just breathing could hurt.

"The obedient little husband, aren't you?" Carol observed from the landing above. "She must be dynamite in bed, to have you so totally hooked."

"Enough, Carol." Two words took a lot of energy.

"I can see how it all works, though. She's got you for a stud, and you get to spend her money. Good job, Zach. I never thought you had that much ambition." She looked down at Shelley. "Considering how many times I heard my brother say he'd never get married, I guess getting pregnant was the only way to spring the trap."

His chest hurt, and his head had started pounding.

But he straightened up, gathering the energy to protest.

Shelley beat him to it. "I *trapped* him?" Folding
her arms across her chest, she raised a skeptical eyebrow. "Do you really think I couldn't live without
another husband in my life? Someone who would
complicate my decisions, mess up my schedule, tell
me how to raise my child? If anyone is trapped..."

She stopped on a deep, deep breath and, without
another word, passed the stairs on her way down the
hallway. Her heels tapped briskly on the wooden
floor as she approached the kitchen. In the silence
she left behind, Zach could hear his mother inviting
her to stay for pot roast and Shelley's polite refusal.

Then she stalked back down the hall, stopped at
the closet and picked out her coat. Before he could
move, she was at the front door. "I assume somebody can give you a ride home, Zach. See you later."
And she shut the door firmly behind her.

Zach sank down to sit on a step. Turning his head,
he stared up at his sister. "Satisfied?" She was looking a little shell-shocked. "You single-handedly destroyed a relationship that took me eight months to
build. I think it would have been less of a problem
if you just cut my heart out with Mom's butter
knife."

He dropped his head back against the wall and
closed his eyes. After a few seconds, Carol's bedroom door slammed shut. Zach sat there for the rest
of the ball game, wondering which of his brothers
would give him a ride home.

Wondering if his wife would be there when they
did.

THE THIRD TIME she passed the same run-down strip mall, Shelley realized she'd better start paying attention to where she was going. She was lucky she hadn't had an accident. Her mind certainly hadn't been on driving a car. Her mind had been...

Stunned. Vaporized. She hadn't dealt with teenagers before. She hadn't realized they could be so...so vicious. Would Allyson react like that one day?

Or even next weekend, when she came to visit?

The prospect hurt so much, Shelley pulled out of traffic into a parking lot. She could barely see to drive.

She still couldn't quite believe what had happened. Zach had said nothing. *Nothing.* No defense of himself, let alone her. Why would he let those accusations slide by?

Maybe because he believed them. Did Zach use that ugly word himself, in his mind? Did he think she'd "trapped" him?

A noise off to the left—a broken bottle and some shouts—dragged her out of her misery. A group of men or older boys, too far away in the dark to distinguish, walked her way. They were shoving each other, making gestures, drinking out of brown paper bags. Getting close.

Her hands slipped on the plastic levers as she flipped off the interior light and pulled the car into Reverse. Backing up caught the group's attention— she heard comments about the Mercedes as she wheeled around and catcalls as she checked for traffic. With a squeal of tires, she shot out of the parking lot, not before a couple of hands pounded on the rear hood. Breathing hard, she drove as fast as she could through the traffic, trying to get away.

Finally, she saw a sign for an entrance onto I-70. The only option was the westbound lane, and the next exit was five miles farther. But at least she'd have a direction. A glance at the clock startled her—she'd left the Harmons' almost two hours ago.

Another forty minutes brought her to Zach's house. The windows blazed with light. Shelley sat for a few minutes parked at the curb, just watching. Was he alone? Would she have to face more accusations? Or would his stony silence be the only sound?

The car got colder as she hesitated, until finally her feet started hurting and her hands were almost numb. It wasn't good for the baby for her to sit here much longer. She couldn't afford to get sick this close to delivery.

A dog barked somewhere in the neighborhood as she shut the car door. Holding her coat closed, she hurried up the driveway and across the walk. She'd just put a foot on the first step when the door surged open. A man stood silhouetted against the light inside.

"Where have you been?" Zach asked. "I was about to call the cops."

CHAPTER EIGHTEEN

SHELLEY STEPPED past him into the house. "You *are* the cops." Her spine ached with weariness. Her head had started to pound.

Zach shut the door behind her. "Having just left the hospital, even I would need help. It's a big town."

Looking around the living room, she felt displaced. Was this home? "I know. I just...wasn't paying attention." She slipped out of her coat. Before she could turn, Zach took it out of her hands and went to the closet.

"Are you okay?" He stood by the door, hands in his pockets, a frown still in his eyes.

"Sure." She brushed back her hair, wishing she didn't have to lie. "Why not?"

"Because—" He stared up at the ceiling, then lowered his gaze to hers. "Carol didn't mean the things she said."

So much for her hopes of being defended. "Oh, I think she probably did." Without glancing at him, Shelley walked through the dining room into the kitchen. "Have you had dinner?"

He followed. "I've been waiting for you."

"I'm not very hungry. I'll heat you up a pizza, if

that sounds okay." She opened the freezer, but couldn't seem to read the box labels.

Zach gripped her shoulder and turned her around. "For God's sake, Shelley, are you trying to drive me crazy?"

He didn't lift his hand, and the sweet pressure pushed her closer to tears. Finally, she looked at him. "No."

"Then talk to me about this." His face was pale and drawn.

"I don't see much to talk about." She managed a shrug. "We *are* married because I'm pregnant. We didn't tell anybody in your family, and that hurt their feelings. We don't know how things are going to work from here. End of discussion."

She tried to turn back to the open freezer, but he held her in place. "I did not marry you to spend your money."

"I know that." The oven buzzer signaled the temperature she'd set. She looked up at Zach, unwilling to beg, desperate to be free. This time he let her go. In silence, she fumbled a pizza out of the box and into the oven.

He waited to speak until she straightened up again. "But there's no denying my income doesn't come close to yours. Maybe we should work out a prenuptial agreement."

"Two years, maybe even a year ago, I would have agreed with that idea." She took a deep breath, released it on a sigh. "Now I think it's just an insult to both of us. Drop it, Zach."

She started to leave the kitchen. He stepped up

behind her and put his hands on her shoulders. "Shelley, we can do better than this."

"Not tonight we can't." His warmth behind her, the closeness of his body, threatened all her defenses. In another second, she would make a fool of herself. "I'm really tired. I need to lie down for a while."

At last, he loosened his grip. "Okay. We'll talk tomorrow."

"Sure." Trying not to run away, Shelley walked carefully down the hallway toward her room. Once inside, she shut the door as quietly as possible, then lay down on the bed with her clothes on. Too tired to undress, too disappointed to think, too numb to cry, she escaped into sleep.

ZACH GOT out of bed Monday morning to find Shelley dressed for work and on her way out the door. Tuesday and Wednesday were the same. She went to the office early, then brought paperwork home to deal with in the afternoon and evenings. Her concentration kept her quiet, almost unreachable. With two weeks of mandatory leave left and no idea how to break the silence, Zach did some reading—history and professional journals, plus a couple of childbirth books he'd bought before the shooting. Those got him thinking.

When Shelley came home on Thursday, he had lunch ready—burritos and a salad. She sat down at the table with the same distant smile she'd used on him all week. "This is good."

"Thanks." He drank some water to wet his dry throat. "Listen, I just realized—babies need cribs and stuff. Clothes."

She didn't look up from her plate. "Yes."

"Do you already have those things?"

"Not many." She shook her head and speared some salad. "Dexter took the baby furniture."

"Well, we'd better get moving, then. There are only three weeks left, right?"

His words seemed to reach her through a fog. She stared at him, looking puzzled. "I guess we should do that."

"How about this afternoon? We could go shopping, pick up some supplies."

"Are you well enough to go out?" She still cared about that, at least.

"As long as I don't have to chase down anything faster than a rock."

Her face warmed a little. "Okay."

Zach grinned for the first time since Sunday. "Okay."

An hour later, he stood in the center of a baby boutique called Tiny Town, overwhelmed. "I had no idea there was this much stuff."

"Babies are big business."

"Maybe I need to restructure my investments."

She smiled at that. "Could be. Where do you want to start?"

"Um—cribs?"

The salesman smelled money and gave them all of his attention. Zach tried to anticipate Shelley's taste. "This one's nice," he said, gesturing toward a creation draped with a tent of white cloth.

Her head cocked as she contemplated. "You like all those yards of eyelet and ruffles?"

"Don't you?"

They gazed at each other, testing the waters. "It's okay," Shelley conceded. "But I don't think it fits the house."

Zach sighed in relief. "What did you have in mind?"

She led him to one of the first cribs they'd seen, simple and uncomplicated in a natural-finish wood. "This would work in that yellow room."

"Okay. You like the chest, too?"

"And the changing table."

"How about a glider?" the salesman slipped in.

"What's a glider?" Zach followed him to a display of chairs. "You mean rocking chairs?"

The salesman gestured widely. "No one rocks anymore. They glide."

Zach glanced at Shelley, saw her trying not to laugh. "Okay. Do we have to sit in all of them? Must be a thousand."

She surveyed the selection. "This one," she said after a few minutes, and walked to a plainly styled chair in a wood that matched the crib. "This is good—not too high." She looked up at Zach. "Want to try?"

For the very first time, the image of him holding his own child came into his head. "Yeah, sure," he said faintly. He sat down, but the chair could have been lined with tack points, for all he noticed. "Feels great."

"I'll have that added to your order," the salesman said. He stopped just short of rubbing his palms together in glee.

The search for sheets and blankets and towels increased the salesman's satisfaction. But Shelley didn't like any of the curtains or crib skirts. "I can have those made. I was thinking old gold and purple stripes."

"If you say so." Zach surveyed yards of pastel, bunny-flecked cotton. "Sounds okay to me."

Then there were the clothes.

"This small?" He held up a long-sleeved suit that might have fit a Chihuahua. "Really?"

"Allyson was seven pounds, eight ounces, and nineteen inches long."

He estimated the length between his hands. "The size of my mom's Christmas roast."

Shelley laughed. "Charming, Zach. Really charming."

Hearing her laugh felt like a victory. "I try. So what do kids in the diaper set wear these days?"

A lot, it seemed, especially in winter in Denver. Hats. Socks. Sleepers, Shelley called them. Buntings.

"Buntings?"

"A little zip-up blanket jacket to keep them warm."

"Oh." Another blinding thought occurred to him. "Do you know…" He swallowed. "Boy or girl?"

"No clue. I don't want to know." She shook her head, but her eyes sparked with excitement. "They said that if they could tell, they'd keep it a secret."

"Oh." A person took shape in his mind—Shelley's blond hair on a blue-eyed little girl. "Should we get some clothes for both, just in case?"

"What we've got will work for the first couple of months. Then we'll know what to buy." She had a mind like a steel trap when it came to shopping. "Now we need to get a car seat."

He felt more at home with the technical elements of car-seat safety and stroller design. Shelley, bless her, let him do most of the talking. Who knew shopping could be this much fun?

They didn't argue at all until they stood at the checkout counter. The cashier gave them a staggering total. He pulled out his credit card. Shelley pulled out hers.

Zach shook his head. "I'll take care of this."

Shelley looked up at him. "We spent a lot of money. Let me do it."

"Not a problem." He put his hand forward, card extended.

Her fingers closed around his wrist. "You weren't expecting this kind of expense." She kept her voice low, but the intensity came through.

"Shelley." Zach let some firmness into his voice. "Later, okay?"

She moved back and he paid the bill, arranging to have everything delivered. As they crossed the parking lot, her quick footsteps tapped out her agitation.

Once the car doors were closed, Zach sat quietly watching Shelley's profile as she stared at her hands wrapped around the steering wheel.

"I really wish you'd let me take care of that bill," she said finally. "There's no reason for you to ruin your accounts and your credit this way."

"I'm the father." Zach fastened his seat belt, wincing as the bandages pulled on his chest and back. "That gives me an interest in what goes on, and a responsibility."

"But I probably make three times your salary in a year."

"You buy the luxuries—silver spoons and gold-plated rattles. I can handle the baby basics."

Shelley bowed her head and rested her forehead on her knuckles. "This baby has already cost you enough. You shouldn't be saddled with the bills as well as a responsibility you never wanted."

Zach reached toward the vulnerable nape of her neck, the shining strands of hair feathering there. "I'm over that hurdle. You need to move on, too—unless you don't want to give up the protection you get from believing it."

Before he could touch her, she straightened up, still looking ahead. "This isn't about me."

"No, it's about us. There has to be an us for the whole situation to work."

Sighing, she started the engine. "You're impossible."

"Only because I'm right."

She cast him a troubled glance, then put the car in Drive. Neither of them said much on the way home. Or at dinner. Or the rest of the evening. Shelley went to bed with only a subdued good-night.

Zach tried the same trick, without success. He tossed around for a few hours, then finally got up and wandered into the kitchen. When he came back down the hall at 2:00 a.m., his wife was awake.

"Zach? Are you okay?"

"Sure. I woke up starving." Sublimating, the psychologists called this process. What kept him awake these days was Shelley. She straightened his bed when she came home in the afternoons and her scent stayed in the room, weaving through his dreams. Since he couldn't go in to wake her up, couldn't make love with her, he tried to satisfy his hunger with a sandwich.

But now...now she stood at the door to her room, lighted from behind by the bedside lamp. Under a long, full gown, the shadow of her body shaped the white cloth—her breasts, her full belly, her long, gorgeous legs... Zach's mouth went dry. The rest of him went on alert. He couldn't think of a single word to say.

Like a piano wire stretched past endurance, tension vibrated between them. Zach could hear himself breathe, could almost hear his heart pound. Shelley stood motionless, seeming not to breathe at all. But her hand tightened on the doorknob.

"Well, then," she whispered. "I—I'll go back to sleep. Good night." She didn't wait for his answer to close the door in his face.

"Yeah, right," Zach muttered. He spent the rest of the dark hours with a manual on changes in department paperwork procedures propped open in front of his sightless eyes.

ZACH CAME out of the doctor's office on Friday afternoon walking easier and moving his arms more. "The bandages are practically gone," he told Shelley. "I can take a deep breath again." He tried, and winced. "Well, almost, anyway."

"Next week," she suggested.

Zach made dinner—his world-famous spaghetti, he said—while Shelley folded and put away baby clothes in the new nursery. They talked a little over the meal, and cleaned up the kitchen together. Not exactly comfortable, but at least not hostile. Afterward, Shelley went to her room to practice her Lamaze techniques. With all the upheaval in the past weeks, she hadn't kept up her breathing exercises. Her due date was just a couple of weeks away. She wanted to be prepared.

She piled pillows on the floor, but getting them arranged just right left her panting from exertion. Relaxing was harder than she anticipated, with Zach moving around the house. She tried to concentrate, tried to keep her breaths even, unhurried. Success escaped her.

And then her leg cramped. She managed to breathe through the pain, which seemed like good practice. But when she tried to sit up, she couldn't bend over the baby. Lying on her side, she couldn't reach her calf to massage the muscle. When she moved her leg to get up, the cramp worsened until she bit her lip to keep from crying.

"Zach?" She called softly at first, hoping for a miracle that would keep her from needing him. "Zach?"

On her third call he hurried down the hall. "Shelley, what's wrong?"

"Come in, please."

Zach opened the door. His eyes widened as he saw her lying on the floor. "Geez, Shelley, did you fall?" He squatted beside her and put a hand on her arm. "Are you hurt?"

"I have a cramp in my leg," she told him through gritted teeth. "And I can't reach it."

Laughter sprang into his eyes, but he kept his mouth straight. "Which leg?"

"Right."

"Lie back against the pillows." He turned and put his palms on the knotted muscle, pressing firmly. "Better?"

Shelley sighed and relaxed. "Getting there."

"Good."

After a few minutes, the pain vanished. "Thanks," she said as her cheeks heated up. "I appreciate the help."

"Anytime." He sat on the floor facing her. "Want to tell me what you're doing down here?"

How much deeper could she blush? "Breathing exercises."

His eyes narrowed. "For labor, you mean? Like Lamaze?"

"Yes."

He stared at her for a few moments. "Aren't you supposed to have a coach for Lamaze?"

"Um, usually."

"Who's yours?"

Make up one, or tell the truth? "Mom took the classes with me back in October, but she works until seven or seven-thirty most nights so I practice on my own."

"Oh." After a long silence, he said, "I could help."

His voice was so low Shelley didn't think she'd heard correctly. "I'm sorry, what did you say?"

He played with the fringe on a pillow. "I could help you practice."

"Do you want to?"

"We could at least see if it would work, right?" He asked the question staring at the floor.

Zach had never struck her as a humble man. Not

arrogant, either, like Dex could be. Just...self-confident.

And yet here he was, requesting the chance to see his child born. From all appearances, if she said no, he'd abide by her choice.

That, more than anything else, made the decision easy.

"We can try," Shelley said. "You might find out you'd rather be on the other side of the delivery-room door."

He looked up with the lighthearted grin she'd first fallen in love with. "I am a little squeamish when it comes to the messy stuff."

She found out what she'd let herself in for soon enough. Zach read the Lamaze-course handbook the next day. That very afternoon, he made her practice. And every day after that.

The Wednesday before Thanksgiving was no exception. He came into the dining room at seven o'clock. "Drop the paperwork, Shelley. You need to practice your breathing."

"I will." She punched in another number on her calculator. "Just let me get this finished first."

"Nope." He took her pencil away. "Allyson's due to arrive in a couple of hours. You're not going to want to practice once she's here." He put his hands on the tops of her arms and eased her out of the seat.

"Okay, okay." She followed him into the living room, where he'd already arranged cushions and pillows. "You're really enthusiastic about this, aren't you?"

"Everyone says it helps—working with the contractions instead of fighting them." He knelt on the floor and held out his hand. "Shelley High-tower...Harmon. Come on down!"

She put her palm against his warm one and let him ease her to the floor. They fussed with pillows a few minutes, then Zach sat back on his heels. "Comfortable?"

"I'll sleep like this tonight, I think."

He shook his head. "Breathe first. Ready?"

"Ready."

"Deep, cleansing breath." He breathed in and out with her. "Again. Now, I'm gonna count six for breathing in and six for breathing out. Go."

Amazing, how easy it was to relax, listening to his mellow voice. While she sat and breathed, he practiced some of the suggestions the book made for increasing relaxation—gentle circular rubs on the thigh, the shoulder, the abdomen. Shelley practically purred. She was so tranquil when they finished the final cleansing breath, she didn't move a muscle.

"Shelley?" His words were just above a whisper. She didn't answer, kept her eyes closed. "Shelley?"

"Mmm?"

"Allyson will be here soon. We need to leave for the airport."

"That's right." She opened her eyes slowly. Zach was closer than she'd realized, just a breath away. The soft light in the living room glinted off his hair and in his eyes. As she watched, he dropped his gaze to her lips. And then looked up again, asking for permission.

Shelley lifted her hand to his cheek. The smallest of pressures drew him forward. Their mouths met, parted, clung again. Zach shifted to brace one arm on the floor on her other side. Then his fingers closed in her hair. The kiss got serious.

After all the pain, the distance, the strangeness, she'd finally come home. Their mouths danced, slowly, then faster, taking and giving in time to the beat of their hearts. Demand was there, yes, and barely leashed passion.

But this kiss did more. This kiss asked for and granted forgiveness. Comforted and consoled. Confessed and reprieved.

Shelley lifted her eyelids when Zach at last pulled back. The tenderness on his face nearly brought her to tears. They simply stared, for a moment, connected by their hands and the meeting of their eyes.

AN HOUR LATER, Allyson pulled away from the flight attendant holding her hand and rushed into the waiting area, straight into Shelley's arms. "Hi, Mommy! Happy Thanksgiving!"

"Definitely." Shelley hugged hard, blinking back tears. "Welcome home, baby."

"Uncle Zach! You're here, too? Cool!" Allyson pulled away long enough to give him a hug. "I had the best seat on the airplane—right up front, almost in the place where the pilot sits. And they let me go in and watch for a couple of minutes, but I had to be real quiet so the pilots could concentrate. And I got soda and cookies and crackers."

"I guess you enjoyed the flight." Shelley glanced at Zach with a smile, caught his grin.

"I think it would be so neat to be able to fly a plane. Can you fly a plane, Uncle Zach?"

"Not one of my skills, Ally Cat."

"Maybe we could learn together. Do you want to learn, too, Mommy?"

"Um, we'll see. Have you got your luggage tickets?"

Shelley showed her ID to the attendant so Allyson could leave, then they went to baggage claim to wait for her luggage.

Allyson didn't stop talking. "You should see Jack—he smiles and he holds things. He doesn't talk yet, though. Claire says that'll take a while. How is your baby, Mommy?"

"Just fine. About ready to meet big sister."

"I get to hold Jack, and he doesn't even cry. And I can change diapers, too." She wrinkled up her nose. "I don't like it much."

Zach laughed. "Join the crowd!"

"But they have to be changed," Allyson informed him seriously. "Or else the baby gets a rash and gets really grumpy."

"Has that happened to Jack?"

"Nope. Claire and Daddy are real careful to keep him dry."

Shelley wished them luck. She remembered diaper rash…all too well.

Zach pulled Allyson's bags off the conveyer belt. "You're now officially here, Ally Cat. Let's go."

Once buckled into the Mercedes and on the way to Zach's place, Shelley knew the moment of truth had arrived. "Allyson? I need to explain a couple of things."

"Okay."

"We're not going up to…to my house tonight."

"Why not?"

"Well..." No way to say this but straight out. "I'm living at Zach's house now."

"You are?" There was a pause. "Why?"

Straight to the point of no return. "Because Zach and I got married."

This pause lasted even longer. "You did?" Allyson's voice sounded small.

"Yes."

"When?"

"About a month ago."

Another silence. "Did you have a wedding like Daddy and Claire's, with everybody dancing and stuff?"

"No. We went to Las Vegas where you can get married right away. Nobody else was there."

"You didn't want anybody there?"

Shelley couldn't answer. From the passenger seat, Zach cleared his throat. "We thought it would be better to get married first and then tell everybody."

"Oh." An even longer silence. "But what about...?" The little girl's voice trailed off.

"What about...?" Shelley stopped the car at a traffic signal and took the chance to glance at her daughter. Wide gray eyes and a puzzled frown predicted trouble.

"What about the baby's dad? Won't he be mad that you married Uncle Zach?"

Zach took the lead. "That's me, Ally Cat."

"Who's you?"

"I'm the dad." Shelley cast him a grateful glance.

Allyson didn't ask for clarification. A long, tense while later, she spoke. "Mommy?"

"Yes?" This would be the worst part.

"I thought you said the baby's dad didn't want to be part of our family."

Shelley felt as much as saw Zach flinch. She drew a deep breath. "You see…"

Her daughter didn't allow her to finish. "Uncle Zach cares about us."

"I do, indeed."

At eight, Allyson was old enough and smart enough to connect pieces of information for herself. "So how," she wanted to know next, "could *he* be your baby's daddy?"

CHAPTER NINETEEN

SHELLEY TIGHTENED her grip on the wheel. She should have said this to *him* first. "I was wrong about that, Allyson. When he found out, Zach..." How could she put the last six months of struggle into words? "Zach told me that he did want to be part of our family."

"So why didn't you have a big wedding? Are you keeping it a secret? Does Daddy know?"

So many tough questions. "I haven't told your father yet. But it's not a secret."

"You coulda told *me*." The sulky voice made no secret of Allyson's hurt feelings.

They were almost home. Shelley let the situation rest until they got into the house and put Allyson's bags in the baby's room. Then she sat down in the new rocker and pulled her daughter into her lap.

"Mad at me?"

Allyson sniffed, sitting stiffly in Shelley's arms.

"I'll take that as a yes." She looked up at Zach, who leaned against the door frame. He gave her a thumbs-up and vanished, pulling the door softly closed behind him.

"I wish I could explain all of this better," Shelley began. "Zach and I had some...problems to work out, Allyson. We did things the wrong way and made a baby before we decided to get married.''

"Why?"

"Because sometimes even grown-ups make mistakes." Shelley smiled ruefully. Maybe especially grown-ups. "But since we weren't married, it's taken us a long time to get to the place where we think we can make a family together. I didn't want—"

Allyson was listening. "What?"

"I didn't want to marry Zach and then go through a divorce like your father and I did. That wouldn't be good for you, or for the baby. Or me, or Zach. So it took a while for me to decide this would be better than not being married.''

Her daughter turned and showed Shelley a reproachful face. "You didn't tell me the truth."

"I did—just not all of it." She picked up a black curl to play with, hoping for forgiveness.

Allyson pulled her head away. "Daddy says only part of the truth might as well be a lie."

"I think that depends on why you only tell part of the truth. If you're trying to keep from hurting somebody, maybe it's not such a bad idea."

"I don't understand."

"Well, I was worried you would be upset if you knew the baby's dad was Zach, but that he didn't want us to be a family. You're such good friends, that might have made you mad at him."

"Yeah." The straight back relaxed a bit.

"Then, when I realized he'd changed his mind, I didn't want to tell you on the phone that I'd gotten married without you. You deserved to be there, and I feel bad that you weren't.''

Allyson twisted her hands together in her lap. "I coulda been your flower girl."

She risked putting a hand on the girl's shoulder. "I know. That would have been so special." They sat in silence for a few seconds. "I did take your baby cap with me."

"You did?"

"I did. So you see, you were there...in my heart."

The girl in her arms sighed. "Okay, I guess I'm not mad anymore." She turned to cuddle around the bulk of Shelley's stomach. "This is a neat house. Are you gonna live here forever?"

"I don't know. We'll see how everything works out."

"Will I have to sleep in the baby's room all the time?"

"This visit. Maybe next time, we can do something different." Which could only mean Shelley would be sleeping...with Zach?

"Okay."

The next morning, Allyson called her dad to wish him happy Thanksgiving. Shelley tapped her on the shoulder. "Let me talk to him when you're finished, baby. I'll tell him...about Zach."

"Okay, Mommy." For an eight-year-old, Allyson was great at keeping secrets. She handed over the phone without breathing a word.

Dex came on the line. "Hi, Shelley. How are you?"

"Just fine. How's life with the new baby?"

"Hectic. We miss having Allyson's help. She's great for running up and down stairs to fetch diapers and blankets. And she keeps Jack entertained for us.''

"I can imagine." Allyson left the living room for the kitchen, where Zach was making a pumpkin pie. "Dexter, I have some news for you. I've gotten married again."

"That's good to hear, Shelley. I'm glad. Who's your new husband?''

"I hope you're sitting down. I married Zach.''

"Zach...Harmon?''

"That's right.''

Dex didn't take long to reach the correct conclusion. "He's the father of your baby?''

"He is.''

"Well." She heard his deep breath. "Congratulations to you both. I hope things work out.''

"Thank you. We're doing our best.''

"Claire will probably want to hear this news from Zach. I'll call her downstairs if you can get him on the line.''

"Of course." Shelley carried the phone into the kitchen. The worst was over—for her. She had a feeling that her husband would not get off so easily.

ZACH'S MOUTH was a little dry as he took the phone and walked back into the living room. "Claire?''

"Hello, Officer Harmon. How are you?" She still sounded tired.

"Great." He probably sounded nervous. "How's that boy of yours?''

"Growing every day. I'm glad I took some time off, though. Babies seem to need full-time attention from somebody.''

He chuckled. "So I've heard."

"I gather from my husband's face that there's something afoot. Want to fill me in?"

"Um, sure." He should have handled this differently, he realized. They'd been good friends for a long time. But now Shelley seemed to be all he could think about. "I'm a married man, Counselor."

"Really?" Her cool lawyer's mind could be heard in the single word. "I thought you had other plans. Who's the lucky woman?"

"Shelley."

The shocked silence said everything. Claire cleared her throat. "You're joking, right?"

"No. I should probably be apologizing, but I'm not joking."

"When did this happen?"

"A month ago, more or less." Zach eased his tense neck and shoulders. He couldn't quite remember life before Shelley. Having her in his house just seemed right.

"I didn't realize the two of you were..." Her voice died away. After a pause, she said, "You're the father?"

"Got it in one."

"Zach." She sounded concerned.

"Don't worry, Claire—it's not the way you think." *I'm in love with her. That's the real problem here.* "This is gonna work out just fine. We're looking forward to the baby, doing Lamaze and everything. Bought all those tiny clothes and a crib and stuff. You and I can exchange pictures."

"But—" He heard her deep breath. "Just for the baby, Zach?"

He couldn't lie to his best friend. "Not anymore. Maybe at the beginning...or maybe not. I always had a soft spot for temperamental ladies."

"Then I wish you both the very best. When's the baby due?"

"Around December fifth."

"Tell Shelley I recommend epidural anesthesia. Makes the whole process bearable."

"I'll do that. Thanks for not going into cardiac arrest at the news."

"I can tell by your voice that you've got high hopes, Zach. Good luck working everything out."

"Appreciate it."

"Is there anything else I should know about?"

"Well, I spent some time in the hospital a few weeks ago. But everything worked out okay." Shelley had come back to him, which was the main thing.

He gave Claire the rest of the details. She sighed. "There's always a surprise with you, Officer Harmon. Shelley has my sincere sympathy. Can I talk to Allyson?"

"Sure. Hey, Ally Cat!"

Thanksgiving Day passed without much more trauma. They visited the Harmons for an early dinner. Carol joined the crowd, though she said absolutely nothing and kept her eyes on the plate she barely touched. They all talked around her, fairly easily, Zach thought. His mother gave Shelley a hug as they were leaving.

"You should expect this baby soon," she warned. "You look ready."

Shelley laughed. "I feel ready. Every day seems like nine months now."

Her newest grandmother gave Allyson her own hug. "Come back to see us, miss. There's always someone here to play with."

"That's neat. I will. And Zach says I get to play baseball next summer."

"Good." Mary Harmon chuckled. "We'll come and cheer for you."

Dinner at Dorothy Owens' house rivaled the Harmons' for noise level. At least no sulking teenagers dampened their spirits. Zach met his in-laws—Shelley's uncles, their families, and her grandparents, up from Phoenix for the occasion. But Shelley and Allyson were the center of attention.

Shelley's mother cornered Zach as he helped clear the table. "So, you've married my daughter."

"I have."

"She looks a little stressed."

With a nod, he headed for the kitchen. "She's about to have a baby."

Dorothy followed. "Are you getting along?"

"Mostly." Shelley's mom cared about her daughter—she deserved some answers. "We're working things out."

She faced him across the open dishwasher. "Is this a long-term arrangement? Shelley doesn't seem to know."

He set down the dishes, put his hands on her shoulders and looked directly into her eyes. "Believe me, Dorothy. I'm hoping to make this a life-long affair."

She took his meaning, gave him a wide smile and a pat on the cheek. "Well, then, be a little more careful on the job, why don't you? Wouldn't want that affair ended too soon!''

AFTER THEY SHOPPED all day Friday and Saturday under cloudy skies, they awoke on the Sunday after Thanksgiving to find it sunny and cold. Zach and Allyson got up early and baked cinnamon rolls for breakfast. When Shelley wasn't out of her room by nine, he knocked softly on her door.

"Shelley? You okay?"

She opened the door, sweetly rumpled but with shadows under her eyes. "I'm okay. Just really, really tired."

"Wrap up in your robe and relax on the couch. Allyson and I have a fire burning and cider warmed up."

Her eyebrows drew together. "You shouldn't be carrying wood."

"I've declared myself completely healed. No arguments. Come join us."

She did as he asked, and watched while he and Allyson played Scrabble. When he glanced up, late in the game, Shelley had fallen asleep again, her cheek pillowed on one hand, her other arm cradling the baby.

Allyson looked, too. "Mommy's tired these days."

"Must be hard to be so small and have to carry a baby around inside you."

"Claire got tired, too. Just before Jackson was born."

The comment shot through Zach like a bolt of lightning. He knew the due date was close. The baby would be here. And then the three of them would be a family.

That prospect didn't worry him anymore. As long as Shelley stayed around, he figured he could handle everything else.

Because he wasn't supposed to drive until he'd seen the doctor again, Shelley insisted on dressing to take Allyson to the airport. They all laughed and teased during the ride, but as the time for departure approached, mother and daughter found less and less to say.

At the door to the plane, Shelley got down awkwardly onto her knees in front of her daughter. "Thanks for being such a big girl." She stroked Allyson's curly black hair. "You've made me so happy this weekend. I love you so much."

Suddenly, the girl's arms clutched around Shelley's neck. "I don't want to leave you, Mommy. Can't I stay?"

Zach saw tears spill over Shelley's cheeks. "Not this time, baby. But you'll come down again the week after Christmas, like always." She sniffed and cleared her throat. "We'll have somebody new for you to take care of and I'll be feeling better and we'll have a great time. That's only a few weeks away, you know? And I'll talk to your dad about next year, getting together more often. This has been kind of a strange few months, hasn't it?"

Allyson nodded, tears hanging on her lashes. Shelley kissed her hard, then started to get up. And couldn't.

Zach put a hand under her elbow. "Let me." She

stood heavily, awkwardly. He wondered for a minute if she was going to keel over.

Instead, she smiled and tapped Allyson's nose. "Now you remember to do all your math problems this time—not just the ones on the front of the sheet. Right?"

"Right."

"And help Claire with the baby so you'll have lots of practice when you come back down." Her voice started to break.

"I will."

Before they could say anything else, the flight attendant stepped forward. "Ready, Miss Hightower? We've got your seat waiting."

Allyson seemed about to balk. Then she sighed. "Okay."

Beside Zach, Shelley tensed, and he wondered if she would call the girl back. But as Allyson walked backward down the ramp, waving, Shelley waved in return, smiling and staying on her feet.

As soon as Allyson disappeared around the curve, her mother turned into Zach's arms and began to cry.

He got her out of the crowd and to a reasonably private corner of the waiting area. And then just held on. All the pain of the last eight years seemed to flow out with her tears.

When she was a little quieter, shaking a little less, he pushed her back just enough to see her face and stroke the wet hair out of her eyes. "Better?"

She shook her head. "It just hit me. The next time I see her, everything will be different. A baby makes such a change and we did this all wrong and she probably doesn't feel like I love her anymore..."

"Now stop right there. That's the last thing Allyson thinks." He wiped tears off her cheeks with his thumbs. "She knows you're her mom and always will be. She's happy about the baby. She knows you want to see more of her. Don't beat yourself up."

Shelley stood for a long minute looking toward the floor, which neither of them could see because of the baby. Then she sighed. "I guess. I just feel so helpless—" She broke off with a gasp.

Zach went on alert. "What's wrong?"

"I'm having a contraction." She put her hand over her stomach and leaned her head against his chest.

"As in, starting labor?" He tightened his grip.

"I—I don't know. Could be those Braxton Hicks things they talk about—you know, false labour."

Here we go. Zach swallowed hard. "Let me know when it ends."

A forever later, she lifted her head. "Better." But her face was paler than he liked.

He put an arm around her waist. "Let's get to the car so you can sit down."

In the parking lot, she'd recovered enough strength to defy him yet again. "You are not supposed to drive. I'm fine."

Zach cast a glance heavenward, asking for help. "Of the two of us, I think the one with a few healing scars is a better choice for driver than the one who might have another contraction any minute now."

Shelley clenched her fists. "The first contractions come hours apart. I can get us home."

"Give up, lady." He held out his hand. "This is one time you don't have control. I'll take the keys."

She looked at him with temper and laughter and—

was he wrong about this?—a spark of passion in her eyes. Finally, she held out the keys. "You win."

"Thank God." With an arm around her waist, he walked her to the passenger side of the Mercedes. "Just sit down and be helpless for a few minutes. You might like it."

"And turtles might fly." But she sank into the seat and put her head back, her eyes closed. Zach drove carefully, avoiding every bump, quick turn, sudden stop.

So when she gasped as they waited at a red light, he was startled. "What? What?"

And then he realized she was having a contraction. She had her hands on her stomach. He drove on, one eye on traffic, one on Shelley. She didn't relax for a long, long time.

In the driveway, he breathed a sigh of relief. "Made it." But when he opened Shelley's door, she was in the middle of another contraction. This time she put out her hand, reaching for his.

"No, don't tighten up," he said automatically. How many times had they practiced? "Loosen your fingers. Breathe in slow. Breathe out, six beats. Relax, Shelley. Just relax."

That got her through. He knelt by the car until she opened her eyes. "That was…intense." she said.

"Maybe we should call the doctor?"

"I don't think so—she said five minutes apart."

"Do you think you can walk in? Do you want me to carry you?"

Shelley lifted an eyebrow. "Do I want the guy who three weeks ago was shot in the chest carrying me? Not likely. I'll walk."

She moved to swing her legs out, then stopped suddenly. Zach waited.

"On second thought," she said breathlessly, "you'd better get that suitcase I packed. Looks like we're going to the hospital."

He stood up so fast his head spun. As he vaulted to the porch, she called out. "Zach?"

"I'm hurrying!"

"No... Well, that, too. But bring some towels when you come out. Lots of them." He heard her chuckle and moan at the same time. "I think my water just broke."

THE PRELIMINARY EXAM took forever and they wouldn't let Zach come in. Shelley stared at the ceiling and tried to stay calm. She was ready. She could do this.

No, she couldn't. Not without Zach.

An impersonal nurse face came to the bedside. "We've called your doctor, Mrs. Hightower. She'll be here shortly."

"Harmon."

The nurse looked up. "I'm sorry?"

"My last name is Harmon. And I'd like to see my husband."

"In a few minutes, when we get you into the birthing center."

"I don't want to wait a few minutes."

"You'll be fine." The nurse patted her shoulder and went away. Shelley contemplated getting up on her own and walking out to find Zach. But another contraction hit and she had all she could think about for a minute or so.

In the midst of the next contraction, the nurse came back and tried to change Shelley's clothes. "Let's just get these pants off…"

"Will you wait until this is finished?" Shelley muttered through clenched teeth. Zach would be able to talk for her. Zach would help her relax. "Zach…"

"Right here, lady." His firm, warm hand took hers. "You aren't breathing, are you? Gotta breathe, Shelley. Six beats in, six out. Relax."

At the end, she sighed. "When did breathing become an Olympic sport?"

He chuckled. "About the time you started carrying around your weight in baby."

"Now can we change those clothes?" The nurse sounded impatient at having her schedule disrupted.

"I'll help her." Zach's tone soothed Shelley like velvet over shattered glass. "Give me the gown and I'll make sure she's ready." She watched him show off his sexy grin, watched the nurse melt.

"You manipulator," she accused when the nurse had left. "You probably used that same spell on me."

"Kinda like the one you used on me." He put his hands to the hem of her sweater. "Let's take this off."

With gentle efficiency, he got rid of all of her clothes. Shelley blushed, wishing she'd cooperated with the nurse so Zach wouldn't see her this way.

But when he'd tied the gown in back and helped her lie down again, he put a hand on the roundness of her belly. "You're beautiful, you know."

"I—" She shook her head.

"Yes, you are."

She wanted to pursue the topic, but her back tightened, and then her stomach. "Here we go again!"

"Deep cleansing breath." She followed his voice. "Now breathe in through your nose slowly. That's right. One, two, three, four, five, six. And out. One, two, three…"

The anesthesiologist came by and talked about drugs. "An epidural will eliminate most pain but not your ability to push."

Shelley shook her head. "I don't think so. I did that the last time. This time, I want to know…everything."

Zach squeezed her hand. "Claire said to tell you that's the way to go."

"He's right, Mrs. Harmon." The doctor looked tired. "After a certain point, we won't be able to offer this."

She managed a smile, though there was another contraction coming on. "Then I'll just have to live with my decision, won't I? Zach…"

"Right here, Shelley. Breathe."

THE OBSTETRICIAN ASKED Zach to step outside during her examination. She joined him shortly. "Things are going well. She's tiny, but she's dilating nicely."

"How much longer will this go on?"

"I'd say three hours. Maybe four."

"You're kidding. How can she hold up that long? I'm about to collapse."

The thin, dark-haired woman patted his arm. "That's what women do, Mr. Harmon. That's the way they're made."

Inside Shelley's room, he found a fretful, thirsty woman. "I really need something to drink, Zach."

"You really can't have anything. Suck on the ice chips in this cloth."

She did. "Not enough."

"Think about something else. Does this baby have a name?"

"I—" She took a deep breath.

"Good job. You're automatically relaxing. Let's work with this one now."

The contractions were getting longer, more powerful. He could see them start on the monitor across the bed, used the graph to help Shelley through them. His chest was hurting some, since he hadn't moved around this much in a while. But Shelley was doing the work. She possessed a strength he could only envy.

"Eight centimeters," the doctor announced about two hours later. "You're getting there, Shelley."

"And it's the last time, too." She tossed her head against the pillow. "Sex isn't worth this. Men aren't worth this. I'm going into a convent."

Zach laughed so hard tears came to his eyes, blurring his view of the monitor.

"Zach? Zach, where are you?" She was already breathing, eyes closed, chin down, her hand reaching for his. He took her hand and held on. "Pant, pant, pant, blow. Pant, pant, pant, blow."

After that, there didn't seem to be a break between the contractions. Shelley got no time to rest, and so he didn't, either. Her back hurt, she said, and he rubbed it with his hands balled into fists. Her feet

were cold—he found the socks she'd packed.
Thirsty. No water. Hot. Cold. Tired.

"I want to push."

Zach headed for the door. "Let me get the doctor."

"No!" She hauled him back with amazing
strength. "You aren't going anywhere. I want to
push."

"Pant, Shelley. Don't push."

"Damn you, don't tell me what to do! You're always telling me what to do." But she panted.

"Fully dilated and effaced," was the next report.
"Should be crowning...ah. There we go. You've got
a baby, Shelley."

"I need to push."

"Give us a minute to get things set."

"Zach..." Her voice approached a scream.

He moved behind her, helped pull her backward
and a little more upright on the bed. Arms around
her shoulders, he held on. "Go ahead, Shelley.
Push."

He'd only *thought* what had come before was hard
work. The true and total definition of labor became
completely clear in the following minutes. He nearly
wept with the desperation of the process.

The last push was like the ones before...impossible and imperative. Shelley groaned
and bore down, her nails digging into his wrists.

She let go so suddenly, Zach panicked. "Shelley?
Shelley, are you okay?" He looked toward the doctor. "Is she all right? What's going...on..."

The doctor straightened up, holding a small

squirming baby. "You've got a good-sized boy here, Shelley."

Within Zach's arms, his wife stirred. "I want to see him." Her voice was faint, but nonetheless proud.

"One second." There was a crowd around the end of the table.

Zach looked down at Shelley, at the sweat on her face. He reached for a cloth. Her eyes met his.

"What's going on? Why doesn't he—"

A thin, angry wail split the air. And then another one.

"Oh," Shelley sighed. "Oh, listen."

The doctor came over with a bundle of blanket. "Meet your son, Shelley, Zach." She put the blanket in Shelley's arms.

Zach looked down at the wrinkled gnome peeking out of the cloth. Dark eyes, open but squinty. A mouth like a flower petal. A shock of wet, brown hair. "I—" He cleared his throat. "Glad to meet you, son. Say hi to your mom."

Shelley stroked a finger over the dark red cheek. "Hi, baby. So sweet." She glanced up at Zach. "He looks like you."

"I'm not sure I'm flattered. He looks like a prune."

"I bet you did, too."

"We'll have to ask." He gave in to a sudden impulse and probed a little way beneath the blanket. A tiny fist, the size of a strawberry, flailed out. "Great right hook. Kid's gonna box."

"Not if I have anything to say about it." Shelley found a foot. "Dancing's safer."

Zach couldn't resist. He put a finger under her chin and tilted her face up. "Is it?" The kiss they shared was a mutual sigh of relief.

"Come to think of it," Shelley murmured, looking down at their son, "maybe not."

CHAPTER TWENTY

HOSPITAL REGULATIONS required the baby and be cleaned up and checked over. Zach wandered out into the hall of the labor and delivery suite. The nurse who'd tried to change Shelley's clothes bustled past. He caught her by the arm.

"He's here. What do I do now?"

She looked at him sternly for a second, then her face softened. "Do you have family to call? Is anybody waiting outside?"

Within an hour, the entire Harmon clan crowded into the waiting lounge. Shelley's mom and her grandparents arrived, were introduced all around. Zach had been given a cigar by each brother and a hug by all the women...except Carol. She'd come, but somehow he never managed to catch her eye. The whole bunch of them trooped to the nursery window to see his son.

My son. Zach said the words to himself over and over as he watched the dark-eyed baby cry. What did he feel? Awe? Fear? His mind and emotions had been shaken up, turned inside out. A brother, a lover, a friend, a cop... He handled those roles fine. He knew what to do.

But nothing had prepared him for the immensity

of being a husband and a father. In the space of a few hours, he was totally and forever changed.

"Mr. Harmon?" A nurse threaded through the group. "Your wife can have visitors now."

"Thanks." He found Dorothy's gaze and nodded. She blew him a kiss, then she and Shelley's grandparents went into the new mom's room.

His brothers and sisters left, promising to be back the next day with flowers and candy and words of advice. The crowd dwindled down to just his mother and himself, staring at the new arrival.

"He's a fine boy," Mary Harmon said. "Strong. Just like his daddy." She linked an arm through Zach's. "Are you okay?"

"Sure." He drew a deep breath. "I didn't do any of this the right way, though."

"You followed your own path—as always. Face it, son, you thrive on challenges and excitement. And with Shelley—with *your* son—you're in for the ride of your life. I know you'll be fine."

He closed her in his arms. "Thanks. Have I mentioned I love you recently?"

"Not recently enough. Now—" she drew back and patted his shoulders. "—I'm going home. Tell your wife I love her and I'll come see her tomorrow."

"Will do." He watched his mother walk down the hall, then turned back to his son, who had fallen asleep. Minutes could have passed, or hours. Claire had told him, but he hadn't understood at the time. Who knew watching a baby could be so fascinating?

"Zach?" He turned at the sound of his name.

Carol stood about ten feet away, her arms wrapped around her waist. "Can I...can I talk to you?"

"Sure. Have you met your nephew?" He beckoned her over. "Kid snores, but everybody has their bad habits."

"He's so sweet." She stared into the glass. "I'm sorry, Zach. Really sorry."

"Yeah?"

"I didn't mean to be so awful. I just—"

He waited.

"I just thought Shelley liked me, like a friend, you know? Not like a little kid. We went shopping and everything, and we talked."

"I know."

"And...and since dad died, I pretty much counted on you to be there. You got me through so much these last couple of years."

He glanced at her sideways. "You helped me, too, Carol. We're family and we love each other."

"So when I found out that you and Shelley...that you'd been...you hadn't told me everything, or even the truth—"

"You were mad." Zach shrugged. "I can understand that."

"Really?" She looked up with tears in her eyes. "I feel like scum."

He put an arm around her shoulders. "Not that bad. Fungus, maybe. Not scum."

She gave a watery laugh.

"But you did say some cruel things to Shelley." He kissed the top of her head. "You're the one who has to undo that damage."

"I'll do anything, Zach. I'll wash all the diapers.

Baby-sitting for life. I like Shelley, I really do. I want her for a sister.''

"Baby-sitting for life sounds good to me. I think you've got a deal.'' He grinned and gave her a squeeze. "I want to check on the new mom. Wait for me and I'll give you a ride home.''

"Sure, Zach.''

When he looked in on Shelley, she'd fallen asleep. He stood for a few minutes, just watching. She wore her own gown and her hair was brushed, her face smooth and clean. Already her stomach was flatter, and the fullness in her face had lessened. She'd be back to her old self in no time.

And where would that leave him? They'd worked together for the birth of a baby. Could they work together afterward? Would Shelley let him into her life? Was there anything she needed that only he could give her?

The answer to that question escaped him. Zach bent to give his wife, the mother of his son, a kiss. And then he left her to her rest.

A STRANGE VOICE woke Shelley to a room in darkness. "Mrs. Harmon? Your baby's here.''

Shelley pushed herself to sit up. "What time is it?'' Every muscle in her body ached.

"About five-thirty.''

"In the morning?''

"That's right.'' A lamp switched on, painfully.

She felt disoriented somehow. Confused. She didn't remember falling asleep, didn't feel as if she'd slept at all.

The nurse came toward the bed. "Here he is.''

Shelley made a cradle of her arms, which was filled with a small, squeaking bundle. "He hasn't had anything to eat yet. You might try to nurse him. Or here's a bottle of water, if you'd like. Do you want me to stay?"

"Um..." Surely she could manage this on her own. "No, thank you." The door dropped into place and she was alone with her son. Zach's son, staring back at her with wide, dark eyes. He was beautiful, the most beautiful thing she'd ever seen, except for Allyson. As she watched, he scrunched up his little face. And let out a plaintive wail.

"Hungry?" She fumbled one-handed with the front of her gown. "Guess we'd better figure something out quick." She teased his mouth with her nipple, as the books had instructed. He didn't notice, and cried harder. "That's not the reaction I wanted, you know." The books counseled patience. "Come on, buddy, we can work together here."

Thirty minutes later, she was crying, too. "At least take some water, okay?" But the baby only wailed. She pressed the call button several times. Finally, a nurse came in.

"Is there a problem?"

Shelley sniffed. "I can't get him to nurse. Or take the water."

"Let me try." Taking her son away, the nurse sat down in a chair and offered him the bottle. After just a minute, she sighed. "That's good, isn't it, little boy?"

Shelley sat up. "He's drinking?"

"Uh-huh."

She flopped back on the pillows. "Great. Just great."

When he woke again at seven, they repeated the program, with the same results. "Maybe I can't do this," Shelley muttered, wiping more tears off her face.

"Nonsense," a different nurse told her. "Nursing just takes persistence. Perseverance."

"Or magic." She watched the baby sleep. "I'm your mom. Why won't you eat for me?"

She didn't realize she'd fallen asleep herself until a knock on the door woke her. "Um…come in." Was this Zach? She brushed her hair back, wondering what in the world she looked like.

But Carol stepped in. Shelley took a deep breath and held it. *I can't do this. Not today.*

The girl stopped at the bassinet. "I told Zach I'd baby-sit for life," she said to the baby, "if you would let everything between us be okay again. I want to tell you I'm sorry. I was messed up…I'm not anymore."

Shelley let her breath out, as the tension left her body. Holding out her hand, she smiled. "Let's forget that afternoon, okay? Neither of us was at her best."

Carol looked at her hand for a few seconds, then finally took hold. "Really? We can do that?"

"We have to. Allyson's depending on you to teach her how to bat next year. And I'm definitely going to need a lifetime baby-sitter. You'll have to go to college in Denver, you know."

Carol laughed, and suddenly she looked like Zach. "Whatever you say, Shelley. Can I hold the baby?"

A new voice entered the conversation. "First rule—let sleeping babies lie." Zach strolled into the room carrying a sheaf of blue and white blooms. "Don't wake them up for love or money."

"But—"

"But nothin'." He stood at the end of the bed and gave Shelley a quiet smile. "How are you?"

"Pretty good." Not nearly as good as he was. He looked rested, he'd shaved and showered and changed. His sweater echoed the blue of his eyes. She remembered the strength of his hands, holding her during childbirth. She remembered his voice, leading her through a maze of pain.

"Well...um...I think I'll be going."

With a start, Shelley broke away from Zach's gaze to see his sister backing toward the door. "You're welcome to stay until he wakes up."

The girl shook her head. "Nah, that's okay. I'm supposed to be at school, anyway. Later, Zach."

"Sure." He didn't move when his sister left. Then he held up the flowers. "Jimmy sent these. He doesn't do hospitals."

"He told me. They're gorgeous."

Zach looked at them with surprise. "Yeah, I guess they are." He put the bouquet on the dresser and came to the bassinet to put a hand on the baby's back. "This little guy still doesn't have a name."

"I know. I—I wasn't sure..."

"Horatio? Horatio Harmon has a certain ring to it."

She stared at him. "Be serious."

"I am. Rudolph's always been a favorite of mine."

"Horatio Rudolph Harmon?"

He nodded. "I like it. H.R.H., we could call him, for short. His Royal Highness."

His nonsense lifted her heart. "Then let's go for it."

Zach grinned. "You're humoring me, aren't you?" Rounding the bassinet, he pulled the chair up close to the bed and sat. "Seriously, what did you have in mind?"

"It's hard to choose." Alone, that was. Suddenly, nothing seemed too hard to accomplish. "Garrett? Tyler? Timothy?"

"Hmm." He picked up her hand and toyed with her fingers. His hands were warm, gentle around hers. "Not Tyler, okay? I got beat up by a Tyler once. Timothy Harmon. Garrett Harmon. Stiff names for such a little bundle."

At that moment, the little bundle jerked, then jerked again. Zach looked at Shelley. "Can I?"

"He's your son. Of course."

His experience with children showed immediately in the sure control of his hands, the easy way he settled the baby into the crook of his arm. "There we go, big guy. What's going on, huh? Wanna catch a hockey game?"

Shelley's throat closed. She'd never deserved this—Zach and their baby together, father and son. What could she possibly do to make this last?

The cry she was learning to recognize broke over them. "He's hungry," she said. "But I'm not having much luck."

"More luck than I would, probably." Zach

grinned at her and put the baby in her arms. "At least you have the right equipment."

"Sometimes equipment isn't enough." But she would try, and keep on trying.

Except the baby—what would his name be?—didn't want to cooperate. Zach handed her the water bottle when she asked, but she couldn't get that to work, either. Going back to nursing, she felt her face heat up. She couldn't feed her own child. Even dogs and cats...

"Hey, Shelley. Calm down." Zach's palm covered the back of hers as she held the baby. "There's no hurry. He's got some fat to last him until he gets the hang of the process."

"That's never going to happen." Her voice thickened with tears. "I've been trying all morning."

"Maybe too hard." Before she realized what he was doing, he'd set the chair against the wall. "Let's get rid of a couple of these." He pulled pillows out from behind her back. "That's better." Slipping off his shoes, he sat down behind her, as he had last night in the birthing room. With a few adjustments, he settled her against his chest, warm and solid. "Better?"

Shelley nodded, afraid to trust her voice. In her arms, the baby still fussed.

"Now just relax. That's right." Zach's hands covered her shoulders, massaged gently. "You're so tense. Kid doesn't want his mom all tense." Shelley held her head up by force of will, as the massage loosened her neck and back. "He's waiting for you to ease up, so he can. He had a hard day yesterday."

Shelley choked on a laugh.

"He did. You try being born. Not an easy thing to do." His hands kneaded, stroked, and she could feel herself flowing into him, as if Zach and the baby and she were all one.

Like magic, a sparkling sensation grew in her breasts. When she looked down, a drop of liquid had escaped her nipple to tremble on the baby's lips. He smacked his mouth, worked around with his tongue. She put up a hand and guided the nipple over his lips, and another drop fell. The baby opened his mouth wide and lapped. After a few seconds, he began to suck enthusiastically.

"Oh, Zach. You did it." She was crying and couldn't help it. "Why did I ever think I could manage this without you?"

"Beats me." His arms tightened. "At least now you know different."

"I don't know much about anything these days. Zach, what are we doing?"

His mouth pressed against her hair. "We're picking a baby name right now. How does Alex strike you?"

"Alex Harmon?" She liked the sound. "Alexander Harmon? That's nice."

"And maybe Henry, after my dad, for a middle name?"

"Alexander Henry Harmon. Alexander H. Harmon. That feels right. I like it. You're a real problem solver today, aren't you?"

"I hope so. Is old Alex there finished?"

"He's gone back to sleep."

"Smart kid. I'll have to raise his allowance." He loosened his arms. Shelley sat up, swung her legs over the edge of the bed and put Alex back in the bassinet. But after covering the sleeping baby with a blanket, she didn't know what to say to her husband.

She knew what she wanted to do. She wanted to lie back against him, to believe that somehow this would all work out and they would become a family—a loving, forever family.

Caught up in her wish, she was startled when Zach put his hand on her arm. "Come back to earth. What are you dreaming about?" His eyes searched her face as she turned.

"N-nothing." She dropped her gaze to her hands, twisting in her lap.

He waited a few seconds. "Okay. Then tell me what I'm dreaming about."

She risked a glance at him—his face was serious, but his eyes laughed at her. Shelley shook her head. "I never know what's in your head."

"Not true. Sometimes you interpret very well." A certain slant to his quick grin told her exactly what he meant. She gave an involuntary chuckle.

"See, you do know. So just extend the talent."

"Zach. I can't. I only know my own thoughts."

"And couldn't mine be the same?"

"No. Oh, no."

"Why not?"

"Because…"

"Because, nothin'." He sat up so that they were close together on the bed. "You deserve this, Shelley. We both do." His arms slipped around her waist. His breath warmed her temple. "The longer we put off taking what we want, the less time we'll have to enjoy it."

She was afraid to believe him. "I don't know..."

"Then let me tell you. I love you, Shelley Owens Hightower Harmon. I don't know when it happened, or how. Maybe two years ago, or nine months, or on our wedding day. Doesn't matter. I want us to stay together. A long, long, long time. A lifetime."

"Zach, if this is just for the baby—"

"Look at me." She couldn't. He tightened his hold. "Look at me, Shelley."

Gathering all her courage, she raised her eyes to his. There was love everywhere on his face, and a kind of hopeful patience that crimped her heart.

In that instant, Shelley stopped trying to hide what she felt. She let her whole heart show.

"That's it." He closed his eyes for a second. When he opened them, his grin widened. "What I see on your face is inside of me. We belong, Shelley."

Could it be this easy? "I drive you crazy."

His warm hands stroked her back. "I like it."

"I'm materialistic and ambitious." Finally, she let herself touch him, his jaw, his nose, his hair. Forget weariness. Every part of her was suddenly, gloriously alive.

He smiled. "You're a soft touch underneath."

She ran a fingertip across his mouth. "I make more money than you do."

"True." He sighed. Then kissed her palm. "I'll learn to live with that. And you have to live with a guy who's satisfied just where he is."

"There are harder jobs." She sighed. "I love you, Zach. More than I can say."

"Mmm." He turned her more fully into his arms

and lowered his head. "I was waiting for that." He breathed the words into her mouth. Into her soul.

Their kiss swept her away...to a winter's night in an anonymous bed with an exciting, unpredictable man. Then forward again...into a future filled with light and laughter. And love.

Zach drew back and smoothed the hair away from his wife's face. "I'd better slow down," he whispered. "The nurses wouldn't appreciate the rating on what happens next."

A rosy color crept into Shelley's skin. But she was still smiling. "I doubt I'm up to much more anyway. And moms and dads shouldn't behave like that."

"Sure they should. Otherwise they wouldn't be moms and dads." He ducked in for another quick kiss, lingered for several. "They just shouldn't get caught."

He stroked the blush over her cheekbones with his thumb, then the slight hollow of her temple, the tremble of her lower lip. Her eyes were wide and dark, and need gathered with the love in his chest. "You are so touchable, lady. I've been crazy for most of the last nine months, dying to get my hands on you. Wanting to make sure you're mine."

"I am, Zach. Forever." She buried her face in his chest and he closed his arms around her with a long sigh of relief.

Happily-ever-after finally looked like a sure bet.

HARLEQUIN®
SUPERROMANCE®

Two women—who are going to be mothers.
Two men—who want to be fathers.

EXPECTING THE BEST by **Lynnette Kent**
Shelly Hightower falls for Denver cop Zach Harmon—but she figures he's done with raising kids. He has to convince her that he *wants* to be a father to their baby....
AVAILABLE IN OCTOBER 1999.

THE FAMILY WAY by **Rebecca Winters**
Wendy Sloan is pregnant by her husband—and mourning his death. She doesn't understand why she's so attracted to the mysterious stranger who's come into her family's life—the man who wants to be a father to her kids. Including this new baby...
AVAILABLE IN NOVEMBER 1999.

Two deeply emotional stories.
Read them both.

Available at your favorite retail outlet.

HARLEQUIN®
Makes any time special ™

Visit us at www.romance.net

HSR9ML99